The Legend
of
Cooper's Landing

A novel by

Katharine Carter

And

John Rottger

The Legend of Cooper's Landing

Printed in the United States by
Mira Digital Publishing
Chesterfield, Missouri 63005

Acknowledgement

I would like to thank John Rottger, who, at a party one night, talked of an idea for a book. As I had never heard of The Knights of the Golden Circle, I came home and researched them on the internet and whilst doing so came up with a story line. John's help in the diving scenes was invaluable due to his past and present experience as a former Navy SEAL Lieutenant.

The scenes of boat chases and crashes were made more spectacular by John due to his later experiences as a stunt man and co-ordinator of underwater movie scenes. It is our hope, the reader finds them as vivid in the book as they would be in a movie.

The shrimping stories have come about from the shrimping community here on the Gulf Coast and watching the shrimpers go out and come back day after day. The shrimping community is full of wonderful stories. I thank them all. The beautiful historical home "The White House" is still in existence and was the source of my inspiration for "The Legend of Cooper's Landing."

John and I would also like to thank our editor whose patience with us is, as always, endless. She has become a good friend and an extremely good mentor.

The beautiful cover was designed by our friend Lloyd Pearcey who lives in Bon Secour adjacent to Gulf Shores. He has designed all my book covers. A lot of the inside artwork and photographs were also supplied by Lloyd, and the final editing also done by Lloyd. Thanks for your patience with both of us.

I would like to thank John's family for my taking so much of his time without complaint, especially his beautiful, warm and friendly wife Mary Ann.

I would also like to thank my husband and son who listen to my never ending chatter on my latest novel and accepting it is something more than a hobby. You are both amazing people.

The beautiful photographs were taken by Lynn Jordan @ www.lynnjordanphotography.com. She lives and works in Gulf Shores and has become a personal friend. Her work is amazing and always on show somewhere locally matted or framed and on her web site, and of course all are for sale. We thank both you and Lloyd so much for amazing artistic work John and I could not attempt.

Katharine and John

The Bountiful Lady Being Tossed in the Storm

Preface

During the Civil War 1863
Somewhere Near Dolphin's Cove, Alabama

He went on deck to see the conditions for himself. The captain of the Bountiful Lady had not been wrong. The Gulf waves swelling and the wind rising, but he was on a mission. "Keep heading north for a while," he instructed the captain. "Perhaps if you skirt the shoreline a little closer, the weather will not be so effective against us there."

He stood by the rail of the deck for some time watching the waves become like steep hills to climb, the wind roaring as if it were an animal bellowing in pain, the rain coming down so hard it bounced off the deck and felt like pellets on bare legs. He looked troubled as the captain approached again.

"We have to take this boat into harbor. We can't be far from Mobile," the captain screamed into the wind. "I can't wait any longer. This storm is not going to lessen. We could all die. We may have left it too late already."

A streak of lightening and a crash of thunder added truth behind his ominous words. The next bolt of lightning rent the sky in two, parting the black sky to reveal the huge waves.

The man nodded his head in agreement. With a sigh, the captain ordered the helmsman to alter course and run with the storm. His only hope was they were not too late in their approach. The boat creaked and groaned as it began its turn to run into harbor with the storm behind it, but on turning, huge waves battered the sides and swamped the boat. One seaman tried to pull in the main sail, but was thrown overboard. His body surfaced once or twice, and he called to the other sailors, but no one heard him. His body disappeared to rot in the boiling, swirling waters of the Gulf.

Others sailors were trying to batten down hatches. As one pulled the hatch with his right hand, the wind blew in the opposite direction first lifting the hatch out of his hand and then slamming it back down, breaking the bones in his wrist and fingers. He screamed in pain, but the sound of his scream was taken up by the wind and dispersed. He grabbed the hatch with his weaker left hand, but the wind caught the hatch, taking the lid directly upright, twisting the wood, and breaking the hinges. The hatch flew upward before being cast into the murky depths.

The man stood for a moment watching the activities of the crew, but then returned below deck, the motion of the ship making him feel sick in the pit of his stomach. Entering his small cabin, he reached to find one of the Mason jars filled with gold and silver and a few jewels. He held on tight to the jar. He could not hold the other eleven, so he left them in the large drawer. The Knights had ordered him to find a predetermined spot to bury all the treasure—reportedly worth millions. The second civil war would not be long in coming. It was imperative that the treasure was buried where no one else could find it. Only a few had knowledge of the coming events—they were called The Knights of the Golden Circle. The members believed the South would rise again to its former glory, and the buried jewels and money would help to finance the uprising. Those in the

Circle who disagreed with the mission or spoke out against slavery were immediately eliminated. Only those who accepted the concept of the Circle remained alive. They had been carefully selected and instructed. "Long live the South," became part of their motto. It was a good way of life that should not be lost. Those from the North had little conception of how good the life had once been. Without a doubt, the Circle would be able to restore that life.

He pulled a sketch from his pocket, and traced it on top of the Mason jar lid. The map was a deception, meant to lead potential thieves astray. When they made land, he would find a burying place for the jars, and he would chisel a similar map on a rock nearby. Over the past years, many such maps had been chiseled into rocks across the States, and dozens of treasure hunters in the future years would be misled. Only trusted members of the Circle would be able to correctly interpret the maps, and they would use the money they found for the good of the South and to promote slavery.

He felt the boat lift and the bow pointed directly upwards. He held his breath and waited for it to fall backward, but it did not. His possessions were thrown around the cabin, battering him as he hung grimly to the cot. The boat dove steeply into the next wave. He fell to his knees and prayed to God to deliver him and the crew safely to their destination. He had been a fool to insisting they stay the course for so long. He could hear occasionally, above the roar of the wind, the captain and crew shouting but he had no idea what they were saying. He felt the water come through the un-battened hatch and swamp the floor below him. The Bountiful Lady continued to creak and groan as she was thrown and tossed around, one minute pointing toward the sky, the next down toward the bottom of the Bay.

Lightning rent the sky, and the thunder continuously roared as the rain pounded down on them. Suddenly all sound and movement stopped, and he threw up all over himself and the cabin. Dare he believe they had all survived? The Gulf waters, however, felt differently, as at that moment, a wave so tall he could not see the crest, picked the ship up and threw it upside down.

For a few minutes the silence seemed surreal. No wind, no rain, no thunder and lightning, just silence and the occasional gurgling sound. He tried to stand on what had been the ceiling of the room he had occupied for the past few days. He was battered and bruised, but alive. He stood unsteadily on his feet with a smile playing around the edges of his mouth. "Thank you, God," he shouted as a large roar and gurgle of water swamped his cabin, as he struggled to get out of the water. He made it out as far as the deck before the ship turned on its end and sank below into the murky Gulf waters. He was thrown from the deck, still holding on tightly to his treasure, but the sinking of the ship caused an eddy in the water and pulled him down with it. Through it all, he hung on to his Mason jar.

The lightning, thunder and rain continued for hours. The storm was a hurricane which had come into Mobile Bay with an unprecedented force, changing the shoreline forever.

Chapter 1

He stood looking out from the shoreline over the Bay of Mobile, cursing his broken down boat once again. How the hell was he supposed to pay for the repairs? He hardly made a living from the Gulf as it was; now his damn boat was in need of a new engine. It had bellowed black smoke on its way back from the last trip, and although he had made it into harbor, it would not be possible to take it out again without repairs. He had even thought of letting the whole thing blow up, but his insurance had run out two months before, and he had not be able to afford the renewal. He knew a lot of the folks in the town were in the same situation. They all were living on the edge of poverty. Fishing had not been good after the oil spill. "Oh yes," he thought, "They say they 'compensated us,' but the fishing never recovered. This whole town is in trouble."

David stuffed his hands in his pockets as he walked back to the house he had been born in, thinking how ironic it was that he had moved back into the house shortly after his mother had died. It was very small house, and it was beginning to look a little dilapidated. The roof leaked, and the walls were crumbling, and David's bank account was almost empty.

His mother had insisted his father build the sunroom, and he thought of her as he put his feet up on the coffee table and looked pensively out over the bay. The bay had provided his father and grandfather with a reasonable living over the years, but it had been a hard life on them all. The shrimping industry was competitive. His grandfather had started the family business with two boats, but one was lost in a storm one night. He had managed to save three of the crew, but two had drowned in the Gulf. The funerals had been held a few days afterwards on the spot the boat went down. He had compensated the families for the loss of their loved ones and found after that he had no money left. His grandfather and father found it hard to eke out a living with just one boat. He, like many in the fishing industry at the time, had not insured his boat for loss at sea—it was too expensive. Still, working 12-hour days seven days a week, he was able to provide for his wife and young son.

When David was old enough, he learned the family business. It was a tough hard life for a sixteen year old. His days were spent on the water, leaving by four or five o'clock in the evening, depending on the tide, and fishing all night. They bought their catch home and tried to sell it to the restaurants in Mobile. Some nights were more successful than others.

David got himself a beer from the aging refrigerator. He flipped the top from the bottle and almost drank it down in one gulp. He went back to his musings.

His father was not happy that David had followed him into the business at such a young age. When he turned sixteen, his father had tried to insist David stay in school. "I want you to go to college," he had told David.

"Why?" David had shouted back at his father. "This is the family business. What am I going to learn at school, never mind college, that will help me learn how to catch shrimp? I just need to know where the best shrimp are spawning, where the shrimp collect together, and how to get the things off the bottom of the Gulf. You can teach me that—college can't." And so David had won the argument. David knew his father didn't have enough money to send him to college. When he was younger, he had hoped for a football scholarship, but he suddenly quit playing in his junior year. When his father questioned him, David admitted he had been seeing a girl at school, and she was pregnant. David gave up high school, football, and his own dreams of college, and married the girl.

It was a year after the child was born, that David found he was not the father of the boy. It was another young man—Tom—who played center on the football field and who had been a good friend at one time. The child grew to look so like Tom that it was obvious to everyone that David was not the father. In the end, David had no choice but to confront his wife, who confessed she had never loved David and that the boy was indeed Tom's child.

David immediately walked out of their rented house. He rented his own place not far away. He missed the child he had thought of as his son, but not his wife. She was a harpy at the best of times, and he suspected that while he was out on the Gulf at night, she was sharing their matrimonial bed with someone else.

When he was able to afford it several years later, he divorced her. He became a secular and solemn man. His routines were the same. He would breakfast in the local café, Marylou's, each morning, where the waitress would not bother to give him a menu and would pour coffee for him as soon as he walked through the door. He would eat his breakfast alone and just nod his head at people who knew him. He would read the morning paper while eating, and, when he finished, he would drain the coffee from his mug, leave the twelve dollars on the table, and walk back to his rented house. He would go to sleep, only arising half an hour before he was due to get to the boat ready to take out to start the next night of shrimping. The only times the routine differed was when a hurricane came in to shore—about once or twice a year. He would board up the house and wait inside until the storm passed.

When his mother died of cancer, she took all the light out of his father's life. David's parents had always been close, his mother doing the books each day and the taxes at the end of the year. She sold shrimp from the house to local residents, kept a clean house, and never allowed a sound to disturb her husband's sleep patterns.

At the age of thirty-nine, David moved back in with his father to keep an eye on him. The two men had little to say to one another as they spent hours together on the Gulf. They spoke of little else but shrimping. During the year following his mother's death, David noticed his father would forget to shout orders at the crew. Several times, he asked his father if anything was wrong, but his father would shake his head and say, no how could there be, he never forgot anything. As the year wore on, David watched his father deteriorate. He not only forgot to give timely orders to his men, but forgot to pay his bills, and once he left a pot boiling on the stove and set fire to the kitchen. David finally took his father to a doctor in Mobile who diagnosed him with early onset of Alzheimer's disease.

David tried to discreetly take over the running of the shrimper. When his father heard David give orders to the crew, he was furious. For the first time in his life, David heard his father swear. "You young bastard! If you can't do what I tell you, I'll fucking kill you. Pull those fucking nets in, you useless pieces of shit." He also shouted at the crew. "You're all fucking lazy. I swear I'll throw you all overboard." He threatened members of the crew, and, once, attacked David with a walking stick. With great regret, David took his father off the boat and refused to let him back on. His father ranted ceaselessly about what an ungrateful son David was, but, in his saner moments, his father understood what David was doing.

Only a few weeks after David removed his father from the boat, David came home one morning from shrimping to find his father slumped in a chair not breathing. An empty pill bottle and an empty bottle of whisky were by his side. The funeral was two days later. Afterwards, David took the crew to the Mighty Shrimp where they got drunk as they related tales of his father. They all agreed his father was one of the best captains a crew could want. It was a sad day when he ended his life, but now they worked for David.

The only thing his father owned outright was the boat. He had a mortgage on the house which David took on as his own.

David walked back to the old refrigerator and saw he had no more beer and kicked the door shut again and softly swore. There was no food to eat and no beer to drink, so he decided to eat at Marylou's. He'd not had breakfast or lunch because he had spent all day on the boat. He really wanted to repair it himself before giving up and going to the local boat yard. He stared down at his hands which were still covered in oil and dirt from the work he had done. He'd wiped them earlier with a rag but they needed soap and water. Perhaps, as he was not taking the shrimper out tonight, a shower would be in order before he went to Marylou's.

It was not busy in the cafe that night, but as he walked through the door, every head looked up in surprise at seeing him there.

"Evening, David," one or two voices muttered. "Not shrimping tonight?"

He shook his head and found a booth further back where no one else was sitting. He sat with his hands clasped on the table looking far out at the distance, continuing his thoughts of earlier that afternoon.

"Good evening," said a soft female voice. "What can I get you?" She laid a menu directly in front of him.

"Usual," he replied without looking at her.

"I'm sorry, I don't know what your usual is," the voice replied. "I'm new here so I have no idea what it is." She rustled the pad and pen in front of her while waiting for him to either look at her and give his order or at least say something.

David did look up into sparkling green eyes. She stared at him with frustration. Was he dumb? Didn't he want to place an order? "Perhaps I should give you a few minutes to glance through the menu," she said, ready to walk away from what was rapidly becoming an awkward moment. It didn't help that she had never done this sort of work before.

As she turned to walk away from the table, he recovered his voice. "What do you recommend?"

Turning back with a sigh, she replied, "I had shepherd's pie yesterday. They are individually made and cooked here and it was really good. Otherwise, I haven't eaten here, and so I can't recommend anything from personal experience. Bacon and eggs seem popular, or hot and cold sandwiches. The quiche looks good. I have no idea what sort of food you care to eat."

Neither seemed aware of the other customers beginning to stare at them. That was probably the most they had ever heard David talk unless it was about the weather or shrimping.

"I'll take the shepherd's pie with peas and corn," David ordered. "And a beer."

"This is a café. We don't have a liquor license. Tea? Or coffee?"

"Coffee then," he said disappointed Marylou's did not have a liquor license. It had been so long since he'd eaten here at night, he had forgotten.

"My name is Morgan if there is anything else I can get you," she said as she walked away to get his coffee, thinking how rude this man was, and hoping he was not a regular. Everyone else had been extremely nice to her. She could feel his eyes boring into her back as she walked away. Placing his order, she turned back with the coffee mug and the pot, and she watched as he turned his head away and looked outside. She poured the coffee and added, "There's cream and sugar on the table." Without waiting for a thank you or even another comment, she walked away to another table, refilled their coffee cups, and chatted easily with the other customers.

David ate his meal in silence, wishing he had bought the morning paper with him. Somehow it felt all wrong to be sitting here with nothing to read and no one to talk to. He watched furtively as Morgan moved around the café and listened to the sound of her laugh. It reminded him of his mother. It had been a long time since he had heard a woman laugh. He left the money on the table before she even gave him a bill and quietly walked out, just nodding to one or two people he knew.

The town center was empty, and David did not know what to do. He was used to being out shrimping at this time of the evening. Walking with his hands stuffed in his pockets he ambled without a destination in mind and found himself down on the pier where his boat was moored. Without thought, he climbed aboard, grabbed a flashlight, and went down into the engine room. He quickly wired up an overhead light, and his hands went to work on the engine. Methodically taking out the plugs and cogs and taking the whole engine to pieces gave him a peace of mind he had not had earlier that day. He cleaned each piece thoroughly and inspected each pipe. He ran a small brush through every one to remove even the minutest particles of dirt. When he was done, he began to reassemble the engine bit by bit. Sweat was pouring from him and he would wipe his brow on his forearm so it would not drip in his eyes. He replaced some tubing that had a hole in it where oil had been leaking. That was what caused the black smoke to bellow from the engine when he had used it last. When he finished reassembling the engine, he looked up to see it was daylight outside. He had worked through the night.

With his heart beating just a little faster and with fingers crossed, he went up to the wheel house and turned the engine over. It coughed and spluttered much as she had the day before, but then caught and thrummed as it ticked over.

He closed his eyes and patted the wheel in thanks. He could go shrimping tonight. He left the engine running while he cleaned himself up. He felt happy and hungry. He had two things to do. One was to inform his crew they would be shrimping tonight, and the other was to eat. He jumped lightly on the pier from his boat and walked towards the boat repair dock. He saw the owner working on a boat in dry dock. "Dan," he shouted out. "No need for me to bring my boat around today. I fixed the engine last night. Keep your fingers crossed it will be alright."

Dan waved his hand in acknowledgement, fervently wishing David had not fixed his boat himself. He could really do with the work. The shrimpers were doing badly, and, as a consequence, so was he. Business had dwindled enormously these last four years. He had no idea how he would ever get out of the hole they were all digging themselves into.

By the time David finished his shower, it was noon. He knew where his crew would be at this time of day if they weren't working. The Mighty Shrimp was open, and his crew members—Mack, Roy, and Ben—were playing a game of pool. He walked over to them and told them, "You will be working tonight, so no more beer. The tide will be early, so be on the shrimper at four. We have a lot of shrimp to catch. Be prepared for a hard night—we've got to make up for last night."

As David left, the three men looked at one another with huge sighs. They would be earning money again tonight and would be able to put food on their tables at home. Each had wondered where the money was coming from. They loved David as a skipper—there was none better. He knew the water, knew the tides, and would take risks where many others wouldn't, but he always remained calm and in control and came out on top each time. However, if the Crimson Tide was unable to run for more than two days at a time, they would have to find employment elsewhere.

The owner of the Mighty Shrimp grumbled to himself behind the bar as he dried a glass. He had heard the men ordered not to drink. They were the only customers in the bar, and he had been open since eleven. They had one beer apiece. How was he supposed to eke a living out of this dying town? Was it any wonder the youngsters were getting college educations and leaving in droves?

The Crimson Tide in Harbor

Chapter 2

Morgan stood on the shore watching the Crimson Tide leave harbor. The sun was low in the bright orange and red sky and dark clouds were beginning to loom overhead. It made for a pretty, but early sunset. She had moved in with her ailing grandfather two weeks before. Both her parents had died two years before in a car accident in Boston. They had been on their way to see the Boston Pop Orchestra when a drunk driver had gone through red lights and smashed into them. The car had almost disintegrated he had been speeding so fast, driving home from an office Christmas party. He and his wife had also died. It had made a devastating Christmas for the two families.

As an only child, Morgan had visited with her grandparents each summer and loved the life and the pace of Oak Tree Town. Her grandfather was a shrimper most of his life, but her father had been determined not to live in Oak Tree Town a moment longer than he had to. He was one of the few who had gone to college and moved away to start a new life. He met his wife at college, and after graduation, they moved to Boston. The life there was fast-paced, and they loved the cultural activities. Her father vowed he would never be dependent on the Gulf to make a living. He worked hard and became a trauma doctor, and she became a nurse. Both worked at the same hospital and their life revolved around busy work schedules and the other staff who worked at the hospital. Morgan had been a surprise to both of them. It wasn't that they didn't want children; they had been so invested in their work they just never thought about the possibilities. Her mother was thirty-five when Morgan was born, and she had not wanted to give up work, so Morgan had been bought up by a variety of home care nannies and the day care center at the hospital. Her parents paid little attention to her, continuing their lives as if she had not been born. It wasn't that they didn't love her—they did. But they also loved the life they lived and were always busy.

The summers with her grandparents were the best part of her childhood. She loved to come to this small town outside of Mobile, set just behind Dolphin's Cove. It was a small fishing community that lived by selling the fish and shrimp they caught. She had only been allowed on her grandfather's shrimp boat once. She had seen how the nets that looked like butterfly wings on either side of the boat were lowered into the water to catch the shrimp from their feeding grounds. She had observed the nets were reeled back in and emptied into the holds. She then watched the waiting crew sort the catch and throw back any fish or shrimp that wasn't wanted. The shrimp were quickly packed into ice so that they would stay fresh. The shrimp boats went out far into the Gulf, and long before the night was over, Morgan had fallen asleep in her grandfather's cabin.

Vacationers were few and far between in Oak Tree Town, but they came by the thousands everywhere else along the white sand beaches of the Gulf, and they loved shrimp. However, the 2010 oil spill changed all that. People no longer flocked to the oil-sodden beaches, nor did they want to wade in the Gulf waters along with globs of oil they trod on or floated by them. The restaurants stopped buying shrimp in quantity. Everyone who made their living from the Gulf was affected. Later, when the vacationers came back and the oil company had made restitution, everyone had thought that they could catch up on their bills and have money to spare, but the recovery was never complete. Many were evicted from their houses as they went into foreclosure. Their bills accumulated interest and a lot of people declared bankruptcy. As a consequence, far from being made rich from the oil spill, a lot of businesses had closed. Fishermen had lost so much from being laid off so long, that they too had either left and tried to find employment elsewhere, or relied on Social Security. Life was hard for those who remained.

When Morgan found her grandparents had been affected as much as anyone else, she tried to send them money. She was doing well in New York with a prestigious job as a museum historian and she shared a rent-controlled apartment. However, her grandfather was a proud man and refused to cash any of the checks she sent. When her grandmother died, she went down to Oak Tree Town for the funeral. She was appalled to find her grandfather was going to give her grandmother a pauper's funeral, and so Morgan had insisted she be involved in choosing the coffin and the service and quietly paid the funeral director for it all. She found out how much her grandfather owed in hospital bills and paid those off too. Her grandfather assumed the bills would come to him eventually, so he had no idea she had done so much.

When she suggested he might like her to stay and look after him, her grandfather had muttered, "I've looked after myself all these years and will continue to do so, thank you. You go and get back to New York and your life there." Morgan had accepted him at face value and flew back to the life she had made for herself.

Morgan was in a relationship with one of the professors at the museum and she was very fond of him, but after eight years, their relationship had not progressed. She had been really happy to move in with Gareth after they had known each other for two years, but as the years passed and no marriage proposal came, she became disillusioned. She wanted to have children, and Gareth had said he did too, but as the years went on their relationship became stale. She flew back from the town of Oak Tree and stood in the middle of her sterile living room. Gareth was not at home— probably still at work—and the more she stood there, the more she felt ill at ease and as if she did not belong. She remembered the tidy cottage her grandfather lived in and knew it's worth was nowhere near that of this apartment, but she loved the cottage more. It looked across fields of grasses and wild flowers, and the town of Oak Tree and had been home to his family for many generations. The furniture was shabby and old, but the wood had worn and weathered so beautifully that it shone like mirrored glass. The pace of life in the town and cove was much simpler and easier than it was in New York. As Morgan gazed around her upscale apartment, a thought jumped into her head. Even though she had paid the outstanding bills for her grandfather, she still had money invested from her parent's estate that could keep her going for a while.

She walked into the bedroom and saw the bed was perfectly made up. Gareth hated an unmade bed and probably employed a cleaning company to come in and look after the place while she was away. There was not a thing out of place—no dust anywhere. She opened the closet and saw his clothes hanging one side and hers the other, nothing mingled. She walked through to their bathroom. He had his cabinet, and she had hers, nothing was out of place here.

As she looked she realized it wouldn't matter who the hell lived with Gareth in his apartment. It would never be any different. It would always look pristine. There was no real love and warmth wherever she looked. "I guess I must have been another collectable," she mumbled to herself, and swiftly, before she changed her mind, she got two more suitcases and threw in as much as she could from the closet and bathroom. She wrote a swift note goodbye not giving any reason just; "this is not the life for me anymore. Thank you for all you have given me. Have a good life."

Taking one last look around and seeing how neat everything was, she suddenly before she could change her mind, swept everything off Gareth's desk onto the floor. With a smile on her face, she quietly closed the door on her way out

She called a taxi cab and went outside with her cases. It wasn't long before the taxi arrived, and with one final look up at the building where she had lived for the last six years, she got into the cab and instructed the driver to take her to the airport.

Chapter 3

The engine had purred for some weeks now, and David had gotten back into the rhythm of his life. Dan, the owner of the boatyard, had stopped by several times asking David if he was after a new engine yet.

But David was more than happy to say to say, "No. The boat is doing just fine."

One night, as David and his crew headed out on the Crimson Tide, he saw the same woman who had served him in the local café all those weeks ago; she was sitting on the bluff overlooking the water. She had brought a chair with her, and she lazily watched the water as the tide went out. David was always busy on the Crimson Tide during departure from the cove, and when he turned back to look again, she had disappeared. He shrugged his shoulders and continued out over the Gulf for a good night's shrimping.

Following the 2010 oil spill, the shrimp were returning to the Gulf, and they were large and good to eat. David had no difficulty selling everything he could catch to the restaurants in Mobile. He wished he had two or three boats, and then maybe he could earn a decent profit and make the necessary repairs to the house and buy a new engine for the Crimson Tide. He was saving up, but as of yet, he was getting nowhere with his quest. His crew listened to David as he shouted out the orders for the night and directed them to take a slightly different path than the one of the previous night. None hesitated to carry out his orders—the instinct he had for fishing was beyond question. The crew had worked for his father for years and, although David was just a youngster to them, they didn't hesitate to do as he requested. They went further out in the Gulf than they had previously, but came back that night with the Crimson Tide laden with good shrimp. It was a profitable night for all of them.

They pulled ashore in the early dawn. David planned to follow his usual routine and go to the café for breakfast, but the sight of the woman on the bluff the night before made him change his mind; he had thought about her for most of the night. He went home, took a shower, set his alarm, and then strummed his guitar for a while in the sunroom before falling asleep. When he walked into the café that night, all conversation stopped as he made his way to the back booth where he had sat before. Again, one or two people acknowledged him as he walked past. He waited patiently for Morgan to appear, and as she walked over to the table, he smiled and said, "Good evening. What's good on the menu tonight?"

She had not forgotten this rude man, and so she tentatively smiled back and said, "There isn't anything on the menu that's not good."

Smiling back, he asked, "Have you tried the entire menu since I last saw you?"

"Not quite everything," Morgan replied.

"Well what do you recommend tonight?" David asked getting a little impatient. He was not used to small talk and had no idea how to talk to a member of the opposite sex.

"Stew's good." Morgan replied, noting the impatience in his voice.

"Then I'll have that. Thanks."

"Coffee?"

"Yes, sure." He looked down from the frank appraisal she seemed to be giving him.

She turned and walked away to place the order and was amazed to see that almost the entire café had been listening to their conversation. She grabbed the coffee pot and a mug and passed back through the café, stopping at a couple of tables to fill their cups. When she got to David's table, she set the cup down and started to pour.

"I saw you up on the bluff yesterday when I was going out in the shrimper. Do you often go up there?" David asked tentatively.

"I like to walk up there and think sometimes," she replied, trying to be noncommittal.

"I thought I was the only one to do that," David smiled back at her. "I'm David by the way. I live in the house that looks over the end of the bluff. It's a nice view over the water which has pretty sunsets most nights."

Morgan smiled back and asked, "Is there anything else I can get you while you wait for the stew?"

He shook his head and looked out of the window, disappointed she did not want to stay and talk. He turned back and watched as she walked away with her pretty red hair bouncing on her shoulders. Her green eyes were like a cat's, he thought. Then his mind turned back to the

Crimson Tide. He noted on the journey back last night, the engine began to splutter again, and he was concerned the engine would not last much longer. He figured he still didn't have enough money saved to pay for a new one, and he knew that Dan in the boat yard was not in a position to let him pay in installments. There was no guarantee that he would be able to make monthly payments anyway. "Fuck. Life has a way to piss you right off," he thought.

His thoughts were interrupted by Morgan placing a dish on the table in front of him. "Your stew," she said. "Would you like some bread with that? We have some really good French bread I could bring you." He nodded his head and she walked away and came back with it. She stood for a moment, before asking hesitantly, "You looked really upset just now. Is everything all right?"

"It would take too long to tell you right now all that's wrong with me and this town, but if you're really interested, I'll meet you up on the bluff one day and we'll walk and talk."

"Perhaps," she replied. She didn't really want to meet with this odd and gloomy man, even if he was attractive. She turned and walked away and attended other people and did not return to his table until it was time to give him his bill.

He quickly checked the amount and set some money on the table. "I'll be up on the bluff tomorrow morning around nine, if that's okay with you," he said as he got up.

She nodded her head, and replied "if I can find the time," and she busied herself with collecting his empty plates. When she looked up, he had left the café.

Morgan went home after she finished her shift. She wanted to ask her grandfather about David, but, unfortunately, he was asleep in bed. She sat down on the couch and slipped off her shoes, rubbing her sore feet. She never had sore feet at the museum even though she was often on them for hours at a time, but these shifts at the café were much harder.

She did not know why she did, but the next morning she got up at six thirty and took a shower. She did not particularly take care over her appearance—she didn't bother with make-up or drying her hair—but, nevertheless, when a man showed her some interest, her curiosity was piqued. She threw on a pair of shorts and a blouse, made her grandfather breakfast, and set out through the town toward the bluff. The tide was in, and the sun was shining, making the rippling water sparkle in the early morning light. April was one of her favorite times of the year—it never got too hot, nor was it too cold. Although it was only eight thirty, the sun was reaching up in the sky and warming everything up.

As she continued to walk, she saw a lone figure pacing on the bluff. The tail of his shirt was blowing in the breeze, and his hands were stuffed in his jeans pockets. He was barefoot. She smiled as she saw he had taken two chairs to the edge of the bluff and put them side by side. He was waiting for her.

She walked confidently over toward him as he stood stock still. She looked up into a pair of deep brown eyes that had crinkles around them from years of being in the sun. He stood at around six feet tall which somehow pleased her as she had to look up at him when he was standing. He had blonde streaked brown hair, which showed off his eyes. His body was wiry from years of fishing and pulling nets. He held his hand out toward her for her to shake and she noticed as she did his hands were strong and weathered. "Good morning," he said, wishing he had spent many more years practicing the social skills he so desperately felt he lacked at this moment.

"Hi," she said. "In case you've forgotten, my name is Morgan."

"No, I hadn't forgotten," he replied.

"Could we walk for a little way, David?" She asked. "It's such a beautiful day. Is it possible to get down to the beach from here?" She was thinking how nice it would be to walk on the sand without shoes.

He nodded his head and pointed to the path that ran from the bluff down to the beach. Then he led the way. He stayed a shoulder in front of her in case she slipped or fell. He remarked with pride to her, "As a boy, I walked this path many times scrabbling over the uneven pathway. Some of the people who stomped their feet through the grass and the earth making the pathway hard were my ancestors."

It took a while for them to meander down the path, and when they reached the beach, Morgan removed her shoes and headed for the water. "Wow!" she smiled, running back out of the oncoming wave. "That's cold! I thought the Gulf was always warm."

"You won't be able to go into it until around mid-May," he answered laughing at her retreat from the wave. "It takes a while for the sun to warm it up." They ambled along the beach with the sun beaming down on them warming their skin. "What bought you to this part of the world?" he asked after a lengthy silence.

"My grandfather. He's not particularly well and getting on in age, and so I gave up my work in New York to come down and look after him." She walked backward facing him so he could hear what she was saying.

"Who's your grandfather?" he asked knowing that he probably knew him. This town was small, and everyone knew everyone else.

"Paul Johnson. He used to be a fisherman, but not anymore. My grandmother died a short while ago."

David nodded his head and remarked, "Doesn't sound like the Paul I know. He's a very independent, hard-headed person. I think he'd rather cut his arm off than accept help."

"That's my grandfather," she acknowledged. "I came to stay with him and my memaw every summer for years. I guess it's my turn to do something for them now."

"I'm sure your grandpa could do with some financial help as indeed most of the fishing town could," David said as he stuffed his hands in his pockets as they continued walking. The water lapped around his ankles, but he seemed not to notice how cold it was.

He looked at her as the sun shone on her red curls, and he admired the freckles sprinkled across the bridge of her nose. He stood and watched as she tried to walk in the water again but just darted out of the way of a wave coming in on the beach. He thought how attractive she looked, but he did not know how to tell her.

Laughing, she walked over to him and asked, "So why did you stay in this town that, by your own admission, seems to be dying?"

"I'm a man of the Gulf. It's in my blood. It's all I know." He could see she was scrutinizing him, so he looked out over the water. "Look at it," he said taking his hand out of his pocket and waving it toward the view. "The Gulf has a mind of her own and allows no one to be her master. If anything, she allows you a short time to fish in her waters or cruise around her territory but she will smash you with all her might and take you under her waters and keep you there should you disregard her warnings. She is an impossible mistress." He smiled as he looked back at her, but when he saw the surprised look on her face, he blushed and remarked, "Not that I know anything about mistresses of course—just this one!"

Morgan was so easy to talk to, and David found he liked spending time with her. "I put some chairs up top if you'd like to sit," he remarked nodding his head to indicate the bluff.

"Okay. And when we're up there you can tell me why this town is dying on its feet, and I'll see if I can come up with some suggestions for getting it back to its former glory," she said with a smile as she struggled to walk up the steep incline. David turned and held out his hand and helped pull her up the worst parts. When they reached the top, he found he was reluctant to let her hand go. Unlike his, her hand was soft.

Morgan liked the feel of his strong hand holding hers. His hands were obviously working hands that had weathered over the years he had been on the water. She could see they were used to holding onto a wheel and directing a boat to the place he wanted it to go. She could envision his hands had spent years pulling in shrimping nets. At the top of the bluff's path, he let her go and she found she was disappointed. They made their way to the chairs he had placed there. Sitting side by side, he remarked, "If you are cold, we can go to the house and have coffee."

She shook her head and said, "I like to be outside. I'm shut up in Marylou's enough during the day and evening. I like fresh air, and it's a beautiful day today." They were quiet for a few moments, so she continued. "How come this town is slowly dying, and what makes you think it can't pull itself around without help?"

He looked sideways at her for a moment. He wanted to keep her by his side longer, so he began to talk. "This was once a good, healthy fishing town. It was usual for each fisherman to have several boats and they reeled in many good fish to eat. The shrimping has always been amazing. As more than one fisherman found, unless he had a fleet of boats going out, the competition became fierce among other boats further up the coast."

He could see she was interested in his tale so he continued. "We did not keep up with the times and open up warehouses like other fishermen did," he surmised. "They were keeping their fish on ice so they could pack them and distribute them all over the country, supplying supermarkets and open markets. The more we fell behind, the more our town began to die, little by little. Our youngsters preferred to go to college and left us and the town behind." He stared hard out at the Gulf but continued, "Even worse, we could not afford to insure our boats and if one was lost, we couldn't buy another."

"Then the oil spill happened. Who would have thought it could wipe out our town? But it almost did. We got further and further into debt and the more we were in debt, the higher the interest rates became. More and more fishermen went into bankruptcy—they lost their houses and everything they owned. Most of the fishermen received settlements, but it took a long time, and many of them did not get enough to stay in business. Many left to start life over again somewhere else. Marylou's has suffered from lack of business, and so has the boatyard, the supermarket, and so on. You get the general drift; the effect spiraled throughout the town. It has left us with mostly older people and few youngsters to follow in our footsteps. Oak Tree is a beautiful place. There are trees with moss hanging from them that give an eerie feeling in the fog, but they are like sentinels in the sun. The town is small, but a great place to bring up kids. We have a school, but even that is in danger of closing if we don't attract young families to live here." He turned and looked back at her. "The truth is the town needs to expand and instead, it is shrinking. Neither I nor anyone else has the answer to these problems. I'm sorry, you'll probably want to leave Oak Tree Town as quickly as possible now I've told you all that." He continued with a smile. "I hope you don't."

"It's all so sad," Morgan replied looking out over the Gulf. She shivered at the enormity of his tale and standing up, she said, "I would really like that coffee now if it's all right with you."

"Of course." he said standing up and holding his hand out for her to take. He did not let it go on the short walk to the cottage. Just outside the rear door to his cottage stood a beautiful golden dog.

"Oh!" Morgan gasped with surprise, you didn't tell me you had a dog, what's its name?" she bent down to pet the dog, who pulled away from her but didn't go far out of her reach.

"I call him Mutt. He's not my dog, but he turns up here every day at about this time to be fed. I usually give him some of what I eat and some water and he curls up under the house or somewhere, and goes to sleep, to return and do the same thing the next day. He's been doing that for a couple of years. No one knows where he comes from but he seems to have attached himself to me."

Morgan stood up and the dog looked expectantly at them. David looked down at the dog said, "I'll be back in a few minutes."

As they entered his home, a gasp of surprise came from her. "Oh, David, this is beautiful," she cried.

He smiled back at her. "It used to be. It was my father's house and his father before him but, it's just one more thing beginning to fall to pieces and I don't have the money to fix it. Just one more thing many of us can't afford." He busied himself putting on the coffee. "I've been doing all the talking. What about you, Morgan?"

She laughed at his question and said, "I will tell you more about my parents one day, but they were killed in a car accident. After that, I was the only person left to help my grandpa, so I moved in with him. There's not much more to tell. No I am not married, nor in a relationship I must say I'm not really after one either. But if it is a friend you're wanting, well, you have one here."

David was willing to accept anything at the moment, so he was happy to reply, "That's fine with me. I was married once a long time ago and thought I had a son, but it turned out she didn't love me at all and the boy wasn't mine." He looked down as he ladled the coffee into the machine. "Maybe one day someone will come along again. Who knows?"

They took the coffee into the sunroom and sat with the sun shining down on them, drinking coffee and happy to be at peace with one another until she looked at her watch and jumped out of the chair with an apology. "Oh, gosh, I'm so sorry! I was supposed to be at work five minutes ago. I'll have to run. Thank you so much. I had fun today. Perhaps I'll see you soon in Marylou's?"

David nodded his head as she dashed out the door and stood and watched as she all but ran across the bluff and into the town. He wished she had not gone, but it had been a good start today with Morgan, and he really liked how comfortable he felt talking to her. It had been so long since he had talked like that to anyone, he felt he had almost forgotten his social skills altogether, but he found it easy to say what was on his mind when he was with her. He sat in the sunroom and picked up his guitar and unconsciously strummed a love melody.

The tide was in, and he would be heading out on his boat before it went out again. He thought it would be too awkward to go into Marylou's for lunch and so he went to the refrigerator. He found enough meat to make a big sandwich and put it between two pieces of bread with tomato and cucumber. He sat out in the sunroom and ate slowly, thinking how quiet it seemed now. He saved half of the sandwich for the mutt outside. He could still smell the scent of her skin in the air and getting impatient with himself for being foolish, as quickly as he could he departed for the Crimson Tide.

Jumping on board, he saw his crew had turned up. "We'll leave early today as the tide is in and go beyond our usual fishing grounds," he told them. "We need a good catch again." They readied the ship to depart.

Ben mumbled with a grin as he passed David. "Nice scent boss, must be new it sure don't smell like no shrimp I ever smelt."

David just smiled.

As they left the harbor, David wondered if she was watching the Crimson Tide leave. He soon became a speck on the horizon as he passed his usual fishing grounds.

Little did David know that the mutt, after eating the half sandwich David had given him, crawled under his father's old red truck and settled down for the night to wait for David to return. He would have liked to jump on the shrimper with David, but he had never been invited. He would wait for his master to come home again.

The wind sprang up, battering David's boat, and the engine began to cough again. It had been a rough night, and the catch had been anything but plentiful. They all were tired. David had bought the Crimson Tide back nearer his usual fishing grounds, but still the catch eluded him. They had pulled the nets up time and time again to throw most of it back. How could this happen to him when he needed the money more than ever? He had told the crew to lower the nets once more and they would drag them in the hope they would get something. They cruised slowly, dragging the nets, when one net suddenly pulled down. The crew became excited thinking they had a big catch that side. The men struggled to pull the net in, but something was wrong –

it could not be lifted. It seemed to be wedged on something. No matter how many times they tried, the net would not come back up. As David and his crew leaned over the side to pull heartily on the net, the engine suddenly coughed and spluttered one last time and went silent.

"Fuck!" David shouted, and he kicked the anchor on the boat hurting his toe, causing him to cuss again. "What the fuck is going on?"

He went back to the wheelhouse but no matter how many times he tried he could not get the engine restarted. He smashed his fist into the steering wheel, which broke the skin, leaving him bleeding profusely, but did not dent the wheel. The crew had given up on getting the net in. They looked at David, and Ben, who was the eldest, dared to ask. "Should we cut the net loose, boss?"

David tried hard to hold his temper. After all, it was not the crew's fault this had happened, but he knew if he cut the net loose he would not be able to afford another. Besides, the engine could well have completely blown up now.

He shook his head at the crew and told them to leave it for now. "Drop anchor, guys," he said.

In the distance, he could see another boat coming back in from a night's fishing. As they neared he flashed his light at them, and then spoke to the captain on his marine radio. The boat pulled up and lay nearby. It was the Morning Star from the next fishing village. David asked their captain if he could take his crew back to shore. "It would be a kindness from you, if you could, Jack," he shouted, "Then I can stay here and see if I can get the engine to start in the morning."

Jack was only too happy to help. He knew how hard it was for the small fishing community. "I'll call back tomorrow," he said, "and make sure you're all right then, David."

"Thanks," David shouted as Jack bought his boat nearer and his crew hoped on board the vessel. The boat moved away, and David was left on his own. He went down to the small galley and took out a hidden bottle of whiskey. He went back out onto the deck and sat overlooking the water, swearing alternately at the Gulf and God. The emptier the bottle got, the angrier David got. "Why the fuck?...... Why?" he would scream into the wind. "The fucking net is caught on something that won't give it back to me.......... And now the fucking engine has given up on me. Why me God? What the fuck have I ever done to you?............ Fucking engine." He got up and paced up and down the deck. "I'll put a fucking hammer through it." He threw the empty bottle into the Gulf waters and, closing his eyes, he began to cuss the wind, before slipping down on the deck and falling asleep.

Chapter 4

David woke the next morning with a terrible hangover. He rubbed his head, stood up and put his finger in the air to find which way the wind was blowing. He went aft to take a leak, trying hard not to fall over the side. He looked around the mighty Gulf and could not see a single boat. He was all alone with his problems.

David kept diving equipment onboard in case repairs were needed under the boat. Reluctantly, he walked down into the cabin and reached for the bag. He sat on the bench seat, and pulled the items out one by one—the mask, the fins, snorkel, his weight belt regulator and gauges. He started dressing by putting his legs into the wetsuit one at a time and pulling it up, putting his arms through and zipping it up all the way to his neck. He picked up a pair of fins, the weight band, and regulators and he carried them all up to the deck.

On deck, he pulled on the net to ensure it was still stuck. It flapped a little in the breeze, but still did not move. He reattached the net to the mechanical winch, which he began to wind. Still, the net did not budge. "Bastard!" He shouted into the wind. The word just blew back at him, but still he continued to mutter and curse to himself.

He made his way forward to get the air tank. He fell over a rope, and cursed again. He got up and picked up the rope and made his way to the side of the boat. He attached the weight belt around his waist, tied the rope around the top of the belt and placed a long sharp knife in the belt. He put on his fins and made sure the tank of air was firmly on his back. He still had a bad head from the whiskey, and so he double-checked his procedures. Before putting on his mask, he drank two entire liter bottles of water. The he moved toward the back of the boat, which was the easiest place for him to enter the water. Feet first, in wide stride, he went into the Gulf. He surfaced, and taking his mask from his face; he rinsed it in the salty water. Then he spat into it and rubbed the spit around to prevent fogging. He put the mask back on and moved around the side of the boat. He grabbed the trapped net and began to make his way down under water. At first the water was clear and he saw dolphins playing near the shrimper, avoiding the net. Much to his surprise, they swam around and headed down in the water with him. David went hand over hand down the edge of the shrimp net until the rope around his waist suddenly pulled taught. He had not reached the bottom yet and the water was somewhat murky here. He debated with himself whether it would be wise or not to cut the rope. He had no idea if he could go much further down, or how much further down he had to go before reaching the place his shrimp net was caught. He could cut the rope and risk not finding his way back, or he could cut through it and find whatever was holding the net. Making a quick decision, David sliced through the rope and, holding onto the net, made his way further down, still surrounded by the school of dolphins that were chattering to each other.

Abruptly he came to the bottom of the Gulf and put his feet firmly down, sending up a cloud of sand that fogged the water. Eventually the sand resettled, and he pulled on the edge of the net but could not loosen it. He tugged again and again with no success. He did not want to cut the net, so his only other option was to find the spot where it was caught. He moved around the sandy bottom until he came across the top of what appeared to be a mast of a ship. The net had caught on the mast and had wrapped itself around it. If the mast was still attached to a ship, David surmised, this was the reason why he could not pull the net up. The ship would have to be buried underneath a ton of sand because he could not see much more of it. The dolphins swam over to the mast with him. He was used to dolphins but had never been surrounded by them before. They darted back and forth almost guiding him, he thought fancifully, to the mast.

He pulled out his knife and cut through the thinnest part of wood. It was soft and beginning to rot. He slipped the knife back into his belt, and with brutal strength, he grabbed the mast with both hands, and broke it. Almost immediately, his net began to go up toward the surface with a piece of mast still entangled. David tried to catch it, but could not. The dolphins once again surrounded him and encouraged him to go down to the bottom. They seemed as if they were not giving him a choice of where he could go. He could see

Some of the pod of Dolphins

something buried in the sand, and out of curiosity, he took out his knife again and began to dig as the dolphins swam around him.

His digging began to uncover a jar of some sort. Curious, David dug further down in the sand to see if he could remove the entire jar. It was firmly imbedded. David checked his air supply and saw the gauge was in the red zone which indicated he was in danger, and so once again he began to tug and dig until eventually the sand released its treasure. "Got it!" he yelled into his mask.

Tucking the jar firmly under his arm, he began his ascent to his ship as quickly as he could. As he began, his belt got caught in the jagged edges left on the mast of the shipwreck pulling him backward to the murky bottom. It also cut a large chunk out of his hand and he began to bleed profusely. With all the strength he could muster, he untangled himself from the mast and swam away from it. He looked up and pointed his body to the top of the water. He flapped his fins as hard as he could, and surrounded by the school of dolphins that occasionally pushed him with their snouts, he popped out of the water like a cork.

He hauled himself up on the deck, pushing the jar in front of him. He was completely out of air and wondered if he would get the bends from going down so far. David lay on the deck, trying to get his breath back. He was exhausted. He laid there for a full half an hour before he felt able to sit up.

He finally had the strength to examine the jar, and he wondered about the bones that encased it. He tried to get the top off of it, but found he still did not have the strength. Cussing because he could not open it, he stepped over to the manual winch and slowly wound the net aboard, cursing more, because it still had a part of the mast attached to it and he would have to carefully remove it. One thing achieved, even though he still had a mighty hangover. He searched the horizon but there were no other boats in sight. It was too early for the shrimpers to be out. Wondering, he walked into the wheel house and turned the key to start the engine and to his astonishment, it coughed and then started first time. David slowly limped back into the harbor at Dolphin's Cove. The school of dolphins escorted him.

As soon as he tied up the boat, David called Jack to let him know that he returned. "Don't worry about trying to find the Crimson Tide, I managed to limp home with her," he said. Thanks for rescuing my crew last night. It was a great thing to do, and I'm sure they were most grateful." David wished him good fishing for the night and put down the phone. The Crimson Tide had been bellowing black smoke again when he returned, and he knew there was another oil leak. There was nothing else for him to do but go home right now.

He picked up the heavy Mason jar and tucked it under his arm. Then he walked on to the pier and on up the hill to his house. No one else saw him and if they did, took no notice.

When he arrived at his house he put the jar into the sunroom, collapsed on the couch, and promptly fell asleep. He missed the tide that afternoon. His crew was surprised when they arrived on the pier prepared to go shrimping and found the Crimson Tide tied up—but no David. Mack tried the engine, but it did not start. Obviously, there would be no shrimping tonight.

David awoke around midnight, somewhat startled to find it dark outside. He never thought he would have slept for so long. He heard a light tapping on his front door, so he got up, ran a hand through his tousled hair, and went to the door.

"Morgan," he said as he opened the door wider for her to come in.

As she came through the door, the yellow mutt followed. She looked at David's somewhat flushed face and said, "I was concerned about you. I understand your boat broke down last night, and one of your nets was caught and that you stayed on the Crimson Tide overnight. The next I heard you had returned this morning, but I haven't seen you in Marylou's, and no one else has seen you all day. The Crimson Tide is still docked, so I came to see if you were all right as soon as my shift finished. Are you were coming down with the flu or something? You look a little flushed. Are you all right?"

David was first stunned that so many words came out of her mouth so quickly. That shifted to amazement that somebody cared enough to knock on his door at nearly midnight. His amazement turned to absolute awe when she started to ask if he was okay, and then it turned to amusement when she thought he looked a little flushed. "I've just woken up," he replied walking through to the kitchen and putting the kettle on. "I seem to have been asleep all day and part of the night. I had to dive down this morning to see if I could untangle my boat's net. I did it, but stayed down a little too long. I was worried I might get the bends, but instead I just seemed to have exhausted myself. What are you doing wandering around Dolphin's Cove at this time of night on your own?" he continued as he put some tea bags in mugs.

"Hmm," Morgan replied. "I didn't walk. I went into Mobile and bought myself a car this morning. Even I'm not brave enough to walk at night." She smiled at him as he put a mug of tea in front of her. "Thanks." She drank the wonderfully flavored brew, but after a moment she became impatient and she asked, "Well, are you going to tell me? What was the net caught on?"

"I'll do better than that," he laughed. "I'll show you. Bring your tea."

They walked out to the sunroom, followed by the mutt.

"The net was caught on a mast," he said as she raised her eyebrows in surprise.

"From a sunken ship?" she asked.

"I don't know." He answered. "Here's the piece of the mast it was caught on." He picked up what looked like a long piece of driftwood. "I have no idea whether the mast was attached to a ship or not, but I took the coordinates the old fashioned way. As my GPS was not working" He looked as her eyebrows rose up in the air obviously not understanding what the old fashioned way entailed. "It's called dead reckoning," he smiled as he continued, "and might not be totally arcuate, but should not far off. As my engine was dead, I wrote the coordinates down and will put them into the GPS on my shrimper later. Then I'll see if I can find any more of the ship on the bottom. I'll need to get more air tanks, as well. I only had one and it wasn't enough. Actually, if it hadn't been for the dolphins that escorted me down and stayed with me all the way up to the surface, I think I would have died. If it weren't for them, I certainly wouldn't have found this jar." He picked up the Mason jar from the table and held it out to her.

Morgan stared at the jar which was covered in barnacles and pieces of seaweed and what looked to be the bones of someone's hand. She sat down on the floor, and the mutt flopped down by her side. She gently touched the top of the jar and said, "There's a drawing on top of this lid. Have you seen it? Do you know what it means?" Her finger idly traced the pattern on the lid.

He sat down on the floor beside her and looked at the lid his net had been caught on. "I had no idea it was a pattern, maybe even like a map if you turn it around. Maybe it's from a pirate ship, and there's a map of treasure on the top, and we'll all be rich." He grinned at her at the turn of his thoughts, but was surprised to see how serious her face was.

"Really, David? I want to come and take some photos of this in the daylight. This is old and might contain something valuable or historic. Please don't open it yet. I want to find out more about it." She stood up abruptly. "I have to go," she said. She took her cup to the kitchen sink, walked to the front door, and shouted out, "I'll be back early in the morning. Don't open your treasure. Goodnight." And she shut the door behind her.

David was startled by her abrupt departure, much as he had been by her abrupt arrival. He continued to sit on the floor and stare at the jar. Indeed, something had been chiseled in the lid—but what? Deciding he was still tired, he went upstairs to his bed. He was asleep in seconds. The mutt, for the first time in years, fell asleep inside, away from all the elements and insects, curled up in an armchair in the sunroom.

Chapter 5

Morgan awoke early the following morning, and without bothering to brush her teeth or wash her face, she went straight down to her computer and booted it up. She found a website that gave her a list of thirty ships that were lost in the local area of the Gulf. She was still studying the list when her grandfather came into the room a couple of hours later.

"You're up early, Morgan," he muttered. "Is everything all right with you?"

She scratched her neck before acknowledging he was in the room and answering. "I'm looking for ships that went down in the Gulf some years ago." She sighed as she turned her computer off. She turned to him, said, "It's what I did at work. I had to research any project I was working on, and it would seem I have a project here to work on."

Paul looked at her with raised eyebrows as he asked, "What do you mean you have a project here?"

"Nothing, Grandpa. I found a small treasure on the beach yesterday when I was walking with David, so now I'm looking it up to see if it has any meaning," she replied quickly back tracking as she didn't know if David wanted anyone else to know of his find.

"You seeing that boy?" Paul grumbled.

"Depends on what you mean by seeing, Grandpa. He and I have become friends and we walked the beach yesterday while he told me what has happened to this town and why it is dying," she replied, trying to minimize any significance of her relationship with David.

"He's divorced, you know." Paul said. "He never stuck by the girl who had a baby by another man. Married her, and then left her. Not a good thing." Pausing he continued, "You put on any coffee yet?"

"No, Grandpa. I'll do so now," she replied walking out to the kitchen as Paul followed. "He seems a nice man to me," she said. "He's lonely though. Doesn't talk to many people and seems to like being on his own." She put the water and coffee into the pot and turned it on. He's talked to me a little, and I like him." Seeing the look on her grandfather's face she continued, "That's all, Grandpa. Nothing else."

"He wouldn't want to share his life with anyone else. He's been on his own far too long and he's become a solitary man. I'd leave him alone if I were you," he remarked before sitting on a stool and rustling the morning paper, thereby dismissing any further conversation with his granddaughter.

Drinking coffee and making breakfast, Morgan thought about David. She hoped that he had not opened the Mason jar. The pattern or map on the top was intriguing, and this morning she was determined to take photos. Morgan would have liked to have phoned him to make sure he had left the jar intact, but she didn't have a number. Hmm, she thought again. This town is so small. I guess the easiest way to contact someone is to simply knock on their door, like I did last night.

She set a plate down in front of Paul. He looked up from his paper and remarked, "You must be in a hurry, you sure the bacon is cooked?"

"Grandpa, you're being rude now. There really is no need for it. I have a long day at work today, so, yes, I am in a hurry. I'll leave you to eat your breakfast, and please make sure you put the dishes in the dishwasher when you're finished. I'll see you later. Bye, Grandpa."

Kissing him on top of his head, she grabbed her phone, camera, and laptop and walked out to her car. She was anxious to get to David's and drove as quickly as she safely could. She knocked impatiently on his door.

"Oh you're here," she said as David finally opened the door. "I hope you haven't touched that Mason jar."

"And good morning to you," he replied as he still held the open door in his hand. "Yes, I'm feeling much better today, thank you, and no, I have not touched the Mason jar." He closed the door and followed her quickly disappearing body into the sunroom. "Have you had breakfast? Coffee? Can I put some on for us?"

"Hmm, yes," Morgan replied as she undid her camera and put the jar into a better position and light to be photographed. She took no notice of David as she busied herself with getting the right shots of the jar to compare them to photos on the internet. The mutt stayed in his comfortable chair and just watched what she was doing.

David took that as a sign he was dismissed and went to the kitchen, and appeared a little later with toast and coffee, by which time Morgan had gotten her laptop out and was sitting on the floor with it. She was obviously frustrated as she could not connect to the internet. "Don't you have an internet connection here?" she asked as he thrust a cup of coffee into her hand.

"Nope, can't afford it," he replied.

"Well, just how the hell do you expect me to chase this if you don't have a server?" she sarcastically said to him. "God, you're so frustrating."

He waited for her temper to abate a little, and then explained to her, "The library has a server and you can use that any time you want. I don't have a computer either because, honestly, it wouldn't help me fish any."

She stared at David, realizing that the look on his face was David being honest. "Well I'll go to the library then," she replied closing her computer.

"Toast and coffee first," he replied pushing the toast at her. "Patience is a virtue—not one you seem to have been blessed with this morning. I haven't touched the jar, and I don't intend to for the time being. Now you can ask me if I had a good night last night."

Morgan wanted to laugh, but did not and politely asked, "Did you have a good night last night?"

"I began to, but some red haired woman came and knocked on my door somewhere around midnight to see if I was all right and woke me up from a very nice dream, and would you believe the same woman came knocking on my door very early this morning to see if I had woken up yet? Perhaps that woman should have a key so she can let herself in or out, if she is going to continually come around here."

Morgan was not sure how to take these remarks until she saw a small smile on his face. He was trying to be witty and so replied, "What a good idea! Perhaps you'd like me to move in while we try to solve this puzzle too. Do you have a spare bedroom, or would I have to share yours?" She smiled sweetly at him and pushing her point she continued, "I could sleep in the bed while you shrimp and you could sleep in a second shift while I work."

"And what would happen if neither of us are working?" David asked. "Would that mean we would be sharing the bed at the same time?" He was pleased to see that he bought a blush to her face.

Morgan looked down and replied in a mumble, "I don't know you well enough to consider such a thing." And looking up she continued, "I've just left a relationship and I'm not looking for another."

"So I gather," he grumbled.

"I need to get to the library," she said to break the tension. She snapped her laptop shut and got up to head for the door. She tried to pass by him, but there wasn't a lot of room, and they found themselves within inches of each other. He looked Morgan straight in the eyes, and put his hand on her arm to steady her as she appeared to be falling over her own feet. She pulled herself away from David's hand, but as she walked to her car, she could not get rid of the sexual tension that had risen between them in that moment.

Morgan sat at a table near the back of the library, trying to concentrate on the list of ships that had gone down in the last century, but David's face kept appearing in front of her eyes. She saw his brown eyes holding on to her green ones. She shook her head to try to get rid of the image, but instead she began to daydream until she heard a voice whisper in her ear, "Are you getting anywhere or just day dreaming, Morgan?"

How did he know? she wondered, before looking directly up into his beautiful brown eyes. He was leaning over her shoulder and his head was inches from hers. She sat as still as a mouse wondering if he was going to kiss her. He looked at her and then at her mouth before tracing the outline with his thumb. Abruptly he stood up and moved away from her, breaking the spell.

She shook her head slightly, disappointed that he hadn't kissed her and then reprimanding herself. She looked back up and said, "There are several ships that could have been carrying all sorts of treasures that went down, so I'm thinking I need to find out a little more about the carving in the lid. It's so unusual, and I do believe our answer is going to lie in deciphering that. I need to go back to New York to the museum where I worked. I think they would be helpful to me, and I can't do this over the phone. I wonder if MaryLou will allow me to have a week off from my job. I've only been there a few weeks. I guess she might fire me, but if I am to discover what this means, I need to go." She sighed as she shut her computer down and looked up at David.

"I don't think it will be worth losing your job over, Morgan," he said. "I appreciate what you're trying to do, but it's not as if we found any treasure, is it? It's probably all a big joke." He stood tall as she scraped her chair back and stood up.

"No, David. You're wrong. This could potentially be worth something. Just give me a week and I'll prove it to you."

He stared at her and suddenly said, "I can't use my boat because the engine has blown. I'll come with you. If MaryLou will let you go, we'll leave tomorrow." He looked at her, willing her to accept the proposition he put forward.

Hesitating, Morgan replied, "I have friends I can stay with in New York. I don't think they would like it if I took you with me, David. Couldn't you work on your boat while I'm away?"

"I could, but it would be pointless. The engine is dead, and I need a new one or a new boat—neither of which I can afford. I have enough money to pay for both of us to go to New York. I'd like us to go together. After all, it's my Mason jar." He stared hard at her trying to get her to accept his proposition. He had not thought about going to New York until she said she was going, and he just hoped that he would have enough money in his bank to cover all their expenses.

His stare never wavered. Finally, Morgan's did. She looked down at her shoes trying to find an excuse for David not to go, but couldn't think of anything. It was his find after all, and she could not take off and find out what is was against David's wishes. She looked back up to find he was still staring, and although she racked her brains as the seconds ticked by, she could not find an excuse. Eventually she said, "Well, I need to go and ask MaryLou first."

"I'll come with you," David said. He took her computer from her and grabbed her free hand. He walked slightly in front of her and led her with just a little propriety out of the door and along the pathway to Marylou's. As they walked he said, "I hope we can leave tomorrow. I've never been to New York, but I've seen it on television, and it looks as if it is enormous with so many buildings and streets. I guess I'll have to rely on you to guide me around and take us to some nice restaurants, if that's all right with you." He looked sharply at her to see if she objected.

Morgan was still struggling with trying to find an excuse to go to New York alone, but there he was, walking through the middle of town, holding her hand and looking for the entire world to see as if he was her other half. She did not mind that he had taken her hand—she really like the feel of her hand in his—but it set a precedent. She was also concerned because every time he came near her, she felt sexual tension between them, and she really did not need that at this time. Besides, if she went back to the museum, she undoubtedly would see Gareth, and how would she explain one man to the other? She had not told Gareth there was anyone else, because at the time she left, there wasn't. But there was no denying there was a sexual chemistry with David, and, furthermore, she felt David knew it too.

She was bought firmly back to the present when he asked, "You're just not listening to me rattling on are you, Morgan? Not replying to my comments is really annoying. Is this because you would rather I didn't go with you? Because honestly I would really like to go."

They stopped as they had reached Marylou's café, and David had let go of her hand. The disappointment was in his eyes as he stared without blinking at Morgan.

"I need to go and find out if I can go first," she replied rather than giving him a straight answer. "Wait here. I'll just be a moment."

She walked quickly into the café and found MaryLou. "Something's come up," she told her. "I need time off, MaryLou. Maybe a week? Would you mind? I promise when I get back I won't take any more time. It's important to me." She looked at MaryLou with pleading in her eyes.

"Just go. It's not as if we're that busy. When you return to Oak Tree Town, come and see me. I'll hire you again. You're a good waitress and patient with people like David who's lurking outside waiting to see if you can have the time off."

"Oh," Morgan said, "We just need to find some……."

MaryLou cut across her. "Ain't none of my business what you and he do. I don't want to know. But I'll tell you this, he's a good man. He deserves a bit of happiness. Tell David I'll see to the mutt that hangs around his house. I'll make sure he has fresh food and water while you're both away."

"Thanks. I'll make sure I tell him." Morgan replied as she made her way out of the café.

David smiled as she came back outside and said, "Well?"

"It's a go. MaryLou says she'll look after your mutt too. She's so nice," Morgan replied. "I just have to tell my grandpa I won't be here for a few days. If you don't mind, I'll do that by myself. Perhaps we could meet first thing in the morning. I'll pick you up in my car. I'll try to get a flight around midday so we can have breakfast first."

David left to go to the bank, and Morgan went back to the library so she could book the tickets on her credit card. She would hold David to his end of the bargain of paying for the tickets. She phoned her girlfriend Mary and told her she would be coming back for a week. Without any encouragement Mary offered to put her up for the week. Morgan replied. "I'm coming with a male friend—David. He and I are not sleeping together, so I think a hotel might be better for him at least. But if I don't stay in the same hotel, he won't easily find his way around. He's a small town fisherman. Can I let you know if I can't find a reasonable hotel?"

"Of course," Mary replied. "He must be handsome if he's just a lowly fisherman. Would I like him? Can I take your fisherman from you?"

Morgan knew Mary was just teasing, but she actually felt a little jealous at Mary's suggestions. She laughed with her longtime friend and replied, "If you can take him from me, you are totally welcome."

"Watch out, girlfriend. I might just try if he looks sunburned and muscled as well as handsome. Make sure I see the two of you. When are you coming to New York? Look forward to it. Gotta run, I have a date for tonight and he's at the door. Love you. Bye."

Morgan disconnected the call. Staring at it as she realized David was all the things that Mary had said. Years of shrimping had given him a great physique; his muscles rippled under his tee shirt. He was permanently tanned from spending so much time on the water, and, although he wasn't traditionally handsome, he was extremely pleasant to look at, with fabulous eyes that were quite mesmerizing. She shook her head trying to get the vision of him out of her head. She was in trouble, she realized—she was more than a little attracted to this man. It had been less than two months since she had walked out on Gareth and during their relationship she had never been attracted to anyone else. She had walked out because she was bored. She headed toward her car deep in thought, her head slightly bent, and did not see the person she slammed into—David.

"God, I'm sorry. I wasn't looking where I was going," she said automatically before she looked up into his eyes. Mesmerizing, she thought to herself. It was a good word to describe them. "I'm sorry what did you just say?" she asked embarrassed to be caught day dreaming again.

"I asked if you booked the tickets," David said, still looking down into her eyes.

"Yes, I did. We leave tomorrow at eleven-thirty. I can leave my car in the long-term lot. We really need to leave here at around nine-thirty."

David nodded his head and asked, "Is there anything else we need to do today, and how much do I owe you for the tickets?"

"No, there isn't anything," she replied loading her laptop into the passenger seat of her car. "You owe me $1,010.00 for the two. We have our return tickets booked for next week." She shut the passenger door and looked at him as he pulled out his billfold.

"Thanks for booking the tickets," he said as he paid her in cash. I'll see you tomorrow then— eight-thirty?"

He wanted so badly to lean in and kiss her, and, as the thought ran through his head, he found his body beginning to pull toward her. With determination he pulled back. They were on Main Street, after all. "Goodbye for now then. I'll see you in the morning for breakfast at Marylou's."

Taking a deep breath, Morgan replied with a smile, "Look forward to it." She walked around her car and got in the driver's side. Her hands shook slightly as she started up the engine and drove back home. She was not looking forward to the imminent conversation with her grandfather, but knew if she did not tell him where she was going and with whom, it would be a lot worse when she came home.

"Why David?" Paul asked, when she told him. "You hardly know the man, and you're off to New York for a week with him? I must say, Morgan, I hadn't pegged you to be going away with the strangest man here in the village. I know he's a good captain on his boat. There isn't one of his crew that wouldn't do anything for him. But you—you hardly know him. So why, Morgan?" he asked crossly.

"Grandpa," she wheedled. "We're just going to see if we can find any information on my little find. There's nothing David can do here until he gets a new engine in his boat. He was with me when I found my little treasure, so he's as interested as I am in seeing if there is value in it."

"What was this little treasure?" Paul asked becoming very suspicious as she had not shown him what it was.

"It's just a coin, Grandpa. Nothing special." Morgan replied.

"Well, where is it?" he asked.

"David has it at his house. I doubt it is worth anything, Grandpa, but who knows?" She smiled at him hoping he would drop the subject.

"Well, I think it's all wrong for you to be traipsing off to New York with a man you hardly know. Next you're be telling me you're sharing a hotel room with him," he grumbled.

"Absolutely not!" Morgan replied with a frown. "I won't be away long, Grandpa, and you tell me you're perfectly capable of looking after yourself. So what is really troubling you?"

"Nothing. Nothing at all," Paul replied gruffly. "I can manage for myself for a week or forever if that's what you want." And he walked out of the room, ending the discussion.

Chapter 6

Morgan was pleased when the plane landed in New York. She had seen David grip the armrest in the plane on take-off and landing. He had obviously been hesitant about flying but had said nothing to her about it. He had let out a loud sigh when they landed safely, and she smiled at this. They both raced from the plane and made their way out to collect their luggage, and then Morgan pointed David in the right direction so they would come out of the airport near the taxis. She raised her hand and one pulled up smartly by her side. David held the door for her before getting in himself. They were driven to a smaller hotel she named in the hope it would not be too expensive. It was off the main streets and this tended to bring the price down a little.

The taxi dropped them at the front door of the hotel, and David paid the driver. At the front desk, they found the hotel had only one double room left, and David, without asking her if it was okay, accepted the room. They were given a quote for a six-night stay and as David did not have a credit card, Morgan put the charge on hers.

A bellboy picked up their luggage and showed them to the room. David handed him ten dollars, and the bellboy discreetly left. Morgan looked at David and said, "This is highly inappropriate, David. I didn't think we were sharing a room. I'm going to phone my girlfriend Mary—she said I could stay with her for the week." She looked at him for a response, but he was busy looking out of the window.

"How did you ever manage to find your way around such a huge city?" he asked looking back at her. "I would never be able to find my way around. I can sleep on the floor or in a chair. No big deal. You can have the bed." He picked up his case and set it on the luggage rack and opened it.

Morgan felt wary of sharing a room with someone she felt such a sexual attraction to, but nodded her head at David realizing that in the long run, it would save time and money for both of them. She took out her phone and tapped Gareth's number. As always, he answered his phone without looking at the caller ID.

"Gareth Hunt," he said.

"Gareth, this is Morgan," she said hesitantly.

There was a few seconds of silence before he replied, "Morgan, how nice to hear from you. How are you?"

"I'm good, thank you. How are you?"

"Lonely, actually. Some young lady walked out on me with no explanation or anything—just a note to say goodbye. Would you know that person?"

"I'm sorry, Gareth. When I flew back from Oak Tree Town the last time, I stood in our living room, and I just knew I didn't belong there with you. I felt it in every bone of my body. I wanted a different life than the one we had. I want children and a home—not a pristine apartment. You promised me marriage and children, Gareth—and then never gave me either one."

"But we were so good together and enjoyed the lifestyle we lived. I thought you were happy, Morgan. Now you're telling me we were not? What happened?"

"Gareth, could we not do this over the phone? Could we meet and talk?" Morgan asked. "I'm in New York and I would be happy to have breakfast or lunch with you tomorrow. If possible, I also need your help at the museum."

"Then have dinner with me tonight," he replied.

"I can't, Gareth. I'm here with a friend from Dolphin's Cove, and we are trying to trace some history on a find he made."

"He? Your here with a male? Are you involved with a 'him' already? Because I won't help you if are."

Morgan's face was burning with embarrassment. "No I am not, Gareth. Could we please talk at a different time? I need to use the facilities the museum afforded me when I was working there. You could make that happen for me, Gareth. Will you? Please?"

The silence on the other end of the phone was deafening, so Morgan continued, "Please, Gareth? For old times' sake?"

"I guess, although I have to say I am not happy about helping you after the way you left me, but yes, I will, Morgan. Meet me at the employees' entrance tomorrow at nine thirty, and I'll make sure you have a visitor's pass. Or did you need two?"

"Yes please, Gareth. One for David Morris-James. Thank you. I promise we'll talk before I leave to go back to Oak Tree Town," she said, softening her voice. "Goodbye for now, and thanks again." They disconnected the phone.

David was leaning against the window watching Morgan. "Old boyfriend?" he asked. "Obviously none too happy you're back in New York with another man."

Still embarrassed, Morgan answered a little sharper than she meant to. "I am not here in New York with you, David. We are together trying to find out about a Mason jar. That's it. End of story."

"Really?" he asked, a smile on his face. "Then let's go out for dinner. I'm hungry." Slinging on his leather jacket, he preceded her out of the door. He called the elevator and took her hand when the doors opened. There were other people inside, so she said nothing.

David refused to eat the fish the restaurant offered on their menu, saying it wouldn't be fresh, and had spaghetti bolognaise instead. He had asked a lot of questions on the way to the little bistro a few blocks from their hotel. He had stared in the windows of boutiques on the way and could not believe the price of clothes. It had been years since he had treated himself to some nice clothes, but then again, he'd never had reason to buy any. He looked Morgan up and down. She had not changed out of the jeans she had been in all day and he speculated she dressed down because she knew that he had no fashionable clothes to wear.

His outfit didn't seem to make a difference in the restaurant. The food and service were both good. The clientele seemed to be mostly young professionals out for a night on the town. The men's voices were louder than the ladies', and with a smile on his face he commented, "MaryLou would throw them all out for being so noisy!"

Morgan had laughed at his remark but agreed with him. They enjoyed a leisurely glass of wine at the bar before returning to the hotel. Morgan pulled out the photos of the Mason jar and some papers, sat cross-legged on the bed, and spread everything out. She pointed to some photos for

David to look at. He found it awkward to stand peering over her shoulder, so he cleared a place on the bed to sit.

Morgan traced the outline of the pattern on the jar and remarked, "It must have some sort of meaning, David. It's a distinct pattern, and one I've never seen before. I'm hoping Gareth will have some idea. This is what he specializes in."

They poured over the photos and papers she had bought with her until she, full from dinner and drowsy from the wine, at last fell asleep where she was. David smiled as he watched her sleep. He got up and pulled a blanket out of the closet. He moved all the papers to the bedside table, and he removed Morgan's shoes. He turned off the light, and then taking off his own shoes he laid down on the other side of the bed. He pulled the blanket over them, and he too went to sleep.

Morgan woke up late and rolled over. She gasped when she realized David was on the bed with her. She looked down and saw they both had their clothes on, so with a sigh of relief, she jumped off the bed and ran to the bathroom. She locked the door and took a shower.

David had heard Morgan get up but kept his eyes shut. He waited until she went into the bathroom to get up, then he found some clean clothes for himself.

In a few minutes, she came out of the bathroom, brushing her wet hair. "Good morning," he said.

"Good morning," she replied. She nodded toward the bathroom. "It's all yours."

He went into the bathroom and took his shower. It wasn't until he was getting out, that he realized he had not brought his clean clothes in with him. He came out of the bathroom with just a towel wrapped around his waist.

Morgan was flustered. It was not that she was unused to seeing a naked man—she had seen Gareth many times like this—but he did not have the body that David had. On first glance, she had been tempted to walk over to David and lay her hands on his chest, and explore his body under the towel.

David saw Morgan's reaction and putting his head to one side looked at her with amusement, knowing what was probably running through her head.

Grabbing the materials they would need later at the museum, she took a deep breath and said rather embarrassedly, "I'll wait for you down in the lobby." And she made a hasty exit from the room.

David noted that Morgan had on a very nice pant suit and blouse. It irritated him that not only had she taken the time to pack nice clothes, but that she had dressed in them today to see Gareth. He put the jeans he was going to wear back into his suitcase and pulled out a pair of dress pants and shirt and grabbed his leather jacket.

Breakfast was a rushed affair in the hotel restaurant. David signed the tab as Morgan went out front and asked the doorman to hail a taxi. A taxi screeched to a halt in front of them, and she climbed in and gave the address of the museum while David got in the other side. The driver pulled away from the curb and joined the stream of traffic on the street. The taxi stopped and started, stopped and started as the meter ticked over. David sat clenching his hands, trying to take interest in what was around them, but began to feel car sick from the motion. Looking at Morgan he said, "Did you battle traffic every day when you lived here?"

"Yes. It was something I was just used to, you know?"

"No, Morgan, I don't. There is no way I could get used to all of this. I hate it already and I've only been here for the one day. How anybody can work in this confined space where traffic stops and starts, I do not know. It wouldn't be for me." David kept quiet the rest of the forty-five minute journey. He could have walked the distance in about the same time—and enjoyed it more.

They got out of the taxi a full thirty minutes before they were to meet Gareth, so David suggested they get some coffee at a small café across the street from the museum. Morgan sat at a table in the window, fidgeting and watching for Gareth to appear. David was unhappy that she seemed anxious to see him.

Morgan had no idea that the night before they left for New York, David had stared at the Mason jar for so long wondering what was in it, that in the end he picked it up and turned it around in his hand. The lid had a very jagged edge to it. He pushed his thumb under it and pushed hard, and the jagged edge stood up in the air. He peeked through the opening he made and saw something shiny. He turned the jar upside down and shook it. Some sand fell out, and then, much to his surprise, a small hermit crab. He shook again, and several coins tumbled out. The coins obviously were old. He had never seen any like them before. But in all honesty he thought to himself, they probably have no value either. They were shiny from being in salt water for so long. He had debated with himself whether to put the coins back in the jar or in his pocket. In the end he had put four in his pocket. Sitting in the café, he was now playing with the coins inside his jacket pocket, looping them continuously through his fingers.

Morgan suddenly grabbed her belongings and said, "There's Gareth now. He's looking for us, come on David. He won't hang around long." And she rushed out in front of him, crossing the street before David even left the café. He watched as she tentatively approached Gareth who pulled her into a big bear hug.

David crossed the street and the two men eyed each other. They were almost the same height, but Gareth was a few years younger than David. Gareth wore a business suit with a tie and had one of those cute little handkerchiefs in his breast pocket. He let Morgan go and turned toward David. Morgan introduced them and the two men shook hands. Neither one smiled in greeting.

"I have your visitor's pass here," Gareth said, handing it over to David. "It has to be worn at all times you are in the museum."

David was surprised at Gareth's accent. "Thank you," he said as he took the badge. "You're originally from England?" he asked.

"Yes, I was. I have been living out here in the States for ten years now. I got my master's degree in Stanford, having done my bachelor's degree in Oxford near London."

His accent was still perfect, and he used it to his advantage with the women, David thought as they walked through the museum's employee entrance.

Gareth smiled down at Morgan and asked, "What are you looking for here? Is it anything I can help you find? It would be fun working together again. I have to say, I have missed you both here and at home." He put his arm around her to guide her in to his office.

David rolled his eyes and followed them. He had no real reason to dislike this man, but somehow he felt uncomfortable around him. Maybe it was because Morgan had lived with him. He put that thought away in his mind to examine later. Morgan sat in one of the visitor's chairs, but David preferred to stand with his hands shoved in his pants pockets and his feet spread just slightly apart—a typical stance when standing on deck.

"Well. What is it that I can help you with?" Gareth asked Morgan sitting on the edge of his desk and smiling at her as if she was a grand prize, and totally ignoring David.

Morgan removed the photos from her purse and handed them over to Gareth. "I want to know what that drawing is and where it came from and how old it is." She looked up at Gareth as he quietly looked at the photos.

He gave them back with a very serious look on his face and inquired, "Where did you get these, Morgan?"

She didn't want to tell Gareth about the Mason jar, so she remained mute and raised her eyes to David. "I found the drawing on an old jar lid," David explained, "and Morgan thought it might hold some historical significance."

Both could see the excitement rising in Gareth's face as he suddenly stood up, "Follow me!" he commanded.

They walked through the back corridors of the museum until they reached a door that Gareth opened for both of them. They proceeded through to a display from the Civil War, ignoring most of it. Gareth stopped at a display bearing the words Knights of the Golden Circle. "Have you never seen this before, Morgan?"

"No. I didn't really specialize in the Civil War," she replied, somewhat surprised that she had never noticed this exhibit.

"Take your time and read all about this Circle and all that it entails. Call me when you have finished." He abruptly turned and walked away from them.

Walking back to his office, Gareth made some phone calls. Wow, he thought, this could potentially be the jackpot. If it was a Mason jar that was found, it could be worth millions by now. He wondered if they had the jar. If so, had they brought it with them? Or were they being cautious, leaving it at home? He would find out from them later. His plans were definitely going to change. He had hoped to take Morgan out for dinner tonight alone, but he changed his mind and would take both of them.

Knights of the Golden Circle
Poster

Chapter 7

October 1864

The horse's hooves thundered through the dark night, the rider urging his mount to go faster. The rider was fully aware that at any time he could ride into a camp of his enemies. He knew if he was caught, it would be certain death. He whispered to his horse to fly faster with the promise of oats when he arrived. His horse knew the path they flew along well, and, at his master's urging, tried his best to gallop faster. His hooves and heart pounding, the faithful horse kept going.

Horse and rider came to a halt a short time later by a large hunting cabin built in the forest some years earlier. Tonight a meeting was to take place, and prominent people were expected, including the rider. The rider threw himself from his horse but taking the reins, gently led him around to the stables where a handler was waiting to take the horse and rub him down. The rider said, "Rub him down well and give him extra oats. We have travelled far today, and he has not let me down." He kissed the sweaty horse's neck and ran his hands down his quivering flank before abruptly turning and striding away to the cabin.

He was recognized immediately as he walked through the door, but in case he was not, he stood tall and placed his right heel in the arch of his left foot. He crossed his right arm over his left arm and tucked his right hand underneath.

He crossed his left hand over his right arm and put four fingers onto the arm. Immediately everyone in the room stood and did the same. Only then did greetings break out.

"General Lee, it's good to see you! You must be thirsty after such a long ride. Have a keg."

"Thank you, Jesse," he replied, taking the tankard and taking a long quaff of his brew. "That feels much better." He removed his coat and threw it over a bench before backing up to the fire to warm his nether regions. "It's a dastardly night out there tonight with all the rain pouring down," he said to no one in particular as he continued to drink his ale. "I came damned close to going into some enemy camps this night, but my blessed stallion never let me down. Are we all here, or are we waiting for more?"

It was George Bickley who replied, "No, you were the last as expected because you had the furthest to come. We can start the meeting as soon as you are ready."

General Lee finished his keg and looked around the lodge. There was not much light except for that thrown out by candles strategically placed so they wouldn't start a fire. The candlelight gave an aura of secrecy as shadows were cast into the corners. The first person here would have checked to make sure no one was lurking in the shadows to overhear this meeting tonight. A circle of chairs had been placed in the center of the room. He placed his keg on the bar and joined the others.

They sat down, and George Bickley, being the founding member of the Knights of the Golden Circle, opened the meeting with calls for their dues. Each member gave forth whatever they had in their pockets. Buckner Stith Morris collected the coins. He counted the coins and said, "This is to be buried along with the other treasure we have collected and raised so far. But there is much news to be discussed tonight."

John Wilkes Booth stood up and looking around at all the faces told them, "Our mission was originally to make Northern Mexico, Cuba and the West Indies into slave states, dividing the area into twenty-five separate states. Our objective was to make the aristocracy of slave owners the wealthiest, and therefore the most powerful, influence in this country. I am sad to say.....we have failed in our mission." He waited while people murmured among themselves at the news. When it had quieted again, he continued. "The south will surrender soon, but all is not lost. The flickering of candles cast ominous shadows across the group. He pointed his finger at the men one by one as his voice rose. "The money we have raised and buried will remain where it is. We still have friends in the Northern states—Ohio, Illinois, and Missouri—who still are against the Civil War. They would like to see the South remain as it was—with slavery intact. We will therefore continue to raise as much money as possible within the Knights of the Golden Circle and we will finance a second Civil War." One candle sputtered and went out.

There was silence for a moment as the men absorbed what Booth had said. Then, suddenly, there were calls of "Aye, Aye." "You're right then, John." "It's what we'll do; we'll have another Civil War."

Robert E. Lee stood up and remarked, "Another war would be fine by me. However, with all that's happened to our troops—so many of our young boys dead and dying—I wonder how quickly we will be able to find us an army to fight again. We've lost so many. We have no supplies or food. No horses. No morale among the rank and file. How quickly are you talking of a second Civil War? And will it be possible?"

Franklin Pierce rose to speak. "We know how badly the South has suffered. It will take a few years before we are able to finance a new war. By that time, we should rightfully have enough young men grown big enough, and willing and able to fight for the South."

A murmur of assent went around the group but General Lee sat down, not entirely convinced this was possible. After all, he was the one still fighting the Northern armies.

"I have another piece of bad news," Buckner Stith Morris said, "but as it was Sam Houston that bought it to my attention, I'll let him tell you."

Sam stood slowly. "As you know," he started slowly, the candle light flickering shadows across his face, "Our friend Asbury Harpending and other California members of the castle in San Francisco outfitted the schooner Jim Chapman as a confederate privateer. It was to run in the Pacific and raid boats for gold, silver and jewels to add to our growing collection. Word came to me a short while ago, the night he was due to leave harbor that all were arrested, and the schooner has been seized. Asbury was killed immediately. Through friends in San Francisco, I have found the source of the rat who squealed on them before they left, and he and all of his family—mother, father, wife, daughter, and two sons—were murdered. There's no one left in the family to tell more tales. The schooner had potential to raise more funds for our cause. Our thoughts go out to all of those in our castle there that were captured." He sat down and a silence fell over the group while they thought of those that had died and been captured. This was part of their law. If anyone so much as mentioned the possibility of their existence, they and their families were disposed of. Life came cheaply.

Lambdin P. Milligan was the next to speak. He rose slowly. "I have no real news to tell any of you. I keep on with publicly ridiculing our Indiana Governor, Oliver P. Morton. I know I have difficulty moving around as freely as I did before, as I am being looked at with great suspicion. I continue to harbor any so-called rebels who come into my state, and I make sure they get out safely. This is the only way we will make the South grand again—by helping those who need us and by raising as much money as we can. I personally have ensured that as much as a million dollars has been buried these past two years. But it's going to take a lot more than that—we must continue to raise as much as possible."

He sat down to murmurs of, "Congratulations!" and "Well done!"

Buckner Morris rose again and said, "As a former mayor of Chicago, I am continuing to try to free prisoners from Camp Douglas. There are so many of our men from the South held there, and I do my best to ensure they are well looked after, although that tests my patience as much as it does the prisoners'. I also try extremely hard to get them released and of course, when any escape, I am only too happy to harbor them."

General Robert E. Lee rose to speak. "The war is not going as we hoped," he said as he looked around. "Morale is at its lowest and so many injuries have been sustained. But as I have ridden around, I too have managed to raise a lot of money for our cause. I even started two castles in Virginia and Texas and one in Alabama. Hopefully the money raised will be wisely spent by this council."

He sat down again to silence. Everyone knew it would not be long before the South surrendered but they did not want to hear about it yet.

The last in this group to speak was Jesse James. "I am honored to be a part of this group. In Ohio I am wanted as a common criminal. No one knows why my brother and I ride and rob trains and banks that hold Union gold. We don't keep the stolen money. We can live on the money we make from our farms. We bury most of the stolen money for the Knights of the Golden Circle. We ride with a bounty hanging over our heads, but we feel it is worth the risk. When we finance a second Civil War, my brother and I would love to move here and enjoy all the South has to offer, including slavery." He sat down to murmurs of, "Well done," "You do well for us, boy," and "You will not be forgotten; we will make sure of it."

Buckner Stith Morris rose to speak again. "For many years we discussed the possibility of assassinating Abraham Lincoln if he was elected president. Well, he has been elected and has been sitting in office for a few years now, and we haven't done a thing about it. It is time we did. This is not a mission I would give to just anyone. It should be one of us. I don't think this plan should be broadcast to all out castles. We need to discuss this tonight. It is becoming urgent. We need a volunteer."

He sat down to silence as everyone stared at him. It had been suggested many times before that President Lincoln should be disposed of, but no one had thought they would be able to carry it out. It would help their cause in the long run if the anti-slavery president was assassinated.

General Robert E. Lee was the first to speak out. "I would have been happy to carry this out for the castle here, but I am kept at war and not available for carrying out such an act. Besides which, I could be killed on the battle field at any time."

Other heads nodded in agreement with him and Jesse James added, "You're more valuable to our cause on the battle field, General Lee. What good would it be for our cause if you were caught and were rotting in jail? I myself would volunteer, but having said that, I am so well known that I doubt whether I would get anywhere near President Lincoln."

No one else spoke for a while and people lit and puffed on their cobs while they were thinking.

It was John Wilkes Booth who finally looked up and said, "It would take me a while to prepare for the assassination, but I think maybe I could get close enough to assassinate President Lincoln. Perhaps before I try, I could spend some time with Texas Ranger Ben McCullock who I believe to be an excellent marksman. I could ride to Texas and spend time with him and come back a better shot, maybe good enough to hit the target. I have the time and the money. McCullock is a part of a castle in Texas, and I have met him a couple of times. Is there anyone here with a better idea or who would want to take my place volunteering for this mission?"

One by one the members of the castle shook their heads. Booth was known to keep his word and they had no doubt whatsoever that if he promised to do something, sooner or later it would be carried out. It was decided upon then. John Wilkes Booth would assassinate the President of the United States for the South and for liberty.

When the meeting was over, the members stood up and showed their mark of trust by repeating their mantra: "For the South, liberty, and slavery. For our brothers who have died for our cause, and for those that still fight for it. May we succeed. We are the Knights of the Golden Circle."

The noise rose as friends greeted each other and tankards of beer were enjoyed along with full pipes. As the smoke rose toward the ceiling and voices became animated, one lone voice from Lambdin Milligan was heard to ask, "Why did Buckner ever start this movement? I thought he was from Chicago."

Buckner Stith Morris heard the question and turned with a smile on his face to Milligan. "Good question to ask, Lambdin. You have obviously not heard that my first wife was born and raised in Kentucky. Evalina was a full blown southern lady and I became her dedicated follower. We moved to Chicago for my career—not because either one or the other of us liked the place—we didn't. My career has kept me there, which was unfortunate in some ways, but very fortunate in others. Unfortunate, because we both loved the South with all our hearts. We enjoyed a very pleasant and peaceful way of life and embraced everything Southern. Fortunate though, because as Mayor of Chicago, one of the busiest cities I was kept in the loop politically. My wife and I were wealthy back then, and we concentrated on finding people like ourselves and encouraging them to fight for the South as it had been. We knew if we could expand slavery to Mexico and the other continents we would become fabulously wealthy. President Lincoln would never have been voted into office, and, basically, we would have ruled the world. Now our treasures are buried, my first wife is dead, and it would seem as if our goal has to be changed. All of us here want what I want, and if they didn't, they too would be assassinated as they know too much!"

Raucous laughter filled the room. Over the years, they had learned enough about Buckner to know he was not joking—as the rat in San Francisco had found out. It was not just he who was killed for his betrayal, but his entire family. Such retribution kept the castles intact and secretive. The evening wore on, and one by one as the candles flickered and died, the Knights left the lodge as they had arrived—alone. Only one carried the money collected which was to be placed in sealed Mason jars and distributed for burying.

Chapter 8

Morgan had specialized in genealogy, which is why she had no idea at all about the Civil War and coins and drawings dating for that era. Therefore, she grew increasingly excited as she and David stood in front of the exhibit and looked at the items on display—old clothing, coins that had already been retrieved, and documents about the Knights of The Golden Circle. The Knights had buried so much treasure, starting when the first group, called a castle, was formed by Buckner Stith Morris in 1854. It seemed he had been a Mayor for Chicago before the Civil War. He had been forewarned of the impending war and disagreed with it. His first wife was from Kentucky, and they had lived the simple, expensive and elegant life of the South before the war with black slaves picking their cotton and looking after their well-bred horses. They had enjoyed their time with her extremely rich family, and planned to return to the South when Buckner was near retirement age and continue with their privileged life.

Morgan stood and admired the dresses from that era and almost jumped with surprise when she first saw a drawing that almost exactly matched a photo of the drawing she had bought with her. David was on the other side of one of the glass cases in the exhibit, and she ran to him, grabbed his hand, and pulled him with her to the drawing. Her face radiated excitement as first she looked at the exhibit and then at David. "That's it!" she cried looking at him. "You've found treasure!"

David put his finger to his lips and shushed her. Morgan did not understand why he was trying to silence her. She searched his face thinking he would have been pleased at her discovery, but far from it. He seemed somewhat angry.

She opened her mouth to say something to him, but instead he placed his lips on hers—kissing her as if his life depended on it, pulling her hard into his arms. She had not seen Gareth skulking around trying to hear what they had been talking about. David had seen him and did not trust him.

He eventually let her go. She stood looking up at him wondering why he had kissed her, but there was no answer written on his face. He was looking beyond her over her shoulder. "David......?" she asked tentatively.

Eventually, he looked at her. "Let's go to lunch, now," he said. He grabbed hold of her hand and began to pull her away from the exhibit while she protested. "I haven't seen enough of the exhibit yet, David. Why can't we stay?"

He didn't answer her but just continued walking, following the exit signs. He was almost free and clear when Gareth emerged suddenly in front of them, blocking their path. "Are you going to lunch?" he asked, "Because if you are, I'd really like to join you, and we can talk about what you've seen at the exhibit this morning."

Morgan opened her mouth to reply but David stepped in. "Could we possibly meet tonight? We can talk then, but Morgan and I have some very urgent business to attend to right now. How about the little boutique restaurant we visited last night? The food was good. Morgan will make us a reservation there for eight if that's okay. She'll call you and let you know later. Thanks for this morning." Taking Morgan's hand firmly in his again he walked out of the museum and hailed a taxi. He opened the door and shoved her inside before getting in himself.

Morgan spluttered in anger at David. "What the hell....? What happened, David?" she tried again in a minutely quieter voice.

"Don't start........"

The cab driver came across the two angry voices and asked, "Where to, Miss?"

She gave him the name of the hotel and turned in her seat so that her back was towards David. She folded her arms across her chest and maintained silence through the rest of their journey. This pleased David as he was able to form his thoughts into good arguments.

When the taxi pulled up at the hotel, Morgan stormed out, leaving David to pay. He threw a bill at the taxi driver and chased her through the lobby, just managing to catch the elevator doors before they closed behind her. They went up to their room in silence.

Inside their room, she exploded. "How dare you, David! Why did you make such a fool of us both? Gareth has done nothing but try to help us, yet you were rude and evasive. What the hell is going on and why did you kiss me?" she finished, standing in the middle of the room, hands on her hips, looking as fierce as he had ever seen her.

He wanted to laugh at the posture she had assumed but instead he asked, "Can we change the tickets and go home earlier?"

"What....?"

"I want us both to go home. Can we change the flight?"

"I don't understand, David," she said, her shoulders looking as if she were weightlifting and her back ramrod straight.

"I think Gareth is going to try to cheat us of the value of anything we have found. He disappeared from the exhibit and did not return for some time, and when he did return, he was trying to overhear our conversation."

"Perhaps he was jealous of you," she shouted back to David, "Although I have no idea why."

"That wasn't it at all," replied David, turning and walking to the window. He stuck his hands in his pockets and looked out at the city. "I have a gut feeling about him. He was up to something, and he came back to see if we were excited about the drawing, but he was watching us from the shadows." He turned and looked at her and saw some of the fight go out of her shoulders. "I don't want him to know we have a Mason jar full of coins."

Morgan jumped in. "How did you know it was full of coins? Did you open it, David?" She walked over to him and studied his face.

He put his hand in his pocket and pulled out one of coins he had taken out of the jar. "I pushed the ragged piece up on the lid and shook the bottle as I saw something shiny in there. This is one of the coins." He handed it over to her and continued. "It's gold, Morgan, and from what I saw this morning in the exhibit, it may be worth a lot of money—just this one coin. I have no idea how many more are in that jar, or if there are any more jars on the shipwreck. We need to do a lot more research before I could declare this find, but one thing I am certain of, I don't want to share this with Gareth."

Morgan looked at the coin and then at David trying to contain the excitement she felt. "Did you realize if you sold this, David, the money could help you repair your boat? If there are lots more, you could order a new one."

"I think you're getting too excited over this, Morgan," he said holding his hand out for the coin. "We need to do much more research before I'm confident that I've made some sort of find. My problem right now is that you've shown those photos to Gareth long before I wanted you to. Is it possible to look all this stuff up on line if we go home?"

Morgan looked at David. She was disappointed that he was not interested in staying in New York.

She tried to choose her words carefully and replied, "Gareth would be able to authenticate your coin and obviously we could sell this one if you would like. I could make up a story of half-truths, half lies and tell him I'm selling the coin for my grandfather from his collection because he needs the money to cover my grandmother's hospital bills."

David sat down on the chair looping the coin through his fingers, wondering if this was such a good idea. He tried, but could not come up with anything different. "Okay, we'll go with that idea tonight and see what happens." He replied on a sigh. "Call the restaurant and make a reservation for tonight at eight, and then phone Gareth and confirm that's what we'll do."

Morgan did both, and then looked at David and said, "I could go and visit with my girlfriend, Mary, which would get me out of your hair for a while. It seems as if we're not very happy in each other's company today."

"Just because we don't agree with everything doesn't mean we've fallen out with one another," he retorted. "Are you still in love with Gareth?" he asked abruptly.

"No, of course not!" she bit back, and then she started to laugh and continued, "Actually, I thought he was a bit stuffy today and extremely condescending to us both. I'll have to remember to tell him that tonight." She remained quiet for a moment and sat on the edge of the bed. Feeling that David was not going to say anything else, she reached for her computer and idly typed David's name in for a Google search.

This is what she had done for years—researching other people's family trees. Morgan had never tried to trace her own family history; somehow she didn't feel it was right while she still had a family member alive. But David would be a different kettle of fish, she thought. The search would keep her occupied if they were not going to be spending the time at the museum. She noted he put his feet up and had his eyes closed as if he was going to sleep. She hit Enter after David's name and address, and his family history began to appear. She found his mother and father and grandparents both maternal and paternal. She chose to follow the maternal side of the family first. The wives had come from Oak Tree Town, as had David's father and grandfather. All the men had been fishermen, and all the wives were daughters of fishermen. It was no wonder it was so finely ingrained into his blood, she thought. Now the site she was using required payment to continue. She took out her credit card and continued. She was interested in finding out if she could get anything at all that could potentially interest David. She knew he didn't care particularly where he had come from, only telling her his father and grandfather had been fisherman, but his great grandfather on his mother's side came from Ohio. He had been a farmer. His wife had come from a farming family in Alabama and they had moved near Birmingham. The grandfather's name was Henry James.

It takes a great deal of time to trace a family back accurately and she had already been working on this for three hours when David woke up and asked, "What are you doing?"

"Nothing much. Just wasting time," she replied quickly, shutting her computer off. They both got ready for the evening ahead, David far more quickly than Morgan, who took over the bathroom to do her makeup and dress. When she came out, David looked at her with admiration in his eyes, and putting his head to one side, he said, "Green suits you. You look really pretty."

Morgan had not blushed for years but found herself coloring up immensely and quietly said, "Thank you." "David was not looking bad either," she thought. He had put on khaki pants, with a dark brown shirt and his brown leather jacket was waiting on the arm of the chair. His muscles bunched beneath his shirt, his stomach was flat, and his arms were in perfect proportion to the rest of his body. She found herself wondering what it would be like to be held in those arms, to be comforted, and to be loved.

David roused her from her musings to ask, "Is there something wrong, Morgan? You have a strange look on your face."

She shook her head and glanced up in his eyes to see the amusement that was there. He walked a little closer and said, "If you're not thinking of Gareth, then it has to be me."

Morgan did not say a word. David closed the space between them and put his arms around her, and looking into her tawny green eyes to see if she would object, he slowly lowered his mouth and locked his lips on hers. He slowly deepened the kiss, not letting her go. Her arms closed around him, feeling his biceps and shoulder muscles bunch under her hands. Why did she feel as if she had come home? She wondered, and then she lost herself completely in the kiss, her heart pounding, her nerve ends tingling. She wanted him with every fiber of her being.

David pulled back a little and she immediately felt as if he was pushing her away. Morgan wanted to be back where she had felt at home. "We have to meet Gareth," he said. "If we continue this, we won't be dining anywhere tonight, except on each other in bed."

Morgan knew he was right but somehow she still felt somewhat rejected. David could see her reaction written on her face and quietly said, "It's five minutes past eight, Morgan. We really need to go. If you don't want to dine out, call Gareth and cancel."

She hesitated for a couple of seconds. David was surprised that she was wavering, but on a huge sigh, she took her lipstick out of her purse and repaired her lips and nodding said, "I'm ready to go."

David picked up his coat and threw it over his arm. He grabbed her hand, headed out the door, and took the elevator down. The taxi drive took only fifteen minutes. Nevertheless Gareth was in the bar and seemed angry they had kept him waiting.

He gave Morgan a big bear hug for the second time that day, and she tried hard to push him away. But Gareth clung on and she suspected he had more than one drink while waiting for them. He called the waiter over and asked David what he would like to drink. David ordered straight scotch and Gareth ordered a vodka and tonic for Morgan without asking. She looked down at her hands feeling very uncomfortable but she had to get over that. They needed his expertise. She accepted the drink with a smile. "You look beautiful as always," he remarked. "Green always was your color. Have you colored your hair? It looks a little different from before. Maybe some blond highlights?"

She shook her head, "It's from the sun and the Gulf in Dolphin's Cove. It's so beautiful there." She continued with small talk about Dolphin's Cove until their table was ready.

As they sat, Gareth asked, "Have you tried the new pasta dish they're serving here, Morgan? You would absolutely love it. I know you would. I'll order it for you. What do you think you would like, David?"

David's fist was closed under the table, and he would have liked to have put it in Gareth's face right then, but he replied, "I'll have a steak."

Gareth said, "The shrimp here is wonderful, straight out of the Gulf waters. I'm surprised you're not choosing a shrimp dish." He shrugged while smiling. Condescending in manner, David thought. Gareth again called the waiter over and ordered for everyone. He perused the wine menu and chose two bottles of wine to go with the meal.

David was getting angrier by the moment and really wished he had not come. He tried hard not to participate in the conversation because he didn't want to talk to this man. He was therefore somewhat surprised to find Morgan's hand reach for his under the table. She slipped her hand into his and left it there.

Gareth had finished making his impression on the waiter, and he settled down a little and asked, "Has either of you learned anything by seeing the exhibit this morning?"

Morgan jumped in saying, "I was amazed to see so much from the Civil War. There were two things that interested me," she continued. "One was the Mason jar that had the map engraved into the lid. The other was the gold coin we saw."

Gareth looked hard at her and asked, "Why would any of that be of interest to you, Morgan? Have you got some jars or coins?" He picked up his wine and began to drink, and looked at her over the rim of the glass. His eyes had greed and avarice in them, which concerned David. As their meals had arrived, Morgan had let go of his hand so she could use her knife and fork. There was no way to pull her back from the story she had obviously concocted and wanted to get out into the open.

"Actually," she said putting down her knife and fork and looking at Gareth. "When my grandmother died, I found my grandfather had no money to pay the bills. I paid for her funeral, but recently he has had her hospital bills in the mail. I had no idea he was so poor, and he cannot pay them. He asked if I would bring a coin out of his collection and see if it was worth anything." She picked up her wine glass and took a sip before picking up her knife and fork again.

David continued to eat his steak, saying nothing. Gareth asked, "Have you got the coin, Morgan?"

It was David who replied, "I've got it. It's here." And he took one out of his pocket.

"It's the only one?" Gareth asked.

"Oh no, I think Grandfather has several." Morgan replied. "Obviously if he has to, he will sell as many as needed to pay the hospital bills. It seems the sensible thing to do."

Gareth nodded his head as he stared at the coin. "What of the picture of the engraving?"

It was David who jumped in to say, "One of my crew on my shrimper pulled it in with the shrimping net one night. No one has any idea what part of the Gulf it came from. It was just there along with our catch. He was going to throw it back into the Gulf, but I took it from him because I thought it might amuse Morgan. She likes strange objects."

"Well, obviously," Gareth replied dryly, looking David up and down. He sighed and looked back at Morgan. "I can give you a price that the museum will offer you for this coin tomorrow. I can't be any help without the Mason jar and the lid that went on it. If you didn't pull any of those in with your shrimping net, then I guess it really has no value on its own, especially if you have no idea what part of the Gulf it was found in."

David smiled and replied, "No idea at all. My crew member found it as we were cleaning the boat up after we docked. But I'll make sure to tell them to look a little more carefully in the future, although it's a bit difficult when you have nets full of shrimp."

Gareth gave David a frustrated look and asked Morgan, "How is your grandfather doing? Is he managing okay? I expect he could really do without you now couldn't he, Morgan? Are you ever going to come back here to New York? It must drive you crazy being in such a small town."

Morgan took a deep breath and replied, "My grandfather never really needed me, Gareth. I chose to go and live with him because I love the life there. I visited every summer as a child until I was eighteen. I wanted to go back and stay. Grandfather really was an excuse. He's not in wonderful health, but seems to be okay thank you. And no, I am never coming back to New York. If you gentlemen would excuse me, I'm going to the rest room." Pushing her chair back, she rose and left the table.

Gareth looked at David and remarked, "I guess that's your influence that Morgan won't come back to New York."

David shrugged his shoulders and replied, "I don't hold any sway over her decisions. Morgan is her own woman. She does as she pleases."

"Well," Gareth continued, "I guess you must be sleeping with our girl then?" David was getting more and angry with the line of questioning about Morgan.

"I don't see how that can be any of your business," he replied. His grip on his wine glass snapped the stem and the glass cut his hand a little.

"It is my business. I lived with her for six years, and I still love her."

David dabbed at the cut on his hand with his napkin, ignoring the last remark from Gareth, when he heard a voice say. "Please let me pass." It was Morgan, and, as he turned to look, he saw three guys at the bar forming a half ring around her stopping her from moving. Again she asked, "Please let me pass through."

"'Course, sweetheart," one of the men said and stepped back for Morgan to walk through. As she did, one of the men grabbed her butt, and another grabbed her breast. Before she could even scream, David jumped up out of his chair, knocking it over, and ran over to the three men. He threw a good punch and knocked one man to the floor. He picked up a beer glass from the bar and whacked a second man in the head, making the glass shatter. The third man backed away, holding the palms of his hand up, saying, "Don't hit me, Bud. I didn't do nothing." As he backed his way out of the restaurant, David pulled his fist back, to make sure the idiot left—otherwise his fist would connect with the man's face. He did not realize that Gareth curiously had got up to watch the brawl. As he drew his fist back, his elbow connected to Gareth's nose, making him yell out, "Be fucking careful, you stupid idiot!" Gareth sat down again rubbing his sore and swollen nose. Unfortunately for David, the management had called the police as soon as the fight had started.

David's hand had split open when he punched the first man, and so Morgan found a napkin, dipped it in a glass of ice water, and wrapped it around David's hand. An ambulance arrived and the EMT's looked at David's hand but said he would be okay. The two men were taken to the hospital—one to remove glass shards from his head and to receive stitches, and the other for observation for a possible concussion. The police came in and took statements from witnesses. All the patrons confirmed that David had not started the fight, but the two men insisted that David be arrested for disorderly conduct and battery. David walked over to the table to get his jacket from his chair and found Gareth firmly planted in his seat. "Some fucking boyfriend you were when you can't protect the woman you proclaim to still love."

David was put into the back of a police car and Morgan called a taxi to follow. Suddenly she realized that Gareth still had the coin, so she told the cab driver to wait a moment and ran back into the restaurant and asked for the coin. Gareth handed it over to her in silence. Both she and David had left Gareth to pay their dinner bill. As soon as they left, Gareth made another phone call.

Morgan sat in the waiting room of the police station. As people came in and out of the station they stared at her as if she had been arrested for prostitution or something. She phoned her friend Mary and asked for some cash if she needed to bail David out. Her friend said, "Of course, Morgan. If David is assigned to the late court session, he will probably be fined and that will be that. If he needs money I will be happy to pay it."

"Thanks, Mary," Morgan said. "I couldn't ask for a better friend."

Morgan looked up expectantly each time a police officer passed her, but they all seemed to be on other business. After forty-five minutes, she walked to the desk and demanded to see the district attorney. It was not until an hour later the district attorney appeared and, looking frustrated, asked what he could do for her.

"I want to press sexual harassment charges against the two men who are in the hospital."

With a sigh he sat down by her side. "Tell me what happened," he said.

David sat in the jail cell on the extremely hard bunk bed. To his right sat a huge black man who had on a tee shirt on which read Bubba's Shrimp House, which David thought was very ironic, especially as the man reminded him of a much younger Ben who was the eldest of his crew.

Another younger man had come in and asked David, "Could I squeeze my little hinny next to yours? Bubba over there looks as if he would bend me over no problem, but I am fussy." He smiled at David as he sat down and put his hand on David's leg.

David gave him a stony stare until he removed his hand." David looked extremely intimidating.

David was finally called into court for the one a.m. night court session. David, the Bubba's Shrimp guy, and the hinny guy were brought together to a corridor outside a courtroom, and David met his assigned and much-harried public defender. His attorney asked, "Are you going to plead guilty to a lesser charge of battery?" He looked at David. "You'll just get a $250.00 fine, and they'll let you go after completing paperwork. If you don't, they'll bind you over to a trail at a late date, and you won't be able to leave New York until you've gone to court. Your choice! Pick one."

"Guilty," David said.

David was surprised to see Morgan in the courtroom. The judge could not wait to get through his full calendar and did not even look up at David but accepted his guilty plea, and was about to continue when the district attorney appeared and asked for a side bar.

"Your honor, sexual harassment charges are pending against the defendants. They have decided to drop the charges against the defendant David Mason-James."

The judge looked at the district attorney and said, "Did this have to come into my court? Could the charges have been dropped, before it got this far?" He looked sternly at the district attorney and said, "You are in my sights, Mr. Wendell. Make sure you don't do this to me again." Looking up, he shouted, "Case dismissed! You are free to leave my court, Mr. Mason-James. Make sure I don't see you again." His hammer came down a little harder than it should causing silence throughout his court, leaving other prisons to sigh, because this judge was stern and usually unmovable.

David was free again. He and Morgan stood outside the court house, arm in arm, happy to be back together. They flagged down a taxi and went back to their hotel.

"Sorry," David said. "Not quite the way to behave when out in a restaurant, is it?"

"Don't apologize to me David, thank you for rescuing me from those men. I really don't like to be groped. They truly were obnoxious and you came to my rescue. I can't thank you enough."

David looked at her and replied with a big smile, "You can thank me enough tomorrow. I can think of several ways you can say thank you, but I'm too tired to act on them. How about we go to sleep for now?"

She nodded her head wondering exactly what David had in mind. Disappointed she could not say thank you tonight, she went first to the bathroom to get ready for bed. She got into her side of the bed waiting with anticipation and bated breath as David went to the bathroom. She was not in the least surprised when she felt him get into the other side of the bed. It was a far more comfortable way to sleep she assured herself. Then, to her disappointment, she heard him murmur, "Good night."

Morgan awoke with a start the following morning. She found her body wound around David's. He was awake and watching her. Her head was on his shoulder, and her legs were intertwined with his. She had never felt more comfortable. She didn't move, not sure how David felt about her encroaching into his personal space. He clamped an arm around her waist and asked, "Are you awake?"

She reluctantly said, "Yes."

"We're not going to make love here," he stated. "I want to make love to you somewhere that is familiar to both of us, and this place is not it. It's damned impersonal, and I don't like that. It's not that I don't want you, Morgan. I do. Just not here." He kissed the top of her head. "Breakfast?"

"I would just like to stay as we are for a while." She lay as still as she could but knew from David's wriggling that his arm was going numb.

As she got out of bed and showered and dressed for the day, David asked, "I suppose you didn't get the coin back, did you, Morgan?"

"Oh yes, I did. I went back into the restaurant and asked Gareth for it. While you're showering, I'll try to look up the value of this coin."

David nodded his head and disappeared into the bathroom. Morgan slid her laptop out from under the bed and booted it up. After a quick search, she found that 1861 gold coins like David's, were selling at coin shops for $2,700.00 — $3,000.00 if they were in mint condition. If David could get even $2,000.00 for it from a dealer, she thought that would help to repair his boat's engine.

David came out from the bathroom as usual covered in just a towel. She looked over at him and said in a sharper tone than she meant to, "David, that's not fair to me—to come walking out in just a towel."

"Do you want me?"

Her stomach turned over in knots as she looked at him, but seeing the smile on his face, she knew he was teasing.

"Absolutely not!" and she looked away until she heard him zip up his pants. He put his shirt on and began to button it up. She calmly walked over to him, unbuttoned it, and placed her head on his chest. He was startled at first, but then, with a smile, he put his arms around her and just held her.

A few minutes later, he let her go and said it was time to go and eat. They walked to a café across the street from the hotel. They were able to grab a table just being vacated.

The waitress bought them coffee, and they placed their order. Morgan found she felt a little shyer with David this morning, especially when he took her hand and held it in his while they drank their coffee and waited for their breakfast.

"When they had finished eating, David looked at Morgan, "I don't know how much you know about me, or even if you've asked about me in Oak Tree Town," he said, "but, I haven't messed around with a lot of women. Can't say I've had the time or the inclination. It's different with you, Morgan. I want you to know that. Okay?"

"What are you saying?" she asked, feeling a little confused.

"I'm not playing with your feelings, Morgan. Let's get our lives sorted out a little and then I'll show you exactly how serious I am about you."

She nodded her head accepting his words. She thought he was trying to tell her they were exclusive. She would be happy with that for now.

"Do you want to phone Gareth before we go to the museum?" David asked Morgan. "I'd like to go back to Dolphin's Cove this afternoon, if we can get the tickets changed."

"Of course," she replied, and taking out her phone she placed the call. Gareth answered right away.

"Morgan, are you and David all right? What happened last night? Is he still in jail? Do you need me to ride in on a white stallion and rescue you?" he pompously asked.

"Please, Gareth," she replied. "Don't be such an asshole. David is perfectly okay. We got back to the hotel in the early hours of this morning and he and I hopefully will leave this afternoon."

"But I haven't spent any time on my own with you, and you did say we would. You haven't told me why you left yet," Gareth whined.

"I don't want to hurt your feelings, Gareth, but perhaps if you want a real explanation, I will try to give you one when I come in with my grandfather's coin. Will the museum buy it from him?"

"No they won't, Morgan, but I have a friend who collects coins. You know him Morgan and have met with him several times when we've been out on the town. Peter? Peter Rinehart? "

The silence stretched out on the phone as Morgan tried to remember him, but could not. "Sorry," she said. "The name doesn't ring a bell."

"Anyway," Gareth continued, "he is willing to meet with you this morning. He says the coin might be worth around $1,800.00 to $2,000.00 depending on the condition."

"Really? That's amazing. I'm sure my grandfather will be thrilled if I can sell the coin. I'll call him and let him know. David and I will come by in about an hour; perhaps we could meet with you and your friend in the café opposite the museum. Thanks, Gareth. See you later." And she disconnected the call before letting out a whoop.

Startled, David looked at her. She said, "Around $2,000.00 cash for the coin. Will that help?"

"Yep. Truly it will. If nothing else I'll be able to temporarily fix the boat and get my men working. If I'm not shrimping, my crew is not earning, and it's just as hard for all of them. Old Ben who works for me—did you know he's 69? He has a wife and a disabled son he keeps at home and his parents are both alive and living in a nursing home which he pays for. I can't and won't retire him because of that. He used to work for my father, and I'd never put him out of work."

Morgan stared at David and, shaking her head a little, she said, "You're a softie through and through, David Mason-James."

Instead of answering, David just stood up, "It's time to leave to meet Gareth, although I admit, I'd like to put my fist right into his smart mouth and shut him up."

They left the café to head to the museum; David's insisted they walk. Near to their destination, David spotted a coin store which he had somehow missed the day before. On impulse he walked in, leaving Morgan in the open doorway. He asked to speak to the owner, who came out of his office.

"Good morning, I am the owner is there something I can help you with?"

David replied, staring at the owner's bright red jeans and shirt, "Could we talk in your office?"

"Sure, come this way."

Shutting his office door, Peter held out his hand and said, "My name is Peter Rinehart. How can I help you?"

"David Mason-James," David said while shaking Peter's hand. "I have four coins that I found in a trunk while cleaning it out and I have been told by a friend that the coins might be worth something." David showed him one of the coins.

Peter glanced through the window in his office at Morgan who was still outside the open doorway, and sat down ready to negotiate a good deal. The coins were in mint condition.

"I could offer you say… $1,500.00 each?"

David smiled and stood up. "Thanks, but no thanks," he said and turned away.

"Well if you are pushing me, $1,750.00," Peter replied stopping David from walking out.

David turned and stared at the younger man standing in front of him. "Let's cut the bull crap, shall we Peter? This coin and the others are in mint condition. I know this because I have seen others in the museum up the road. There is no comparison. Top dollar or I take them elsewhere."

Peter stared back at David for a few seconds. Folding his lips into a thin line, he slowly nodded his head before opening his safe in the wall and taking out a wad of bills. "I'll pay you $2,000.00 for each coin if you sell me the four. Final offer."

"Done." David replied.

"You wouldn't have more of these, would you?" Peter asked, as he counted out the bills into David's hand.

"No," David said watching the bills and not looking up. "I wish there were more, but this is it."

When David reappeared, it was with a smile on his face. He took Morgan's hand and they continued their walk to the museum.

Morgan waited a moment, but David just continued to grin. "Why did you go into the store, David?" she finally demanded. "Were you just checking on the value of the coin?"

"I sold it to him, Morgan. Actually, I have a confession to make to you." He stopped in his tracks on the pavement and looked at her in the eyes. "You always assumed I had just taken one coin out of the jar. I didn't. I took four, and I sold them to this guy for $2,000.00 each. I lied to you by omission, and for that I apologize." David, seeing that Morgan was about to explode with indignation, continued, "I was afraid Gareth would try pull more information out of you, and I thought it was better that Gareth thought we had only one coin. I really don't want any secrets between us. I am sorry."

"Well," she said as she began to soften.

"I don't trust Gareth, Morgan, and because of that I don't think I would trust his coin dealer friend. I'm glad we found this shop. Now I have enough money to repair my boat and get my men back to work. If you want to, I'll wait across the road in the café, while you see Gareth, but to be honest with you, I'm really not happy about you spending time with him. I'd rather we just went home."

"Could you please just come into his office with me? Then, if it's okay and I think I can handle him on my own, you can go on over to the café and wait for me while I tell him exactly what I think of him."

David reluctantly agreed. He would far rather have just turned around and gone back to Dolphin's Cove.

They picked up their badges at the employee's entrance and made their way into Gareth's office. They knocked on

Gareth's door and walked in. He was on his cell phone and hastily cut his call short.

"'Gotta go. Thanks for the call," He said as he hung up his phone. He looked up without smiling at either of them feigning surprise at the time. "Oh, is it that time already? Come in. Sit down." He made a sweeping gesture toward the chairs in front of his desk. Morgan sat, but once again, David stood with his feet slightly apart, firmly placed on the floor, and his hands shoved into his jeans pockets.

Gareth barely glanced at David, but asked Morgan, "Have you got the coin, Sweetie?"

"No. David has already sold it," Morgan replied as David just stared at Gareth.

The two men exchanged looks of pure hatred, and then Gareth all but spat at David, "David would you mind giving us some privacy so I can catch up with Morgan? I think it would be the least you could do, as you are canceling on my dealer at the last minute. I'll phone him in a moment to let him know exactly how inconsiderate you are. I hope he didn't cancel other obligations for you."

David looked at Morgan who nodded her head and suggested, "Meet me at the same coffee bar we used the other morning. I'll be there very shortly."

"You'll be all right?" David asked.

She nodded her head.

Reluctantly, David left Gareth's office and stood outside the door for a few moments before leaving the museum and crossing the street to the café. He sat at a table in the window so he could watch for Morgan.

David sat idly drinking his coffee, drumming his fingers on the table top, wishing he had never left Morgan and considering going back and rescuing her. Suddenly, much to his surprise, he saw the coin dealer, Peter Rinehart, in his bright red jeans and shirt, walk into the museum's main entrance, and disappear inside. Putting two and two together, he surmised this was the person he was supposed to have had a meeting with in this cafe and obviously he knew Gareth. Would this mean further trouble for them all? He sincerely hoped not.

Gareth eyed Morgan as she sat uneasily across from him in his office. He stood up, came around his desk, and demanded, "Come here Morgan and give me a proper hug! I've spent no time with you since you came back to New York, and I still don't know why you left."

Six months earlier, Morgan would have done what Gareth said. But she was a woman used to making her own decisions now, so she did stand up but did not go anywhere near Gareth. "I left because you did not give me the life you promised me, Gareth. No real home. No children, not even a dog or cat— nothing that would resemble a happy life and home. Yes," she said looking directly at him, "I was absolutely smitten by you when we first met. Now I can look at you for what you are—an arrogant prick! You make sarcastic remarks to people and don't give a damn. You order for people in restaurants without asking first, and, in the end, people perceive you as the totally ignorant, foolish, snobbish, stuffy Englishman you are—the sort of man England tries to get rid of because it harms their reputation. David is twice the man you will ever be. He doesn't have to wear designer shoes and clothes. He doesn't need to hide himself. Obviously you do. I'm glad I came back to

New York because you've made me see what a fool I was too waste so much time on you. I doubt we'll meet again. Goodbye, Gareth." She turned and walked out of his office leaving him feeling rather taken aback, until his cell phone rang again.

"Is it safe for me to come in?" Peter asked.

"Yes," Gareth answered.

In less than a minute, Peter was at Gareth's door. He threw himself into the chair opposite Gareth's desk and grinned from ear to ear.

"Can you believe they walked into my shop? There are a dozen coin shops in Manhattan!"

"Well, yours is the closest to the museum," Gareth answered.

"I might not have recognized Morgan if you hadn't told me about them earlier," Peter said. "I am sure she didn't recognize me." Peter showed Gareth the four coins he had purchased. "I tried to give him $1,500.00 each, but he seemed to know a little of what he was doing."

"You got four coins?" Gareth asked in astonishment.

Gareth stared for a moment and then said, "I don't understand, Morgan told me she had taken one coin from her grandfather's collection. Now you're saying you bought four? One has to wonder what collection her grandfather has, or if indeed the lid on the Mason jar has something to do with all of this."

"Yes – four," Peter said. "I can get $3,000.00 each for these. Don't worry – I'll send you your commission as soon as I sell these. David claims that this is all the coins all there are, but I have a gut feeling from the look on his face there are a lot. Boy, someone is going to be very rich if they have a load more." He laughed at Gareth's startled look and got up. He walked out of the office door whistling, pleased with his purchase.

Morgan ran out of the museum and over to the café without stopping. She sat down quickly in the chair opposite David. He looked at her flushed cheeks, called the waitress over, and asked her to bring another coffee.

"Are you all right?" he asked, concern showing in his face.

"Never better," she answered forcefully. She looked up at David and started to laugh. "I called him an arrogant prick. I think I added in stuffy, snobbish, and all sorts of insulting things. Oh, that felt so good." She picked up her cell phone and made a call to the airline and although it cost another $100.00 to change each ticket, she got them reservations for that afternoon. They hastily drank their coffee and went back to the hotel to pack their cases and leave.

At the airport, with their luggage booked through to Mobile and a coffee in front of them, they both began to relax. Morgan looked at David, "I can't wait to go home," she said. I didn't realize that it meant so much to me, but it does. Oak Tree Town has become my home, and I love it there. I love the slower pace of life and the town which is so small but just,....oh, I don't know—enough—especially against somewhere like New York. I've come to realize I no longer want meals out late at night, talking to people all trying to make their way in such a huge place. I've heard people say before, if you want to be lonely, there's no lonelier place than New York. I don't know why I didn't see all this before. But I'm glad I have now."

David had just looked at Morgan and smiled. He'd known that all his life. Small town living was the best, and to share it with someone and just to live on the coast was amazing.

Morgan made a quick call home to her grandfather, "I'll be home later tonight, probably about nine," she said.

"Well I hope you haven't cut your week short for me," he grumbled. "I've been fine without you."

"No, Grandpa," she replied. "We've finished what we wanted to do in New York. Now I want to come home."

"If you're calling Oak Tree home, does that mean I have to put up with you for the rest of my life then?" he grumbled again.

"No, Grandpa." I'll find somewhere of my own. But it does mean I'll be around all the time and can still keep an eye on you, and cook for you occasionally."

"Well, I guess that will be acceptable," he said with a smile in his voice. "I reckon the two of us could manage that. I'll see you later then. Your bed's all made up. Goodbye. Have a good flight."

"Goodbye, Grandpa. Thank you. I love you." She disconnected her phone.

Chapter 9

Paul heard Morgan disconnect, and he put the receiver down on his house phone. There was a broad grin over his face as he turned back to the television with a lighter heart. His friend Tyler was there to visit for a short while, so Paul laughingly said, "I would never tell Morgan I will be happy to have her back again, but I have become very used to seeing her around the house. She is a far better cook than I am. I've packed on a few pounds since she lived here," he said patting his stomach. "She gives me a reason to get up every day."

"You should get out more, Paul. Go to the bar for a pint or to Marylou's for breakfast. People would talk to you. You've always been a loner, and it's not good to be like that. We all need family and friends. Speaking of which, I need to go to see my family. They'll be expecting me. Do you want me to call in tomorrow?"

"Not tomorrow. Morgan will be back. Maybe the day after?"

"Okay. Think about what I've just said." Tyler got up to leave. "I'll see myself out. No need for you to get up."

As Paul had no intention of getting up, he just nodded his head. "See you," he muttered.

Paul did what he always did when he was on his own and the sun was shining through the window—he fell asleep in his chair. He did not wake up until it was dark and he heard a noise he did not recognize, but all went quiet again and so he closed his eyes for a few minutes more. He still had his eyes closed wondering what he would eat for dinner when he heard another noise. This time he sat up sharply. He was not alone in the house, and there was no way that Morgan would be skulking around. He reached out for the lamp on the table and switched it on. As the light lit the room, he saw two standing figures with dark clothing and ski-masks masking their faces. Only the slits of their eyes and mouth were showing.

"What do you want?" Paul asked sharply standing up, only to be pushed back into the chair by the smaller of the two thugs.

"Sit down, old man," the thug said. "Tell us where you collection is."

"What are you talking about?" Paul answered. His hand slid underneath the base of the chair where he kept the cudgel he had once killed fish with.

"Your collection," the thug repeated, his voice getting louder. "Can't you hear me, old man? We want your collection."

The taller of the two walked over to Paul's chair and grabbing hold of his shirt front, pulled Paul half way off the chair and repeated, "We ain't kidding old man. Tell us where it is before we hurt you."

"I don't know what you're talking about," Paul repeated, only to have the man strike him across the face with the back of his hand.

Incensed these two men were treating him in this manner, Paul grabbed the club and raised it above his head and struck the smaller of the two, but it just glanced off his shoulder. Paul raised the club to try and strike again. He was old and frail and the blow was just a glancing one. Paul shook his head as the man threw him back in the chair and got his gun from the back of his pants belt, and pointed it at Paul's face. "Tell us!" he yelled.

But Paul could only shake his head.

The smaller of the thugs went to the first drawer in the dresser, pulled it out, and upended it—the contents falling on the floor. He continued with the other drawers, kicking his foot through the debris on the ground. He went from one drawer to another tipping each of them, stomping through the contents, breaking anything fragile. He swept his arm over every surface, knocking everything from its place. When he found nothing in the living room, he went back to Paul who was sat in the chair with the gun pointed to his face.

"Tell me old man, or I swear I will hurt you," he ground out through clenched teeth. When no answer was forthcoming from Paul, he pulled out his own gun and smashed it across Paul's face. It broke Paul's nose which bled copiously, and broke a tooth which he spat out. The smaller of the thugs stayed with Paul while the taller one took a turn looking for the coin collection. Paul could hear him in the next room, removing drawers from their places, tipping the contents on the floor, and stomping over them. He went through the entire lower floor area and came back and he asked Paul this time. "Where is it, old man? I'm losing my patience."

"What?" Paul managed to grunt out of his swollen mouth.

"Your coin collection!" the smaller of the two thugs yelled. "Just tell us where it is or we'll beat you up even worse. Maybe just kill you a little."

The taller of the two thought that remark was funny and laughed. He stopped abruptly. "Where is it?!" he yelled at Paul and then smashed his gun butt around his ear.

Still, Paul did not reply and he wondered if this had anything to do with the coin Morgan had taken to New York. There is no way he was going to bring her into this, even if it meant he would die.

While the taller of the two thugs stayed with him, the smaller went upstairs and pulled every drawer out that he could, emptying the contents all over the floor. He then went into the closets and pulled all the men's clothes out and slit all the pockets with the knife he carried in his belt.

He continued into the second bedroom and realized as he tipped the drawers that they held feminine underpants and bras. Picking up a pair of the smaller pants on the end of his knife, he went down to the room where they were holding Paul. "You got yourself a young floozy?" he asked, pointing the underpants still on the end of the knife under Paul's nose. "This ain't no granny pants. You dicking her?"

Paul closed his eyes and said nothing.

"Come on, Grandpa. You can tell us. You giving her one? You screwing the ass of some young thing?" he continued, suddenly beginning to shout. "It ain't right. An old man and a young girl. It's gross. I want to know if you're fucking her."

The taller of the two thugs said. "We're here to get the collection and then get out. Your messing now with things

we shouldn't be. Let's just find the collection and get out."
His cell phone rang and he put it to his ear. He called the
smaller thug into the kitchen whispering, "Hey, Brandon,
the collection might not be here, it could be at another
address. Let's finish up here and see."

"You fucking idiot! You just said my name!" the shorter one
yelled. "There's no way we can just leave him now. Let's
have a bit of fun before we kill him."

Walking back into the living room, the taller of the two
thugs pulled Paul to his feet. He threw him at Brandon, who
caught Paul and spun him around. Then the taller thug
systematically began to beat Paul—fist after fist into his
kidneys, his spleen, his stomach, his chest. Paul was helpless
and failing fast. He would not have been able to stand if it
hadn't been for the thug holding him. When he let Paul go,
he slid onto the floor, and both thugs began to kick him in
the body and the head.

"Thanks for wasting our time, old man," Brandon said. "I
hope you die. You deserve it for fucking with a young 'un."

The taller of the two said, "We forgot to look under the
pictures on the walls. Let's look just in case he's got a safe."
And as Paul lay unconscious on the floor, they went into
each room again and pulled all the pictures from the walls.
They slashed some of the nicer pictures with their knives
just for the hell of it, but they found nothing. They went
back to find Paul unconscious on the floor. "He's as good as
dead," Brandon said. "Let's get out of here."

They left by the back door and drove away quietly for a
quarter mile before turning on their headlights. Then they
left town driving slowly—no point in drawing attention

to themselves. They only had a vague address for David but managed to find the house. They drew up outside the dark house. Brazenly, they got out of the car and walked around to the back door. The taller thug raised the butt of his gun intending to smash a window in the sunroom when suddenly, out of nowhere, a ferocious dog jumped up at his arm and bit as hard as he could.

The dog, growling viciously, began to shake the arm as if it were a rag doll. Brandon was terrified of dogs and ran as fast as he could back to the car. He opened the driver's side door to jump in, but the dog caught up with him and bit his ass. The dog hung on to his hold, shaking the vulnerable skin in his teeth ripping a hole in the thug's butt that would require several stitches. Brandon screamed and twisted away, lashing out with a kick before he could shut the door on the dog. The other thug ran back to the car, dove into the passenger side, and fired off a shot at the dog as he drove away. The old yellow dog howled and fell to the ground. He laid as still as he could so that if other shots was fired he wouldn't be hit again. Later, when he was able, he dragged himself off under the old red truck to lick his wound and die.

Much to Morgan's distress, their first flight was delayed which meant they only had a few minutes between connections, but amazingly, they made the connection and were able to fly into Mobile that night. They made their way out to her car, where David demanded, "Give me the keys, Morgan. I'll drive."

Reluctantly, Morgan handed over her keys. They paid the parking fee, and as they drove out of the airport, Morgan tentatively said, "I know you probably think I am nuts, but I have a strange feeling about going home. Do you think you could drive as if our lives depended on it?"

David looked quickly at Morgan, wondering if she was kidding, but she was not. Seeing Morgan looking a little distressed, he asked, "What's wrong?"

"I don't know," she had replied. "I just have this funny feeling in the pit of my stomach. Probably nothing, but on the other hand, it could be women's intuition."

The drive that normally took thirty to forty minutes, but they got to Oak Tree Town in twenty. They drove straight to Paul's house. "Thank you," Morgan said. "Paul's left a light on in the front room for me, but would you mind coming in with me?"

David was already out of the car removing her case from the trunk. "I wouldn't let you carry this in on your own anyway," he replied with an infectious grin. Holding out his hand to her, he said, "Come on. Let's see if Paul is waiting for you so he can tell you how bad you are for going with me to New York."

They went around to the back of the house, to find the back door ajar. David immediately pushed Morgan behind him. He held his finger to his lips to indicate she should be quiet, and, opening the door a little, he found the light switch and flipped it.

They both stood there stunned at the chaos in the room in front of them. Then Morgan screamed, "Grandpa! Grandpa! Where are you?" She tried to push past David, who held her back. He shushed her again and listened, but other than the television that was still on, there was nothing.

"Morgan," he whispered. "I want you to stay here. We don't know what we're walking into yet. Call the police on your cell phone." He entered the kitchen and looked around. He saw a long, sharp knife on the floor. He picked it up and went into the living room. He turned on the ceiling light and stood, astounded at the mess. Then he spotted Paul lying on the floor. He bent his head down placing his ear over Paul's mouth and shouted out to Morgan to call an ambulance immediately.

"Grandpa?" she yelled.

"Call an ambulance!" David repeated.

Morgan placed the call quickly, she then entered the living room where she saw the unconscious Paul on the floor. "Grandpa," she whispered sitting down by his side of him and taking his bruised and broken hand in hers. "Oh my God!" she cried. "What happened? Grandpa, talk to me," she insisted.

David could only quickly look around before he came and sat with Morgan, putting his arm around her. "This is terrible. I wonder what happened."

They stayed on the floor with Paul, David just rising once to get a blanket to cover the unconscious man. It was not long before they heard the wail of sirens. The ambulance was the first to arrive. The EMTs came in with a stretcher and oxygen. They gave Paul a quick assessment and placed an oxygen mask over his nose and mouth. They lifted him onto a gurney and told Morgan they would be taking him into the emergency trauma entrance of the Mobile Hospital. Morgan insisted she ride in the ambulance with Paul while David stayed with the police.

Detective Lawson introduced himself. After getting the three names he started to question David. "What time you did you arrive back in Oak Tree?"

"About two minutes before we placed the call to you," David replied.

"Was the victim responsive when you first came in?"

"No," David replied.

"Have you any idea why this happened?" Detective Lawson asked.

"No," David replied. "As far as I know, Paul had nothing of any value, much the same as most of us here. Look at this house," he continued. "It's been ransacked as if someone was looking for something." He shook his head. "I don't understand it, and why beat up an old man who couldn't defend himself?"

"Have you spoken to Paul Johnson recently?" Detective Lawson asked.

"Morgan phoned her grandfather this afternoon around three-thirty, I think it was," David replied.

"So this had to have happen after that. At least it gives us a time frame."

"Can you tell us if anything is missing?" Detective Lawson asked.

David shook his head. "I have no idea what he had in this house. I've never been in here before. I went upstairs to get a blanket for Paul, and I can tell you it looks the same there."

The detective nodded his head and said, "Thanks, David. If you want to go to the hospital now, we can continue here and catch up with you later there. Will Morgan be coming back to the house tomorrow?"

David shook his head and replied. "No. She can stay with me for a while. I live in the house on the bluff."

The detective nodded his head saying, "Okay. I'll see you tomorrow. In the interim, please try to come up with an idea of why this would happen to Paul. We'll probably be processing the house tonight. It would be better if neither of you come back here for a while. The police officer I've sent with the ambulance will keep in in touch with me, updating me on Paul's condition, but just in case, here's my phone number. Call me if you need me." He handed his card over to David and walked upstairs, leaving David free to drive back into Mobile and the hospital.

The only thing David could think about as he drove to the hospital was how white Morgan's face had gone. She had been horrified to see the damage to the house and contents but when he eyes looked down on her grandfather, her face turned as white as a sheet. If she hadn't sat down, David thought she might have fainted. He drove as fast as he could all the way there, ignoring the speed limits. He threw the keys of Morgan's car to a valet and rushed through the doors to find Morgan in the waiting room, still looking equally as pale.

"Have you spoken to the doctors?"

She seemed not to hear him.

"Morgan?" he asked again. "Have you talked to the doctors? What have they said?"

She looked up at David, realizing for the first time that he was with her. "David," she said on a sob standing up and throwing herself into his open arms.

He held for a little while and then pushing her from him but holding onto her arms, he repeated his question. "What about Paul, Morgan?"

Trying hard to pull herself together, she told him, "The doctor said Paul had a lot of broken bones, and they have him in surgery now. A rib pierced his lung and the lung collapsed, all from being punched and kicked. Who the hell would do this, David? Why? His nose is broken, and his ear is so swollen from whatever they hit him with, the doctor thinks he may lose his hearing in that ear. I don't understand why. My grandfather has never hurt anyone in his life. Who would do this? Why, David? Why?" Morgan burst into tears again. David held her shaking body and allowed her to cry this time for as long as it took to get the shock out of her system. He sat her down afterwards and left her for a short while to get coffee for the both of them.

They passed the night, sitting, walking to get the stiffness out of their bones, and drinking coffee, David holding Morgan's hand, but not talking a great deal. The night shift departed during the early hours of the morning, and new nurses came in to see them, but had no news. It was not until 10.13a.m. that morning that a nurse came in and asked if they would accompany her to a private conference room. The surgeon, Dr. Thomas, came in and introduced himself, then perched on the edge of a table. He looked tired and he ran his hand through his hair before looking at Morgan drawing his lips into a thin line. "Paul has received many broken bones and those we could, we've set. The broken ribs will heal by themselves, there is nothing we can do for those. He's been beaten to within an inch of his life. He is not a young man, and, honestly, I have no idea whether he will survive this horrible attack. We'll keep an eye on the punctured lung. Hopefully it will seal itself—until then he'll be on oxygen. If he comes around, and, at this point, I am not promising he will, Paul will have lost the hearing in his left ear. The blow he received on his face has also affected the nerves in his left eye. We think he will lose some sight in it. I'm sorry." Dr. Thomas continued, "It all sounds like doom and gloom I know, but the next few days are critical for him. He is still in a coma and we need to see if he comes around from that. If he does, and he is really uncomfortable and cannot stand the pain, we will put him back into a medically induced coma."

"All in all, we have done the best we can for him. When you see him, I think you'll be shocked. I suggest you go and spend five minutes with him and then take yourselves home and get some sleep. It won't do Paul any good if you make yourselves ill, and, really, right now, he won't even know you're there." He stood up and shook both of their hands. Holding onto Morgan's he added, "We'll do our best for your grandfather. I promise. Call me if you think you need me."

"Thank you, doctor." Morgan said. "David and I appreciate all you've done for my grandfather."

"Just follow the nurse and she'll take you to his room. He's in the ICU and will remain there for a few days. There are no particular hours for visiting. Come and go as you please." He turned and left, and David and Morgan followed the nurse. Morgan gripped David's hand as they walked the corridors until the nurse turned into the ICU. Morgan's eyes flared wide open as she looked at Paul, but she bit her lip to stop herself from crying out. She pulled a chair up by the side of his bed and sat down. She took Paul's hand just held it without saying a word.

Thirty minutes later, David said softly, "It's time to leave and allow Paul to sleep and heal as much as he can." He held his hand out for Morgan.

Morgan knew he was right but felt reluctant to leave. "I'm torn between catching up on some sleep and being there when Grandpa wakes," she mumbled, but took David's hand and allowed him to lead her away.

She sat in her car and the tears came again. "I'll have to go and try to clean up the mess at Grandpa's house,"

"David shook his head. "The police won't allow you back in their crime scene," he warned her, "and besides, neither will I. You'll come and stay with me."

The sun shone down through the car windows and Morgan was lulled to sleep by the warmth of the day. Her head fell onto David's shoulder, and her thoughts were about him as she drifted in and out of consciousness. He pulled up in the driveway, and reluctantly he tried to wake her up.

"Morgan," he whispered, "We're home." When she didn't wake up, he tried kissing her, but in the end, it was a howling that woke her up.

"Where are we?" she asked, feeling disorientated.

"Home," David said decisively.

"What was the noise?"

116

"I'm not sure," David replied, "but it came from around the back of the house. Maybe a bird or something is trapped. Should we go and look?"

Reluctantly, because she was so comfortable where she was, Morgan stumbled out of the car and followed David. They went around to the back of the house. Nothing seemed out of place, and so they turned to go inside when the howling began again. The big mutt dragged himself from out from beneath the old, red truck.

"What's wrong, boy?" Morgan said, approaching him with caution. But having dragged himself out from his hiding place the mutt was exhausted and just lay quivering on the ground. He whined as Morgan approached and his tail thumped twice, but he couldn't move any further.

"Careful, Morgan. That's blood on him!" David said. He kneeled down and carefully examined the mutt who whined and lifted his head with deep hurt emanating from in his eyes.

David looked at Morgan, "That's a bullet hole! The poor dog has been shot. We'll have to get him to a vet." He ran into his house and found a blanket. They gently lifted the dog between them and placed him on the blanket and then lifted the blanket up and into the back of the car. They started quickly toward town while Morgan searched for veterinarian offices on her phone. She found what seemed to be the closest one and called the number as they sped in.

The vet confirmed the dog had been shot and would need emergency surgery. David and Morgan stayed with the mutt until he was put under with anesthetic. "Go home," the vet said. "I'll call when I have some news. I need to see what damage the bullet did."

Morgan was on the verge of tears again. "I don't know what's going on, David. First Grandpa, and now this?"

Unfortunately David was beginning to get an idea of what was going on but he wasn't going to share the news with Morgan until she could deal with it. One name kept coming to mind— Gareth!

Morgan had black bags under her eyes and looked exhausted. The most important thing was to get her home and sleeping. When they drew up in the driveway, David told her to stay in the car. He went in through the rear of the house, picked up a big kitchen knife, and went through his house thoroughly. Satisfied that no one was there, he went back out to Morgan and helped her into the house. He hustled her upstairs to his bed, took off her shoes and coat, removed her jeans and sweater, and gently pushed her under the covers. She was asleep before her head hit the pillow.

David went back downstairs and made a couple of phone calls. First he called the hospital—there was no different news on Paul, but the nurse assured him that he was resting comfortably. The second call was to Detective Lawson.

"Can you come over?" David asked him. "There are some new developments."

When the detective arrived, David went out to meet him and showed him the mutt's trail of blood. "There's a little outside the kitchen door and some on the driveway. There's more on the far side of the driveway all the way up under my daddy's old, red truck. The mutt is at the vet's is being operated on. Hopefully they will be removing a bullet from the dog; perhaps you'll be able to match it to a gun."

"Thanks," Lawson said. "You got some idea who might have done all this then?"

"I have no right to be pointing fingers. If Paul comes around, I would like to know if he remembers what happened and why."

"David, you're not withholding vital information from this investigation are you?"

"No. If I find anything out, I'll let you know. In the meantime, if there is anything else I can do let me know later. I need some sleep now."

Detective Lawson nodded his head at David who turned and went back into the house while the police team took swabs and samples of blood. It was a full hour before they left the premises.

David went upstairs to his bedroom and saw that Morgan was fast asleep, but whimpering. He disrobed quickly to his shorts and slipped into his bed as quietly as he could. He warmed up a little before moving closer to her and put his arm around her. Her whimpering stopped immediately, and, in her sleep, she sought the comfort from David that she needed by turning over and snuggling into his arms. She found a quieter, deeper, and safer sleep. David smiled, and he too fell into an exhausted sleep.

Chapter 10

His deep sleep was interrupted by a phone ringing, and he couldn't find the damn thing to answer it. As he emerged from his sleepy state, he realized that it was Morgan's cell phone, and he reached over her and picked it up.

He sat up in bed trying to come out of his sleep. It was the vet. "The operation went well, and your dog is now in recovery," she said. "He was lucky the bullet did not hit any major arteries or organs. An infection had set in because he wasn't seen right away, but we managed to contain that and will keep him on an antibiotic for two weeks. He needs to stay with us for a few days as we have a drainage tube in the open wound. When we have removed it and have sewn the wound up, you can pick him up. If you would like to visit you can any time between 8am and 5pm."

"Thanks," David mumbled. "We'll be in to see the dog tomorrow." He disconnected the call and lay there. His head was still a little fuzzy, but he had been asleep for six hours and that should be enough. He glanced at Morgan and saw she was still sleeping, so he quietly got out of bed, taking her phone with him. He went downstairs and put on some coffee. He walked out to the sunroom and sat looking over the deep grey and blue waters of the Gulf. The sun was losing height and moving well into the west which meant that night must not be far away. The coffee pot beeped to let him know it was ready. He poured a cup and went back to his contemplation.

Nothing violent ever happened in Oak Tree Town or Dolphin's Cove. Now within a period of one day, an old man had been beaten to within inches of his life, and a dog had been shot and left for dead. The two were connected by Morgan and David. Was this a co-incidence? David didn't think so. Morgan and he had just come back from New York where she had fabricated a tale of her grandfather's coin collection, and his address would not have been hard to trace. He sighed aloud as he drank a little more of his coffee and didn't hear Morgan as she approached from behind. She had borrowed one of his shirts and put it on over her bra and pants.

"Any coffee for me?" she asked in his ear.

He smiled at her and said, "Of course." He watched her walk into the kitchen and return with the pot of coffee and a mug. "I don't think I have ever seen that shirt look so good," he grinned at her.

"Did you want some more coffee?" she asked and filled both their cups, took the pot back to the kitchen, and returned to sit next to him on the couch. "I woke up and you had gone," she said, "and I felt cold and afraid."

"I'm sorry," David said, a frown forming between his eyes. "You're here in my home, and I wouldn't let any harm come to you."

"I know," she said looking at him. "I guess I just missed your being there."

"How did you know I was there?" he asked, teasing her to lighten the mood.

"I just knew. I moved to where the warmth was coming from. I had been asleep for a while. I couldn't get warm until you came to bed, and then later the bed began to go cold again, and so I woke up."

"Oh, so now I'm just a warm comforter to you, am I?" he asked with mischief shining in his eyes.

"I felt safe with you there, David," Morgan replied seriously.

He looked at Morgan and replied looking down at his hands. "You can always be here, all the time if that's what you want, but in any case, you have to be here for a while so that we can go back and forth to see Paul. The vet phoned while you were asleep and told me the mutt is doing well. She's seen to his wound and put a drainage tube in and given him an antibiotic. We'll pick him up in a few days. It looks like we're going to be adopting him. I think he could well have tried to stop someone from breaking into this house. I wish he had been with Paul!"

They sat there just sipping their coffee. After a while Morgan said, "We'll have to name the mutt. We can't keep calling him Mutt. It's not nice."

"Do you have a name in mind?" David asked.

Morgan shrugged her shoulders. "He's sort of blonde. How about calling him Clam Chowder or Chowder for short?"

David gave a wiry grin and said, "Okay, if that's what you want. Chowder it will be."

She looked at David and laughingly remarked, "It's your dog, and you should be naming him."

He shook his head and muttered, "Chowder will be just fine."

"I've lost my phone. I wanted to phone the hospital and see how my grandfather was doing. I don't suppose you've seen it?" she asked.

"It's here. I took it when the vet phoned and woke. I left you and bought it with me. I didn't want any calls to wake you."

He got up and took the cups out to the kitchen and refilled them while Morgan made her call. When he took them back to the sunroom, he saw she had tears in her eyes. "What's happened, Morgan?" he asked, quickly putting the cups down and pulling her into his arms.

She shook her head and said, "Nothing. Absolutely nothing. He's not come out of the coma but as far as the hospital knows, he's resting comfortably." The tears began to trickle out of her eyes again even though she was trying hard not to cry.

"I'm sorry," she whispered as he rubbed her back. "You must be fed up with me crying."

He looked down at her and said, "Are you joking? I get to hold you, rub your back and cuddle with you in bed, and, so far, you haven't reprimanded me or my actions. You curl around me as if you were a vine, and I love it." He continued a little more seriously. "I want to take care of you, Morgan. Tears are a part of that." He looked down into her eyes, and, as the sun dipped low in the sky, his mouth covered hers, and she clung to him. He deepened the kiss, and she responded without thought. When he pulled back, he looked at her, "I asked you once before if you wanted me, but I was teasing. Now I'm not. Do you want me, Morgan?"

She stared back at him, her heart pounding, and she could only nod her head. He wasted no time in pulling her by her hand up the stairs and into his bedroom where he kicked the door closed behind them.

He pulled her shirt over her head, and then did the same with his own. He unbuckled the belt on his jeans.

He pulled Morgan with him, and, kissing her gently at first, lowered her to the bed. He pulled his jeans off and climbed on the bed with her. His lips found hers, gently at first, and then, as he was devouring her, his hands roved across her body. His lips left hers, and they traveled across her neck, down to her shoulders, and into the hollows of her shoulders, before going back and traveling a similar path on the other side.

Morgan could not keep her body still. It reacted by itself in the heat of the moment reaching up for David's. Her back arched when he removed her bra and took her nipple in his mouth and began to tease, but still he would not give her what she wanted. His mouth travelled from her nipple to her stomach as his lips followed his hands and he removed her panties. Finding the center of her body where he lavished love on her, taking her to the brink of ecstasy before stopping and starting again. When he heard her whisper, "David.......please......I want you," he lifted his head and took them both to heaven and back.

They both lay for a long time without moving or talking. David thought he had never really made love to anyone before. This is what he truly felt, love—It was a wonderful thing.

Morgan had never had anyone so unselfishly make love to her before. Her body still shook imperceptibly from the experience. She had not wanted it to end. Besides, she thought on a sigh, we can always start again, which is where David's mind had gone. This time their lovemaking was slower, exploring each other's bodies and sweeter for the whisperings of lovers in love, the joining of two hearts, two minds and two souls who belong together. David cried out his love for Morgan in his ecstasy, and she told him of her love as she clung to him afterwards.

They fell asleep entwined in each other's bodies and did not wake until the following morning when they simultaneously heard knocking on the front door and Morgan's cell ringing. David rolled out of bed, pulled his jeans on, went to the front door, and opened it. Detective Lawson was there.

"Good morning," Lawson said. "I hope I'm not interrupting anything." He walked past David and into the kitchen.

David raised his eyebrows, closed the door, and followed. "No," he replied. "I was just going to make some coffee. Would you like some?"

"That would be very nice," Detective Lawson said, removing his coat and laying it over a chair. Finding a stool he pulled it out and sat at the kitchen counter while David went on with the coffee preparation.

"Strong or otherwise?" David asked.

"Strong will be good this morning. I didn't get a call from you yesterday and I assumed you were tired and wanted to sleep the day away, but we need to talk about these cases today before the trail goes cold."

David had nothing to say to Detective Lawson.

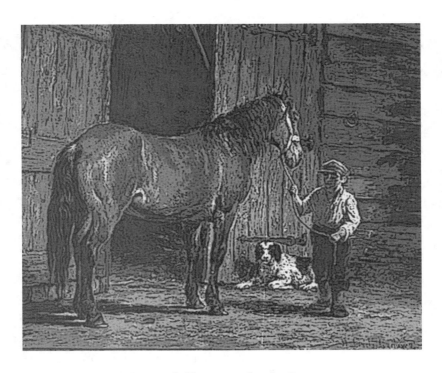

Ben and Champion by the Barn

Chapter 11

October 1864

He had been spotted on his horse not long after he had left the cabin. He knew that for the sake of the others in the castle, he needed to draw this posse away from them, and so he turned toward the coast. There was no one else to help divert the posse. This time he was on his own. He urged his mount to speed. He was in unknown territory, not being used to traveling across country to the coastline. The moon came out from behind a cloud lighting the pathway. He glanced behind him to see how far away the posse was. Not far enough, he thought, and urged his mount to even greater speed now he could see where he was going.

The moon came and went, and he gradually began to lose his pursuers. Jesse rode up into the hills where he felt more comfortable, and he got off his horse. He took the reins and led him over rocky pathways, giving the horse a chance to recover from the hard ride. Jesse looked for a pond or stream, but couldn't find one and decided that he could do without water more than his horse could, so he took a small pan from his saddle, poured his water out of its container into the pan, and held it for the horse to drink. The horse shook his magnificent head and whinnied in appreciation. Softly snorting out of his nose, he allowed Jesse to take the reins and mount again. They rode gently through the hills, hoping the posse would not be able to pick up the trail, and when the moon faded and the sun began to rise in the sky, he rode out of the hills onto flat planes. He had no idea of where he was, but kept riding forward checking every few minutes that no one was behind him.

When the sun rose high in the sky, he got off his horse and walked him. Both were thirsty, and he was hungry and assumed the horse must be too. It must have been well past noon when he finally came across a river. He turned his horse lose to drink and eat grass. He lay on the edge of the water and drank his fill of the clear water which had a slightly salty taste to it, but took the edge of his thirst and hunger. When his horse had its fill, they followed the river downward. It was not long before he came across the occasional small cabin—some with crude home-made boats outside of them. He skirted around them and continued further down the river. As the sun was beginning to sink in the sky, he came across a house that had two smaller buildings in its grounds, standing a little way from the bank of the river. He was immediately drawn to the house, although he had no idea why. The house stood glistening white with huge oak trees surrounding it. Spanish moss draped from the tree limbs to the grounds, giving a slightly eerie feeling, but shading the house. Two children were playing among the trees, and a woman sat on the stoop enjoying the last of the sun.

He dismounted and tied his horse up to the post by the gate. "Good evening, Ma'am," he said to the woman sitting on the stoop. Her children immediately ran to her. "I did not mean to scare you and your children," he said seeing she had stood up immediately, draping her shawl around her shoulders and pulling the children close to her. "I am a stranger here, and my horse and I need some water, and I wondered if you had a pump here we could get some. Or is there a town nearby where I may rest my horse and get something to eat?"

The woman stared at him for a few moments and said, "If you remove your guns and put them away, you are welcome to bring yourself and your horse to our pump. If you would like, you can clean up some and come and share our supper with us. I have some oats for the horse, and my boy can brush him down for you. He's real good with horses."

"That's mighty kind of you, Ma'am. You have a real nice house here if I may say so," Jesse said as he untied his horse. The boy walked shyly over to him and held out his hand to take the reins. Jesse looked at the boy who was about twelve, and, smiling, he asked," Do you think you can manage him, young man?"

"Yes sir, I reckon," The boy replied with a grin. Jesse took out a coin from his pocket and tossed it to the boy who caught it with a grin. "The pump's over here," the boy said, leading the way to the pump and its trough. Jesse took off his hat and put his head full under the pump and washed up as well as he could. He watched as the lad led the horse to the trough and gave him freedom to drink as much as he wanted.

He sat on a tree stump looking at the young man and asked, "Where are we?"

"We're on the Gulf Coast, Sir," the lad replied, "Or at least not far from it. This is the Bon Secour River and it goes all the way into the Bay of Mobile. My dad used to fish these waters but he got caught out in a big storm and died when his boat went down."

"I'm sorry, lad," Jesse said. "It must be hard to be without your father."

"I got used to it," the boy replied. "Been some years since."

"What's your name, lad?" Jesse asked

"Ben," the boy replied.

Jesse stretched out his hand and said, "Mine's Jesse. Nice to meet you." And they shook hands.

Ben took the horse's reins, and, finding a brush, began to clean the horse up.

"You're real gentle with that horse," Jesse said, watching as the boy was carefully brushing the horse.

"He's a real nice stallion. What's his name, Mr. Jesse?"

"Champion."

"That's a real nice name and suits him. I love horses," Ben said reaching up and pulling the horses head nearer his. He softly blew up the horse's nose, and the horse whinnied.

"You sure have a way with them," Jesse replied, smiling at Ben. "Normally he won't let anyone else touch him but me."

"Really?" Ben asked, obviously excited that he had such a way with horses.

They shared a few minutes of silence while Ben continued to brush the stallion that let him do as he pleased. When he had finished, Ben got a bucket and half filled it with oats for the horse. "Is this enough, do you think?" he asked looking at Jesse for approval.

Jesse said, "It sure is. You know your horses, Ben. Is there somewhere we can bed him down with some hay?"

"I'll put some in the barn over there if you think that would do," Ben said.

"You're amazing, Ben. Thank you for taking such good care of Champion for me."

"You're welcome," Ben replied. They took Champion in to the barn and put some hay out for him and settled him down and as they came out again, Ben said, "Oh! There's Mom shouting for us to go in to supper."

"Then we shouldn't keep her waiting," Jesse replied. The two walked side by side into the white house. Upon entering, Jesse removed his hat, and nodded his head at the woman. This is really nice of you, Ma'am. I haven't eaten since yesterday, and your food smells real good."

"Thank you, she replied, "Ben did you wash up while you were out there?" she asked.

"Yes, Ma'am," he replied not looking at her.

"You know you should wash up before eating, Ben, why don't you at least wash your hands at the sink?"

"Yes, Ma'am."

"Sit!" she said to Jesse and pointed to the end of the table.

He nodded his head and sat on the chair.

My name is Annie Cooper," she said as a way of introduction, "and this here is my daughter, Lillian, and my son, Ben."

"Nice to meet you all. My name is Jesse James," and he held his breath to see if anyone had heard of him, but, if they had, they said nothing.

Annie placed the meal in front of him and served her children before taking a plate for herself.

Jesse started to eat as everyone else folded their hands for evening grace. Annie opens one eye and sees what is happening and opens both and raises her eyebrows at Jesse.

"Can you say the evening prayers Jesse or would you prefer that I do?"

"I'm really sorry Ma'am. I forgot my manners. He closed his eyes trying to think of a suitable prayer and eventually said, "For what we are about to receive from your glorious bounty, may the Lord make us truly thankful." And hastily he added, "Bless the hands that prepared this food, O Lord. Amen"

Annie smiled at his prayer. Obviously, he was not used to praying before he ate.

"What brings you to this part of the country Mr. James?" she asked.

"Please call me Jesse," he replied. "I have never seen the coast before and I thought I would just like to come and look."

"Where are you staying?"

"I have nowhere in mind, Ma'am. This was all done on a whim."

"Times are hard for us here," she replied. "You can stay out in the cottage and I'll cook you breakfast and supper every day for a fee," she said breaking some bread and laying it on her plate.

"Well, Ma'am, if it isn't any inconvenience that would be right nice of you," he replied. "The food is really good."

She laughed at him as Ben jumped in to say, "I can look after your horse for you, Mr. Jesse."

"Well now, it seems I have nothing to worry about does it. And what of you, little Miss?" he said to Lillian.

"I can sing for you," she smiled shyly at him.

"Well it seems I am to be entertained all the way around."

The rest of the meal passed peacefully. When he finished eating, Jesse asked permission to go and sit on the porch with his pipe and puff peacefully. Annie nodded her ascent and set about clearing the table and washing the pots. It was not long after, she put her head out of the door and asked if he would like a keg, and he thanked her. She returned with the ale in her hand and passed it over. "Would you mind if I join you?" she asked.

"Not if you don't mind if I keep smoking," he replied, "I'd be right glad to have some company."

Annie sat down, and, after a while, she remarked, "I used to sit out here with my husband. He'd always enjoy a pipe after he'd eaten."

"Young Ben told me he died. I'm sorry. It must be a hard thing to run this place with no husband," he said.

"Sometimes it is," she said. "He built this place, you know. He built it just for his first wife who died after giving birth to Ben. I came from a big wealthy family in Mobile and my parents did not approve of my choice of husband. They said he would never amount to much, so I ran away with him when I was just fourteen, and they cut me off. He worked hard to build this place up and called it 'Cooper's Landing.' We had the biggest and best fishing boat he would take out and go down the river to Mobile Bay and beyond into the Gulf of Mexico and fish for shrimp. He was good at it too. He would come home and wash himself down because he said he smelled of fish," she laughed. "And would you believe? He did too! He was a good man," she finished on a sigh.

Jesse nodded his head and remarked, "You must miss him."

"I do," Annie said with a small smile. "But I have my children and they remind me of him—especially young Lillian. She looks like he did. Ben takes after his father's side of the family. They loved horses too. They didn't ever go near the fishing industry which is such a big part of living down here. I must go and put the young ones to bed," she smiled. "The cottage to your left is the one I keep for guests. There is a lamp just inside the door. Goodnight, Jesse."

"Goodnight, Annie. I hope you sleep well."

But Annie did not sleep well. It had been a long time since she had company come and stay. She was grateful, because it would put some money in her pocket, but that wasn't why she couldn't sleep. Mr. James was a well-built young man with wide shoulders and he had light brown hair which swept his collar. He looked a little haunted in his features which were sharp, but he had dark brown eyes that seemed easy to smile. He was easy to talk to, and she had missed that since she lost her husband. Yes, she thought, I could like this man. I hope he stays around for a while.

She rose early the next morning and got the stove lit and made some coffee. The children hadn't risen yet and she took her first cup out onto the pier over the river.

"Can I pour me a cup of that?" Jesse asked startling her out of her reverie. She wasn't used to having anyone else around when she drank her first cup.

"Oh!" she replied, "I'll go and get you a cup. I usually drink the first cup on my own as the children aren't up. I enjoy the peace and quiet."

"I'm sorry," Jesse immediately said, I'll go back to the cottage."

But she smiled and said, "Wait there. I won't be but a moment."

She was back quickly with the brew, and, sitting down on the edge of the pier, she pulled her dress up so she could dangle her legs in the water. "Come and join me," she said.

Taking off his boots, Jesse sat on the pier next to her and put his feet in the water. They both remained quiet until she said, "Do you hear that?"

"I don't hear anything very much," he said. "Maybe a few birds. I can hear a squirrel scratching, but nothing to disturb the air."

"But that's just it!" Annie said. "This is what I love so much first thing in the morning. The sun is just coming up, there's a bit of breeze springing up, and a few birds are waking to the morning and calling out to one another. There's a big old beaver over there. He's been collecting some twigs. He wants to make a dam, and if he does, I'll have to get in the river and break it up. All this is what I love about the mornings and getting up and facing each day." She sighed and then emptied her coffee cup in one swallow.

Jesse looked at her and asked, "Would you like to share another cup with me?' She smiled back and nodded her head and waited while he went to fetch the coffee. As he walked back, he noted that she had done nothing with her hair this morning except to tie it back with a bow. Her hair was long and chestnut in color, with hints of gold reflected in the sun. She'd dressed in a simple long cotton gown of green which had a darker green sash, and she looked like a very young girl sitting on the pier swinging her legs in the water. It bought a smile to his face. He placed the coffee on the pier and sat down again, and really looked at her face for the first time. She had green eyes. They reminded him of the cat that lived in the barn on his farm. She had a sprinkling of freckles across her nose. He thought most women would believe the freckles unfashionable and should be covered up with heavy makeup, but she wore none. He thought they were lovely and bought out the color of her eyes. Maybe I'll stay for a few days and he relax and listen to the sounds of the morning with Annie, he thought.

After he had breakfast, he and Ben went to the barn and fetched Champion. The horse was well rested and eager to go out again. Jesse saddled him up and told Ben, "I'm going to look around the towns and countryside hereabouts, but I will be back later for dinner." Bidding everyone good day, he rode away.

Jesse could hear the rumble of waves not far away, and so he followed the river, allowing Champion to pick his own way. Eventually he arrived on the bay itself. He dismounted Champion and walked toward the water which came onshore in waves. Kneeling down, he put his hand in the water and tasted it. It was very salty, and he spat it out again and stopped Champion from drinking. It would just make them both thirstier than they already were. He should have remembered to take some fresh water from the pump this morning.

He followed the bay around its shoreline. It was beautiful in its own way but he preferred Ohio, where there were hills and valleys. Much like a woman's body he thought, and then wished he hadn't as it made for uncomfortable riding. So once again he dismounted and tried hard to think of other things, but the only thoughts that came to mind were those of Annie, sitting on the pier and laughing up at him. She was very tempting, he thought.

Impatient with his own thoughts, he tried to focus on the posse that had tried to follow him the previous night. He hoped they had lost his trail and then doubled back on themselves. After all, he had never stepped foot in this part of the country before. Therefore, there was no reason for him to be here, except for one very tempting redhead. He got back on Champion and wondered if there was a way he could get around the other side of the coastline. Time was running short today, so he decided he would find out tomorrow. Maybe Annie would know. He would ask her when he got back to Cooper's Landing.

She was out on the stoop drinking a cup of coffee when Jesse got back. As he had the night before, he flicked a coin at Ben, who caught it with ease and waited for Jesse to dismount. Ben led Champion away to groom him and to give him water and oats. Jesse put his head under the pump before approaching Annie and asking permission to sit next to her.

She smiled peacefully up at him and said, "Sit." As he did, his thigh touched hers. He placed his hat in the region he did not want her to see. They watched as the sun began to sink in the sky. The sky was beautiful—gold, reds, and oranges with a hint of grey clouds. The sunset was stunning, and they both watched it silently.

"It never fails to amaze me," she remarked. "Nature's colors are so beautiful. I could never get enough of them. You must be hungry after being out riding all day. Dinner is ready. Shall we go and eat?" He stood up and waited while she rose. He offered the crook of his elbow, which she took. He liked the feeling of her body being so close to his.

The children were full of what they had done that day. Ben boasted, "I caught the rabbit we're eating for dinner tonight. I didn't have to do lessons with Mom today because it's a Saturday."

Lillian not to be outdone said, "I read with Mommy today. She likes me to read every day. She says it's important to read."

"And so it is," Jesse had replied. "Maybe one day soon, I could hear you read." Lillian had just smiled back at him, not sure if this person could read and would be able to help her say the words. She was only three.

Lillian stared out of the corner of her eye at Jesse during the meal and eventually plucked up enough courage to ask, "Have you come here to be my new daddy?"

"He smiled back at her and replied, "I would love to be your daddy, but I'm afraid not, Lillian. Someone else will have that pleasure, I am sure."

Annie had opened her mouth to chastise Lillian for asking such a question, but when Jesse answered in the gentle manner he did, she closed her mouth again and said nothing to her daughter who seemed perfectly happy with Jesse's answer. Annie thought he must be used to dealing with small children and wondered if he had any.

After dinner, he once again retired to the stoop, and Annie soon joined him. They sat peacefully for a little while until she plucked up the courage to ask pertinent questions. "Who are you, Jesse? And where do you come from? Are you married? And do you have children?"

"That's a lot of questions you've asked me." He took a deep breath and puffed furiously on his pipe for a few moments before saying, "Do you want me to be totally honest? Or would you rather I not tell you the truth?"

"I want the truth," she said without hesitating. "No matter how bad it is. Tell me about yourself, Jesse."

"Firstly—and I don't want you to be scared because I would never hurt you in any way—I am the Jesse James."

"Who's that?" she asked, interrupting immediately.

"I rob Union banks and trains."

"Why?"

"I'm trying to raise money for a good cause which I can't tell you about because if I did, I would have to kill you, and I don't want to do that."

"Oh. Well, I guess I'm glad you don't want to kill me."

"I'm from Ohio where I own and work a farm," he continued, putting his pipe back in his mouth and puffing on it.

"Are you married?" she asked, interrupting once again.

"Yes, I am." He said removing the pipe. "I've been married a year and we have one child—a boy."

"That's why you're so good with mine," she said looking at him and smiling.

"I guess," he replied, looking down at his hands

"Why aren't you at the farm now?" Morgan asked with a frown appearing between her eyes.

"I went to a meeting with the top conspirators of my castle, many miles away from here and when I left, I found a posse following me. I have never been here before, and so I travelled this way for a twofold reason—one was to get rid of the posse—and the second reason was to lead them away from my fellow conspirators."

"I see," Annie said looking out into the dark night. "Will you be here long? Because it doesn't seem as if you were followed. Not that I mind you being here. I don't—even if your name is Jesse James." She smiled at him and then began to laugh. "I guess we just don't seem to hear of people of your notoriety here. You are no different to me than any other man. I like having you here," she continued. "You are an interesting person and good with my children, that's enough for me for now. I must go and put them to bed. Goodnight, Jesse." She rose and walked away, and he could hear the swish of her gown. He wished she and the gown were walking toward the cottage.

The following morning found Annie on the pier with two cups of coffee. "I put yours here next to mine," she smiled up at him as he approached. "It seems you like your coffee in the morning too. Come and sit down with me." He removed his boots as he had the day before and dangled his feet into the water next to hers. Today she was in a simple blue cotton dress and had pulled it up over her knees to put her feet into the water. He admired the shape of her leg and then fervently wished he hadn't.

"The water seems higher this morning than it did yesterday," he remarked, trying to get his mind off the shapely leg.

"You are very observant," she replied. "The water levels change every day with the tides from the Gulf. It is only marginally higher today, yet you noticed."

They continued to watch the sun rise in silence—the colors spectacular in the sky, the sun peeking through the Spanish moss on the oak tree giving splendid shadows here and there.

He finished his coffee and remarked, "This is a place a man could come and set his hat down and never move again. It is truly beautiful and so peaceful here."

Annie studied his face before asking, "Is that what you want to do, Jesse?"

"Right now, I am wishing I could. But 'tis no more than a dream for me. I have a wife and a child who need looking after." He looked back at her with regret in his eyes. He lifted his hand and gently removed a piece of hair that had blown across her face and tucked it behind her ear, his hand remaining motionless on her face.

Annie's heart was racing and she closed her eyes hoping he would kiss her, but he abruptly stood up, "I have to leave early this morning. I've a mind to find the nearest town. Which way should I be riding?" He looked down at her.

Annie stood up slowly and let her dress fall over her wet feet. "If you ride northwest from here and keep riding, you'll come into Mobile. It will take you a good day's riding to get there. Will you be coming back?"

He saw the hurt he had put into her eyes. "I'll be back tomorrow for certain. Make sure you have supper for me. I'll pay you what I owe you now just in case I get lost." He put his hand in his pocket and pulled out several gold coins and passed them over to her.

"Oh no!" she cried. "This is far too much for the little I have done for you." She tried to give the coins back.

He shook his head. "Keep them, Annie," he said, pressing them in her hand. "I'll see you tomorrow." He turned swiftly and, getting Champion from the barn, he mounted him and rode as fast as he could.

As the miles and the day passed, the scenery unnoticed, all Jesse could think about was Annie. She was so tempting, and he would like to dally in Cooper's Landing, but he had a feeling that if he did, he would not return to his wife and family, and that would be just plain wrong. "What is wrong with me?" he shouted to the wind. "I've had whores before—nothing I couldn't just use and leave. Why, oh why, could I not do the same to this woman? She's crawling under my skin, and I want her."

It was late afternoon when he came to the outskirts of Mobile. The city was thriving, largely because of its port. Many ships docked there, and merchants waited eagerly to take their cargo to market. The harbor was bustling with activity. Men strode around in their fancy clothes, and women, dressed in the latest fashion, carried opened parasols so as not to let the sun touch their skin. Young boys ran back and forth trying to earn a penny or two for helping secure cargo, or by selling the latest news on paper. Jesse bought a paper from a youngster and tossed him a coin.

"Thanks, mister!" the boy yelled as he went on to the next customer.

Jesse opened the paper and quickly scanned it. There was nothing about him. He was not known here. He leaned against a post and watched the port activity from behind the paper. "If this was a major port, wouldn't there be a Union ship somewhere around?" he thought to himself, and then he saw the schooner.

He casually made his way along the dock toward the schooner. It was painted black and had five masts. Looking hard over the top of the paper, he became convinced it was a Union ship. It had a European flag flying from it, but the longer he looked the more convinced he became that it was not European. It was well known among the Knights of the Golden Circle that Union ships disguised themselves by painting out the name of their ship before docking in a port and by flying a foreign flag. He watched the activity aboard the ship until well after the sun had set.

He left the dock and found a seedy hotel in a back street to stay for the night. It was not a particularly clean hotel, and rather than taking off his clothes, he laid on the bed fully dressed and put his hat under his head as a pillow hoping to not pick up any fleas. He spent a restless night alternately thinking of Annie and how to rob a schooner. He suspected it might have many valuables aboard. Not being able to sleep, he lit a candle and grabbed the newspaper that he had bought on the street and that was still lying on his hotel room floor. On the second page, he read a very interesting piece that he had missed before. He reread about the visitor from the Union three times as an idea began to form.

Early the following morning, Jesse got up and left the hotel. He walked among the more affluent people in the city looking for a likely candidate walking alone and about his size. It took him a while before he spotted a likely victim dressed in a modern-day suit, then Jesse followed the man for several blocks. They entered a seedier neighborhood that contained factories, warehouses, and alleys. The man was obviously on his way to work. When the timing was right, Jesse stepped up behind the man, and, with one swift blow from the butt of his gun, he knocked the man out cold. He caught him, dragged him into an alley, and stripped him to his under clothing. He tied the stolen clothes into parcel and made his way back to his hotel. He continued to glance behind him, but within a few blocks, he was satisfied he had not been detected.

He changed into the stolen clothes and came out looking a different man. Calling a horse and carriage for hire, he ordered the driver to take him to the docks and to the schooner he had seen the previous day.

He told the driver to wait for him, and walked up the gang plank of the ship, looking neither left nor right. A sailor waited at the top of the gang plank, blocking his path.

"General Robert Anderson," Jesse said to the sailor. "I need to see the captain. He'll know who I am."

"Captain Grant, at you service," the captain said as he approached Jesse, looking him up and down.

"Good morning, Captain. I am General Robert Anderson. May we go to your cabin, so that we cannot be overheard?"

"This way, General." The captain said as he led the way down to his cabin below. When they were seated, captain Grant asked, "Have you proof you are General Robert Anderson? You look extremely young to be holding such a high rank."

"If you survive out in the field these days, and if you show any signs of authority and a sense of war, you are quickly promoted. These are hard times, Captain. If I were caught in the South, I would be put to death immediately. We are fighting battles in Chattanooga at this time and running very short of funds. We need money to buy food and horses as we cannot get supplies through to the battle fields. It is my understanding from my fellow intelligence officers that you are running money and jewels through to our post further up in the North, and I, and other generals, are greatly in need of the money immediately. I have travelled over many miles in peril of my life to get here in time to take what you have back to the battle fields so that our soldiers may survive and prevail."

Captain Grant hesitated for a few moments, until Jesse feigned annoyance. "Sir, I am not used to be questioned about my authority. I am a general in the Union army. Either you are on our side, or I must quickly deal with you and report to my superior, the President of the United States, Mr. Abraham Lincoln, letting him know what has transpired here today."

"Very well," captain Grant said standing up and retrieving a large box in one of his cabinets. This is all I have, you may take it, but I need you to sign for what you have taken."

"Of course, Captain."

He waited patiently for the captain to create a receipt. The small piece of paper stated that General Robert Anderson had appropriated gold and jewelry with an estimated value of 20,000.00 dollars. "Please sign here." He turned the paper for Jesse to sign.

Jesse signed with a flourish—the unreadable signature of General Robert Anderson. "Thank you, Captain." He said stood to pick up the box. The captain, however, snatched the box back.

"Sir, I know I have no reason not to trust you, yet I know this box is full of valuable jewels and coins and I am thinking that I should send some of my men to escort you back to the battle fields to make sure the revenue collected here is being used as it should." He turned to open his cabin door and shout out to the guard outside, when Jesse whipped out his gun and smashed it on the back of the captain's head knocking him out. He removed the captain's necktie and pushed it into the captain's mouth. He found a piece of rope, and he bound the captain's hands and feet. He pushed the captain to the back of the cabin near his bed and pulled the drape over him to hide the body. Straightening himself up, Jesse picked up the box. Walking out of the cabin, he turned and shouted into the open doorway. "Thank you so much, Captain. I will let President Lincoln know of you resourcefulness and the cooperation you have shown his army. May God bless you and all who serve aboard you ship. Good sailing, Captain." He quietly closed the door and, smiling, walked past the soldier on duty and up onto the deck above. He walked straight down the gangplank and got into his carriage which took off at a smart pace.

It was not until he got back to the seedy hotel and changed back into his own clothes that he took a deep breath. He had not realized how apprehensive and daring he had felt. He quickly walked out with the box tucked firmly under his arm and found the stable where Champion was boarding. He tossed a coin to the stable boy, saddled his horse, and tucked the box into his saddle bag. Then he calmly rode out of the stable and out of town. Only when he was in the open stretches of countryside did he urge Champion to gallop as if is life depended on it.

It was sunset as he rode back into Cooper's Landing. He sat for a moment on Champion as he looked at Annie sitting on the stoop. Her smile was tentative. The moment between them was broken by an excited Ben coming out to brush Champion down and feed and stable him.

As was Jesse's habit, he went to the pump and washed down. He removed the box from Champion's saddle and tossed a coin at an excited Ben who was throwing questions at him.

"Did you go to Mobile, Jesse? Was it a sight? I've never been, and my mom says she won't take me. What did you see?"

Jesse smiled at the young boy and wondered what would become of him in time. "Perhaps we could talk of this over the dinner table," he replied. "I need to go to the cottage first before I join you all for dinner."

He turned and quickly walked to the cottage. He looked around the sparsely furnished room and wondered where he could hide the box for a few days. Seeing a couple of beams forming a Y in the ceiling, he climbed on a chair and placed the box as far back as he could in the join, before returning to the White House and dinner.

"I waited for you to come back before serving dinner," Annie said with a hint of a smile. "Why don't you sit down and join us and tell us all about Mobile and how big you found it against our very quiet Cooper's Landing?"

He sat at the table and made them all laugh as he talked of ladies' fashions and parasols, and how the men wore suits and neck ties with ruffles and looked like fops. And then he talked of the schooners and boats in the docks and the cargo they bought in them. "But it seemed to me as if they were mostly taking cargo out rather than bringing it in. I don't think you would like it there, Ben. Of course, I can't speak for you, but the way of life here is so precious and so rare, that if I lived here in Cooper's Landing, I don't think I would ever want to live anywhere else."

"The why don't you stay here with us and be my daddy?" asked Lillian, looking at him with big, innocent, blue eyes.

He reached a hand across the table and caressed her face. "It would be so easy for me," he said quietly. "I really wish I could." And he quickly got up from the table and went outside and lit his pipe. He sat down and wondered what he had gotten himself into.

Annie came and joined him after a while and sat quietly before saying, "You mustn't take too much notice of Lillian. She's just a child, and she doesn't understand. She doesn't remember her father like Ben and I do. She was just a baby when he died. She's finding life a little different in the house with a man around, but she'll get used to your not being here when you leave."

"I'll be here for a few more days yet," he said, looking at Annie, "if that's agreeable to you."

She nodded her head and said no more until it came time to put the children to bed, and she quietly left the stoop without saying goodnight.

He went to the cottage and lay on top of his bed thinking of Annie. He knew if he stayed he could be in trouble, but on the other hand if the captain of the schooner had already reported his imitation of General Anderson and the theft he committed, there would be a bounty on his head in Mobile. He didn't want to take the risk of getting caught. A few days here would be advantageous for him. He got up and moved restlessly around. He removed his jacket and necktie and threw them on a chair. Then he unbuttoned the top few buttons on his shirt. He walked outside and looked at the stars above him and lit his pipe again, which was rare for him. One pipeful was usually sufficient before he retired for the night. As he stood contemplating the bright moon and stars in the sky, he heard a small rustling sound. Looking around, he saw Annie walking towards him in just a nightgown, which Jesse could see straight through in the moonlight.

He stood as still as a statue as she seemed to glide across the grass, the oak tree casting shadows across her body, making her all the more tempting. She looked at him with longing in her eyes. "It's been so long, Jesse, and I've really grown to like you. You can do what you like to my body. All I ask in return is that you treat me gently and with love and respect, and that you give as much back as you take."

His throat had gone dry. How could he resist this beautiful woman? Taking her hand he led her inside. They needed no light as the moon was shining brightly into the room. He watched as she lifted the nightgown over her head and dropped it to the floor. She was naked underneath, and he stared at her body before opening his arms and inviting her in. Time and again he lost himself in her body that night, but he could not slate the thirst he had for her, nor she for him.

In the morning, she slipped out of his bed to put coffee on and to get dressed before the children saw her. She waited for him on the pier with their coffee. They sat in silence watching the sun rise, casting beautiful colors and shadows across the ground. He reached over and took her hand in his. "I want to stay for a few days. Do you have any repairs that need doing on your house or grounds?"

"Yes, there are a few," Annie replied with a smile. The roof needs seeing to, if you wouldn't mind, and the barn we put Champion in needs to be turned into a proper stable. I think Ben would like his own horse, and when I can afford it one of these fine days, I will buy him one."

"What of Lillian?" he asked. "What would she like?" He smiled at the thought of the little girl.

"I think she wants a daddy and can't see beyond that right now."

"And what of you, Annie?" What do you want?"

She shook her head. "I can't have what I want."

"What, Annie? What is it?"

"I want you to stay, Jesse. But I know it's beyond the realm of possibility. So I am content for now with slipping into your bed at night. You made me very happy last night," she said with the merest hint of a blush.

He nodded his head. God, he was so tempted to stay. Last night had put all thoughts of his wife and child out of his head. But he was committed to the Knights of the Golden Circle and his family. Already he had stayed too long. He hoped it wouldn't hurt to stay for a few more days.

Jesse worked hard on the roof that day, repairing holes and cleaning the chimney. Ben stayed by his side most of the day, having first put Champion out in a field to eat his fill of grass.

That night, after the children had gone to bed, Annie returned to the cottage. Removing the nightgown, she slipped into the bed where Jesse was waiting impatiently for her. He sat up and pushed the covers from her body. He studied her outline, tracing it with his forefinger. He kissed her mouth, slowly and deliciously sending shivers up her spine. He kissed her forehead and her cheeks, trailing his lips to her ear and down her neck making her quiver with longing. The pad of his thumb swirled across her nipple making it peak with pleasure, but more so when his mouth followed and his teeth grazed across. She felt bereft when he took his mouth away until his lips ended on her belly button and then he traced his finger lower and his mouth and tongue followed. Her breath came in sort gasps as he found her hot moist center with his tongue. Her body rose in peaks as he bought her pleasure before asking if she was ready for him, and then he pushed into her, plunging in and out bringing them both to a world that neither had experienced before. She cried out his name at the peak of ecstasy, her fingernails raking down his back.

They lay quietly side by side. Neither one spoke of what had just happened. She was in love with this man, and he with her—she felt it deep in her soul. They made love many times again that night always to ecstasy and back, and each time, he drew her further and further into his heart.

The next few days followed the same pattern with Jesse making repairs to the fence, turning the barn into a stable, and chopping wood for the coming winter. When he could find no more to do, he spent a day riding into Fort Morgan on Champion with Ben. He found a horse trader near the Fort, and looking over the stock the man had for sale, he found a suitable gentle grey stallion for Ben. He paid for the horse, a saddle, and some feed. They also visited the trading post and purchased several items, including some tobacco for Jesse's pipe. They rode back slowly, arriving in the evening in time for supper.

He surprised Lillian with some pretty hair ribbons he had purchased and some material to make dresses. Annie had smiled and thanked him for his kindness toward her children.

That night he was waiting for her, and his love making had a poignant twist that she felt in every move and every kiss. She wondered if this was goodbye. After their second time of love making, he lay watching her sleep and pulled a strand of her hair away from her face. Then he fetched his sharp knife and cut the lock from her head. He dressed and retrieved the box, scooping out a huge handful of gold coins which he placed softly on the dresser next to the bed. He removed a large topaz stone on a gold necklace—not for the value—but because it would suit her skin and her eyes, and he placed it next to the money. He found a beautiful diamond solitaire in a simple setting of a plain gold band. He stared at it for a while, and then on the inside of the band with his knife, he scratched two initials—A and J— and he carved a heart in between the initials, wanting her to know how he felt. He steeled himself and took one last glance at the woman he had fallen in love with, the woman who had stolen his heart and soul, and he dejectedly walked out into the night. He saddled Champion and stole away with a heavy heart and a longing which would last his entire lifetime—a longing for a woman called Annie and her children. In honor of what they shared, he had an amulet made containing the lock of her hair. He wore it around his neck for the rest of his life.

Coin From the Knight of the Golden Circle.
One Thrown at Ben

He did not know he had left Annie with child, and, nine months later, she gave birth to a son she called Jesse Mason (for her father) James. Mason-James became a double-barreled surname of which future generations became very proud. No one knew, nor perhaps even cared, that Annie had another child, but Jesse grew up to be a fine young man who loved the Gulf and made his living from it. His brother Ben, who kept the coins tossed at him by Jesse, moved to Mobile and made a living as a successful merchant. He kept the grey stallion until it died of natural causes. He hadn't ridden him in years but he visited with him every day. Lillian grew up to be an opera singer and moved to Chicago. Annie refused to move from Cooper's Landing. She never wore any other jewelry except a golden topaz around her neck and a ring with hers and Jesse's initial carved into the band. She never again saw the man she still loved. When she died at a ripe old age the house Cooper's Landing became Jesse's.

Chapter 12

July 2013

This was the life of luxury. He lay back on his soft bed which had been waiting for him when he returned from the vet's. He lived in the sunroom now.

In the kitchen he had his own water bowl and feeding dish, and Morgan fed him twice a day. "I still like human food," he thought, "but it's great never to feel hungry again. This is my home. This is where I belong. Perhaps when I no longer have this bad pain, my dad will take me on the shrimping boat with him."

The rain poured down, bouncing from the glass roof top, but Chowder just rolled over on his bed and snuggled himself down. He was dry, and he had people who loved him. Life was good.

It was a while later when he heard the car and ran to the front door to greet his new owners. Morgan came in first, and Chowder danced around in front of her waiting for her to get his treat. David followed and bent down and patted Chowder's head. They got Chowder his treat and started a pot of coffee for Morgan. David grabbed a beer from the fridge. They headed for the sunroom, Morgan looking dejected. "I've talked and talked to Grandpa", she said to David. "I just don't understand why he's not coming 'round.

This is the fourth day now. Surely he should be making signs of coming back to us."

David hugged her on his way to the couch. "He'll make it, Morgan. I saw his eyes blinking today when you were talking to him. He knows your voice. You wait and see. Give him another couple of days, and he'll be just fine." He sat down and patted the cushion next to him.

"I'll get my coffee and come and join you," she mumbled still feeling dejected but knowing it was good for David to be optimistic.

She grabbed her coffee and sat down next to David and looked out at the rain still pouring down. "Even the day is miserable," she said. She looked over at Chowder who was trying hard to beg for food, and his antics made her smile. She looked over the top of his head and spotted something both she and David had forgotten. The Mason jar. Getting up, she walked over and retrieved the jar from its shelf. "We've forgotten about this with everything going on," she said smiling at David. "You've already pulled back part of the lid. Shall we take it off and see what's inside?"

David really smiled for the first time in days. "I can't believe we had forgotten it was here, but I don't see why we shouldn't have a look inside. Don't get too excited, a lot of sand poured out when I upended it the last time." He sat up and took the Mason jar from her and tried to unseal it. "I think I'm going to need a large screwdriver to get under the seal," he said to Morgan. "There's one out in the hall closet in a set of them on the wall. Could you get it for me please?"

Morgan quickly returned with the screwdriver in hand, and David put it under the seal and pushed and struggled with the lid. Suddenly, it popped off. "Don't look!" he teased Morgan. "Cover your eyes." He walked over to the coffee table and, kneeling down, he turned the jar upside down.

Morgan heard the soft tinkle of metal and David's intake of breath. "Can I look now?" she asked. And without waiting for an answer, she walked over to the coffee table. Staring hard, she slowly sank to her knees next to him as her hand moved across her mouth.

"There must be fifty coins here!" she whispered. "Oh my God, David! That's almost a million dollars!" Her finger reached tentatively to touch one, but somehow she couldn't. "David, this is crazy."

His hand suddenly snatched the gold from the table and pushed it back into the Mason jar. He was shaking.

"What are you going to do with it, David?"

"I don't know," he muttered. "I really don't know."

He pushed back the carpet and pulled up several floor boards that were loose. Underneath was a large safe. Punching in the combination, he opened it and shoved the jar inside and closed it up again.

He walked into the kitchen and got another beer. His eyes were darting around while he thought. He had not said much to Morgan, and she didn't know where his mind was taking him, but she almost fell over when he said, "I want to get my shrimper repaired. I'll go and see Dan tomorrow."

"You could buy a new one, David," Morgan said.

"No. Absolutely not," he said determinedly. "If I do that, people will know I've come into money. I just want the shrimper repaired. I think there could be more Mason jars down there, Morgan. We have to go and find the sunken ship." He drank deeply from his beer, finishing it. "We can't tell anyone about this, Morgan. No one at all! Promise me, Morgan, this will be just between the two of us." He looked fiercely at her and she nodded her head. "I need time to think."

David was full of surprises today. She didn't know he had a safe at home, and now he didn't want anyone to know of his find. How would he sleep knowing that all that money was under the floor boards?

It was almost time for her to go back to see Paul. She picked up a book from a shelf in the sunroom to read to Paul. The doctors had told her that even though he might not seem responsive, he could probably hear and maybe even understand, and reading to him would be therapeutic. It was a book on local fishing lore, homes, and places.

She got out the casserole dish and placed some chicken, vegetables, and sauce in it. She put it in the oven and turned it on low, leaving it to cook while she was out. She walked into the sunroom, and putting her arms around David's shoulders, she said, "I'll be out for about two hours, and then I'll come back and we'll eat—unless Paul comes 'round, of course. I'll call you if there's any news."

The hospital was busy with multiple emergencies that night. Morgan found her way to the ICU, and the nurse on duty greeted her now-familiar presence. "Nothing to report today, Morgan. Paul is still resting comfortably, although we did notice today his eyes were flickering underneath his lids."

"When he visited Paul this afternoon, Dr. Thomas was not sure if his eyes were moving because he was remembering what happened to him, or if he was coming around. We've kept a sharp eye on him, but nothing has happened since. Don't give up hope, Morgan," the nurse said as she saw the disappointment on Morgan's face. "Paul will be out of here soon. You wait and see if I'm not right." She smiled brightly at Morgan and touched her arm in a reassuring gesture.

Morgan walked in to Paul's room. He didn't look much better than when she had seen him the first day he was bought in. His head was bandaged, his arm was in a sling, and one leg was in traction. She could see the screw that had been put through the bone in his leg to immobilize it. The worst for her was listening to the ventilator. There were monitors doing their job keeping note of his heart rhythms and pulse. Nurses were constantly in and out of his room, and he had the best care he could possibly have, so why was it that he didn't come back to her?

Morgan pulled up a chair on his good side, as she thought of it, and taking his hand in hers, she bent over and kissed his forehead. "Hi, Grandpa. I'm back. Did you miss me? I'm running out of things to say to try to bring you back, so I thought I would read a book to you. Nothing exciting because the doctor said we should try to keep calm. It's a book written by a local artist on the fishing industry and the surrounding areas of the Gulf Coast. I think you may even be mentioned in it. Perhaps it will be of interest to both of us." Morgan cleared her throat as she opened the first page of the book and began to read to Paul. She would stop occasionally to see if the reading was having any effect, but nothing happened. Paul remained asleep. After two hours, she kissed Paul goodnight and left.

David seemed excited the next morning during breakfast. He told Morgan to get her computer out, and she sat down in the sunroom with it open on the floor, and looked at David.

"Try your computer," he said. "Go to your email." It was a thoughtful thing David had done for Morgan. He had an internet connection installed the day before while she was at the hospital. Now she could use her computer any time she wanted.

When she had finished playing with her computer, he insisted they go out together. David told Chowder to jump into the back of the car, and he instructed Morgan to drive to her grandfather's house. "Come on," he said when they got there, "The tape's been removed as it is no longer a crime scene." She walked through the back door and stood with her mouth open.

"Did you do this, David?" she asked staring at the kitchen in which she had spent most of her life. She saw the smile on his face. "You couldn't have done this all on your own! Who helped?"

"I bought my crew over here when you left yesterday—your grandpa's friend Tyler, Marylou and her husband, and some other people from the town. They all came and helped repair the damage. Have we done a good job?" he asked with a smile.

Morgan could only shake her head. Paul would be amazed that people cared enough to do this. "Thank you, David for thinking of him," she said, "and for doing this for me." Morgan walked around the house and knew that Tyler must have been a great help in restoring each item to its rightful place. It was almost as it had been before. She walked upstairs and saw they had removed all the clothing that had been ripped to shreds. Photos had been replaced in new frames. She was especially pleased to see the large one of her memaw had a new frame and was replaced by the side of her grandfather's bed.

They were just about to leave when Detective Lawson came by. "I thought I saw someone in here," he said.

"Do you have any news?" Morgan asked immediately.

"None at all, I'm afraid. This seems to have been a random act of violence. There was neither rhyme nor reason to this. Your grandfather was the only one attacked in the village. It very much looks as if the perpetrators got away with it. We tested the blood on David's driveway, but we have nothing in the data base. The trail has gone cold for us at the moment, but I won't give up. I will still keep looking. How is your grandfather?"

"He's still in a coma, but the hospital has been noticing some different eye movement from him, and they are hoping he might come around soon. I guess you'll need to interview him when he does."

"Yes, we will. Keep in touch," he said and left by the front door. He stood outside and lit up a cigarette. He had a feeling David was hiding something from the police but if he was, he was keeping it well hidden. David had remained strangely quiet when he visited two days after the incident. He had arrived early in the morning determined to get information from David. Instead, David had ignored his questions and claimed ignorance. Although the police had kept David under observation since, they had not seen him do anything suspicious. Now because they had no reason to continue surveillance, Detective Lawson reluctantly had to remove his men. He stubbed out his cigarette with his heel, walked to his car, got in, and drove away frustrated. He hoped Paul would come around and be able to help them.

Morgan looked at David and sighed. "I wish I knew what had happened. It really doesn't matter at the moment, I suppose. The most important thing is for my grandfather comes out of his coma." Her cell rang and she took it out of her pocket and opened it. "Really?" she said into the phone. "I'm on my way; I'll be there in twenty minutes. She looked at David with a genuine smile. "Grandpa's coming 'round. I have to go to the hospital."

"Let's go!" he said, grabbing her hand and heading for the car.

Morgan could not keep quiet on the way there. "It will be so good to get him back," she remarked. "Do you think we should tell him about us, David? He might not be happy to know we're living together." She stopped babbling long enough to look at David and ask, "Are we living together? I guess we're not really because you took me in because of what happened in Grandpa's house." Because David remained quiet, she looked over at him again. "Are we living together, David?"

"Is that what you want?" he asked. "Just to live with me?"

He pulled off the highway, into the stream of traffic on the main road, and concentrated on getting out of the traffic into the hospital parking lot. He pulled up in a spare parking space and looked at Morgan. She looked partly hurt and partly quizzical, not being quite sure what David meant. He asked, "Can we talk about this later? Right now we're here to see how Paul is." He got out of the car and walked around to the passenger side. He held his hand out to her, but Morgan was not sure what was going on and hesitated. David caught her hand in his, and they hurried into the hospital, leaving Chowder on the back seat with the window half way down.

Doctor Thomas was in the ICU, waiting for Morgan and David. He came out of Paul's room and looking at Morgan he said, "I'm sorry, Morgan, your grandfather has come around and is awake. But he has no memory of what happened that night. In fact, his memory seems to be very shaky just now. If he doesn't remember who you are, don't panic. Often a trauma such as he had can cause temporary loss of memory. So once again we have to ask you to be patient with him. We've taken him off the ventilator, and he is breathing on his own. That's really good. He says his arm and leg are not causing him too much pain. The ribs and lung are a different matter. We've put him on a morphine drip which we will administer to him in larger quantities, if necessary."

"Hopefully, we will see an improvement in the next couple of days and then we'll move him to a different room until we can release him. He should be able to have other visitors in the next few days. It will probably do him a lot of good if he does."

Morgan threw her arms around Doctor Thomas. "Thank you so much for all you've done for him," she whispered.

"You're welcome, Morgan. You have my card if there is anything else I can do for Paul—even after you've left the hospital." He turned and walked away to another patient.

Morgan put a smile on her face and steeled herself to walk into her grandpa's room. "Hello, Grandpa," she said.

He stared back at her. "Who are you?"

Morgan pulled up a chair to his bed and taking his hand which he tried hard to snatch away from her, "I'm Morgan— your granddaughter. Martin's daughter."

Paul continued to stare, but didn't say anything for a moment. "I don't know you. Why are you here?"

Morgan turned to look helplessly at David who was hovering in the doorway. She was so unsure of what to say to him. David entered the room and stood by the side of the bed, "Morgan is related to you, Paul. You had a nasty accident, actually if truth be told, you were attacked. Do you remember anything of that night?"

Paul looked at David. "I think I might know you. But what attack? I don't know what you are talking about."

"You don't remember being punched and hit around the head—possibly nearly kicked to death?" David asked.

Paul shook his head. "Is this why I'm here and in pain?"

"I'm afraid so, Paul. You've been in the hospital for a week now and had us all worried. It probably will take you time to get your memory back, but Morgan and I will look after you."

Paul just nodded his head and looked back at Morgan who had sat quietly through the interchange with David. She smiled back at Paul and quietly said, "I read to you yesterday, and I thought today I might continue reading the story if that's all right with you."

Paul just nodded his head. Morgan opened to the page she had stopped at the night before and began to read. Paul closed his eyes and listened to her. David interrupted long enough to say he would be back in about two hours to pick her up. Morgan just nodded her head.

Paul opened his eyes long enough to ask Morgan, "Did you read to me before?"

She smiled back at him and excitedly said, "Yes. I did yesterday."

Paul replied, "I remember your voice. Keep going."

And Morgan did for about an hour when their morning coffee was bought in. Paul drank his through a straw. Putting it down on the tray in front of him he suddenly said, "I remember the Morning Sun Rise. That was my shrimper."

"Yes, it was, Grandpa," she replied. "Perhaps this book will bring your memory back. Do you remember Oak Tree Town?"

He nodded and said, "It's where I live."

"Do you remember me now?" she asked softly.

But Paul just shook his head and added, "But you seem like a nice young lady. Thank you for reading to me. I'm tired now and I think I would like to sleep."

"Would you like me to sit here quietly while you do? I'll come back this afternoon and read you some more if you would like."

"That would be nice," he said. She took his hand again and she held it until he went to sleep.

Morgan walked out to the nurse's station and asked the nurse not to let the police in to see her grandfather unless either she or David was with him.

David was late picking her up but explained, "I've just had Dan tow the boat around to his boatyard. He's going to be putting in a refurbished engine. Hopefully it will be ready in a couple of days. I gave him the eight thousand dollars we got for the coins and another five I had saved up in my bank account. I want to take the rest of the coins to another dealer and have them valued and then sell them."

"I'm sure Gareth could get you a good price," Morgan suggested.

David said nothing until they drew up at his house. Chowder jumped out of the car as soon as David opened the door for him, and ran across the bluff to find a suitable place to pee. They watched as he stretched and ran back to them determined not to be left outside. Warm or not, his place was in the house. He would defend these two to the death.

They fed Chowder, and then ate lunch with Chowder sitting at David's feet waiting for the scraps.

"It's a beautiful afternoon," David sighed. "Let's go for a walk across the bluff."

Morgan changed into shorts. They called Chowder to come with them, and they walked out of the door. Both David and Morgan were strangely quiet. Morgan, because David had avoided most of her questions, and David, because he did not know how to bring her questions back up. They followed the same path they had the first day they walked together. Morgan ran off to get her feet wet in the water which was much warmer now. Chowder ran in the Gulf after her, barking at the incoming waves and birds flying around. He had much improved since he had come back from the vet's. Living in the house had helped terrifically. Morgan picked up a stick and threw it in the water for him to retrieve forgetting he still had stitches, and he yelped as the salty Gulf water hit the wound, but then went after the stick anyway.

David smiled as he watched the two and their antics. Morgan came running over to him with Chowder in hot pursuit. She was laughing with her face turned up into the sun. She turned her back to David and threw the stick for Chowder, and he ran off to retrieve it. She looked round at David who still was oddly silent. He reached out and took Morgan's hand and holding hers asked, "Is that what you want, Morgan? Just to live with me? Or do you want more than that?"

She stared back at him and asked, "What more is there, David?"

David stuck his free hand in his pants pocket and retrieved the small box there. He knelt down on one knee. Chowder had retrieved the stick and ran up, jumping around David, thinking he was playing. David opened the box to reveal a beautiful solitaire diamond. "Morgan, I am not a very romantic man and don't have the words others do, but, I love you. Will you marry me?"

She stared at him for a moment with one lone tear trickling down her face. "Yes," she whispered.

He took her trembling hand in his and pushed the diamond on her engagement finger. "It fits!" he smiled. Standing up and taking her in his arms, he devoured her mouth and whispered after, "I love you, Morgan. I don't want you for a night or a few more. I want you around forever. I want to have children with you and make our home here. Do you think you could be happy here?"

She could only nod her head and hang onto the man she had come to love in such a short time. "We're really engaged?" she asked looking up at him.

"It's what people usually do before they get married," he laughed back. "We'll get married as soon as Paul can get out of the hospital. You need someone to give you away! Until then, I would like to go down and see if there are more of those jars."

"Are we going to take them all to Gareth?" she asked.

He stopped walking along the sand and turned toward her his mouth going into a thin line. "You haven't connected the dots yet have you, Morgan?" he asked, concern showing in his eyes. The puzzled look on her face showed him she hadn't. "Gareth was the only one who knew about the coins, and you told him your grandfather had a collection. Paul and I were targeted. I'm not saying Gareth himself assaulted your grandfather, but I am saying he sent some thugs down here to do it for him."

"No!" Morgan countered. "You're wrong, David! Gareth wouldn't do such a thing........ Would he?"

"Think about it, Morgan," David replied. "I have, and nothing else makes any sense at all. I think it will be a good thing if Paul cannot remember what happened. We don't need the police confiscating the coins."

"If you don't take the coins to Gareth, where will you take them?"

"I've found someone in New Orleans who is a genuine coin collector. He also knows someone who lives in Hollywood who would like to have them for his private collection if I find more than a few. Honestly, Morgan, I think we would be better off leaving Gareth out of all this."

Morgan nodded her head, not convinced that Gareth was responsible. "They're your coins, David. I was only trying to be helpful. You must do what you think is right. When are you going to New Orleans? I don't think I can leave my grandfather for any long period of time yet."

"I'm not in any hurry. I just have to phone my contact in New Orleans, and he'll meet with me any day I choose. Let's get Paul home first and my shrimper back in the water. I need to get my crew back working. I haven't been able to pay them for the time my boat's been laid up, and, honestly, I've been a little more than concerned over Paul. Now I know my crew is running short of money, and they haven't been able to pick up any more work from other shrimpers. I owe them, Morgan—big time."

Hesitantly, Morgan said, "I have some money in my savings account. You could pay them out of that, and then, if you're bull headed enough, you could pay me back when you've sold the coins." They were walking up the side of the bluff when Chowder suddenly ran between their legs, and David nearly fell over him.

"I've just got engaged to you Morgan—not married. I can't take money from you."

"Why not?" she demanded, standing stock still, her back straight. "You can pay me back, David. If you prefer, I'll take two of the coins in exchange for four thousand dollars, and I'll sell those."

It was at moments like this, he loved Morgan more than any other time. She was not the least intimidated by him, having her own thoughts and ideas and demanding at times to have her own way.

Looking down at her from his height advantage, he suddenly picked her up and swung her around. Excited by the play, Chowder jumped around, wanting to join in. "Okay," he said, "I give in. I'll sell you two coins." Then kissing her lightly at first, but then with a hunger he had not felt since coming back to the Gulf, they hurried home and celebrated their love in bed, with Chowder in the sunroom asleep on his warm bed.

Two days later, Paul was lying in the ICU recuperating nicely. There was talk from the nurses of moving him into a standard room soon because he was mending so well. He liked that Morgan read to him every day, and had asked her to buy the daily paper and read that, so the book she had started had been put to one side and she read the paper every day. He was due to start physiotherapy the following day to relearn how to walk and to use the arm that had been broken. Once he was able to bathe himself and walk a little, he would be allowed to go home.

David and Morgan had discussed the possibility of Paul coming to stay with them for the first few weeks after he was released. It would make life easier for both Paul and Morgan as she was to be his caretaker.

David was once again shrimping and the crew members were amazed when he paid them a thousand dollars each for their down time. Ben was especially pleased as he was now able to pay some of his never-ending, outstanding bills.

Chowder's bed was moved up into the bedroom. Morgan felt a little more comfortable with him sleeping by her side when David was shrimping. It gave them both peace of mind. Once or twice, when David was out at night, Chowder paced restlessly and growled, but after a short while, he settled down again and had gone to sleep. That left Morgan second guessing every creak and groan in the house until she was too exhausted to stay awake.

Paul was moved into a new room out of the IC Unit. Morgan drove his friend Tyler to the hospital for a visit. The two men argued over the articles written in the paper, but would end up laughing over the same articles. Morgan saw them interacting and was a little peeved that her grandfather still did not recognize her. She had left Tyler with Paul when the police interviewed him. Tyler would tell her what went on— which turned out to be big fat nothing. Paul maintained he remembered nothing at all of his attack. Morgan had looked at Detective Lawson on his way out. She gave him a sad smile. "He doesn't even remember me," she said. "I wish he did. I'm to take him home in two days. He says he doesn't remember home either. I think David and I will have him with us for the first few weeks until he can take care of himself. If you need to see him again, you'll know where to find him."

Two days later, both Morgan and David bought Paul home. They took him to his own home at first, but he seemed reluctant to walk into it. He shook his head and mumbled, "I don't want anything from here." Morgan walked upstairs with him to his bedroom and Morgan packed up some of his toiletries from the bathroom. When she stepped back into the bedroom, she saw him holding the photo of his deceased wife. He traced the outline of her face with his finger, and tears came to his eyes.

"Take the picture with you," Morgan advised.

Paul looked at Morgan. "You look like her, Morgan. Even when you were a young girl, you looked just like I remember she looked as a youngster. She was the prettiest woman you ever saw. Her hair was like yours, only much redder, and she had freckles over her nose and the cutest laugh you've ever heard. I fell in love with her the moment I saw her and vowed she would be mine. I could not have been happier than on our wedding day."

He looked at his granddaughter. "I do remember you. Do you want me to stay here?"

"No, Grandpa. I want you to come and stay in David's house with us. I can look after you there."

"You're not living with that man are you? He'll never amount to much, Morgan. You could have had your pick of any man. Why him?"

"It's nice to have you back, Grandpa," Morgan said with a smile. "Feisty as ever!" Laughing, she planted a kiss on his cheek and led him out of his house, back to the car, and to David's house, which she had come to think of as home.

Every other day, a physiotherapist came to the house to work with Paul—much to the amusement of Morgan and David, as all Paul did was moan and groan. Slowly but surely, he was regaining his strength. It had been five weeks since David and Morgan had returned from New York. She had several calls from Gareth, but just ignored them. David felt it was worth leaving Paul for a few hours while he and Morgan took the shrimper out without the crew. He had placed quite a few air tanks on board and had checked his diver's suit. They went out a long way into the bay, hidden from the coastline, and David punched in the coordinates that he'd written down into his GPS.

He went down on his own into the clear waters of the Gulf, and swam until he hit the bottom. Because he had two tanks of air this time, he could spend longer looking around. He tried to find the mast of the boat. Instead he found a lot of beautiful fish that swam up to him with interest, but then swam quickly out of his way, and he found seaweed growing from rocks, but didn't find anything close to a mast. He swam further away from the boat, kicking his fins, all without success. He saw some beautiful red snappers that were so good to eat swimming around him almost as if they were teasing him because he had no way of getting them out of the Gulf. He had to swim quickly to one side when a huge marlin came and looked around, scaring the red snapper away. He checked his tanks and saw he was running low. Disappointed he had found nothing else, he went topside to see that his shrimper was several hundred feet away from him. He swam back to the boat, disappointment in every stroke he took. He was sure he had put the coordinates in to his GPS correctly, so why hadn't he found the wreck again?

Morgan helped David climb back on the boat. He took off his diving gear and dejectedly sat down on a bench. "Nothing," he said. "I didn't find the damn wreck. I don't understand why, Morgan. I put the right coordinates in the GPS." He sat quietly for a while, and then, making up his mind, he said, "I'm not giving up. We'll come out again. I have to get back today—it's almost time for me to go shrimping." He turned the boat around and headed for the shore.

Chowder was pleased to see Morgan when she arrived home. She opened the door for him and instructed, "Go and find David. He's on the boat." Chowder ran down to the docks and jumped on the shrimper. Ben saw him coming and had laughed at the dog's antics in getting there. "You taking him with you today, David?"

"No," David replied. "I'm happier right now with him staying with Morgan and Paul."

Ben nodded his old head and replied. "A wise decision! It was a bad thing that happened to Paul. You don't want it to happen to him again—or to Morgan. Did you ever find out who attacked Paul?"

"No. The police never did find the bastards, but if I do, I'll take them apart. They kicked and punched the old man like he was a target. I don't understand anyone's mentality that would hurt a harmless old man."

David shook his head and as he and Ben got the boat ready to take out, Ben looked at Paul and said, "I got me a gun, Boss, if you want to keep one at home and if you want help to kill them bastards, I'm with you."

David smiled at Ben, and, putting his arm around the old man's shoulders, said, "I know I could count on you Ben, but let's hope this comes to nothing." He turned to find Chowder had made himself at home on the shrimper, so he ordered, "Go home, Chowder, and find Morgan."

The dog's tail dropped as if he had done something wrong, but as David said, "Go on, Chowder," he jumped from the boat and made his way back home. He found Morgan calling for him from the wide-open door. He ran into the house and sat, expecting a treat. He gobbled it down, and then Paul called him over to his chair. He curled up at Paul's feet, feeling life was really good.

Paul improved so much after going home that David asked Morgan, "Can you leave him for a day, and we'll go to New Orleans?"

Both David and Morgan were really excited to meet up with the coin collector. They left very early in the morning and arrived in New Orleans at ten. The coin dealer, Geoff Wright, waited for them at a hotel on Bourbon Street.

He was in the foyer as they walked in. Introducing himself, he told them he had booked a room for the morning so that they could have privacy while they conducted their transaction. "I've also bought in the collector from California that I mentioned. His name is John Standing. He already has quite the collection, most of which he has purchased from me over the years. Rather than my buying these coins from you and then selling them to him, I'm quite willing to take a fee for introducing you, and then it's up to you both to come to some arrangement." He walked toward the room he had arranged for them and continued, "Usually I would be only too happy to buy. However from the quantity you mentioned, I thought it might be better to find someone who is wealthy enough to pay a good price for them." He led them into the room, and they saw John Standing for the first time. He stood with his back to them, hands in his pants pockets and looking out of the window.

John turned to them as they came in, and Geoff made the necessary introductions. They all shook hands. Morgan noted his suit was tailor made, his shoes were good quality leather, and his briefcase, lying on the coffee table, also was of high quality leather. He stood tall—around six feet four—had a mustache and beard that suited him well. He had a lot of grey in his hair and lines in his face which would indicate he was in his late sixties.

John immediately said, "I have no credentials to show you, but I am an authentic collector, and I have a driver's license here to verify who I am. And, of course, I have been a client of Geoff's for years."

David tentatively shook hands with John, who seeing how hesitant he looked, took a magazine out of his briefcase. "Maybe this will put your mind at ease," he said with a smile. David immediately saw John's photo on the front page. He was an entrepreneur who had amassed a fortune over the past thirty years. The article on the inside suggested there was no one who could touch him in his ventures into space, airplanes, electronics, and real estate.

"I hate to push myself forward as it would seem as if I'm bragging," he said. "I just wanted you to know that no matter what I see today, I can afford to purchase the coins from you. I'm not here to waste your time." There was a knock on the door and John said, "I took the liberty of ordering some coffee and rolls. I hope you don't mind." He opened the door for the waiter who wheeled in a cart.

Morgan had stood all through the introductions and suddenly her instincts told her she could trust this man. She took off her jacket and sat down ready for negotiations. After all, two of those coins were hers.

After the waiter had left the room and everyone was seated with coffee, Morgan pulled out the Mason jar from the tote she had bought with her. Very carefully, so as not to disturb the bones on the outside of the jar, she un-wrapped it and set it on the coffee table. No one said anything for a moment, and then John stood up and walked around the coffee table studying the jar from all angles. He took his glasses out from the inside pocket of his suit jacket and put them on and walked around the jar again.

David watched for a moment or two and then said, "We put the coins back in the Mason jar and reattached the lid. We kept one of the coins out, so that you may see they are genuine."

John, never taking his eyes from the jar, nodded. He hunched down and looked at the bones. "Have you taken this anywhere for DNA sampling or authentication?"

Morgan replied, "No, we haven't."

John Standing stood back up and began to pace up and down looking extremely excited. "Is this the only one?"

David was a little more reticent about his find, and hesitantly replied, "Yes."

"I understand you have sold several of the coins to a dealer in New York, which is a pity, but it can't be helped now. Can Geoff look at the coin you kept out?"

David passed the coin over, and Geoff proved to be as excited as John. "It's real all right. Is the jar full of them?"

"I am willing to pay you a million dollars in cash this morning without opening the Mason jar again," John said firmly.

David shook his head, "I think we should open the jar so that you know I am not duping you. It is, after all, a two-way street."

"No, John," replied. "I trust you, and besides I know where to find you." he smiled at David. "We're both honest businessmen, and Geoff, although he doesn't know you that well, had you investigated. He vouches for you. I am going to take this away and have the entire thing authenticated. Then I would like to get in touch with you again if that's all right with you."

"Of course," David said.

"Now, John said, "I think we have ignored Morgan long enough. What are you going to do with all this new found wealth, Morgan?"

"It's not my money," she smiled. "It's David's, and I think it is up to him as to what he does with it."

"Wouldn't you like to move to somewhere more exotic?"

"I don't know," she replied, wishing he would stop asking her questions. "I guess David and I haven't given thought to that, nor talked about it."

"Well," John said, as he rose up once again and placing his glasses back into the inside of his jacket. Just as carefully as Morgan had un-wrapped the Mason jar, he rewrapped it. "My chauffeur is outside, and my plane is waiting at the airport. Your money is in this briefcase, David. Check it before I leave. I left the keys in the lock, and my card is also in the briefcase. If you find any more Mason Jars, call me. Oh," he continued turning back and looking at them, "if you would like me to help you invest any money let me know. I would be happy to advise you both." He held out his hand and shook David's before turning to Morgan and said, "Perhaps I could have a hug from you? It would put us on a friendlier and more personal note."

David and Morgan began the drive back to Dolphin's Cove in stunned silence. Locked in the briefcase behind them was one million dollars, less the $10,000.00 dollars they had paid Geoff. Neither had ever seen that amount of money before, nor had they thought what they could do with that amount.

John Standing had boarded his plane and taken off for California. He was excited because the coin was authentic, and because, unknown to the other two, the jar itself might be worth a lot of money because of the bones around the outside. When he arrived back in his home, he would start a search for ships that went down in the Gulf near Mobile and see if he could track which boat had held the treasure

Shrimp Boats in Harbor

Chapter 13

When they got home, David placed the bounty in his safe under the floor boards. Paul was already in bed, but Chowder had given the two a warm welcome home. Morgan had laughed and said, "Anyone would think we've been away for months instead of a day!"

David still seemed quiet and was obviously pondering on something. Having put the coffee on for them, Morgan joined David in the dark in the sunroom, overlooking the beautiful waters of the bay.

"Will you tell me what you're thinking about, David?"

"I've been given a huge responsibility with this money. I could just up and leave here with you, and we could live a good life on what we have. But I have a feeling in the pit of my stomach that it's not the right thing to do. This town could thrive as it did years ago if money was infused in to it one way or another, but I don't want to be hailed as the town savior either. I'm also thinking I want to dive again and see if there are any more of these Mason jars to bring up from the sunken ship. The coordinates were wrong, and I don't know why, but I can dive again and again until I find the wreck. It can't be far away from the coordinates I put in the GPS."

"What are you thinking of, Morgan?" he continued. "You lived in the big city and loved it. Perhaps John Standing can help us, and we could move to a city of some sort and see what we think. We could live high on the hog and enjoy ourselves."

Morgan thought for a few moments before very carefully saying, "I know we're engaged, David, and I do want to spend the rest of my life with you, but the money is yours, and I think you should do whatever you feel is right in your heart. I would live in a mansion with you, if that's what you want, but I would be just as happy to live here with you. Give some thought to what you want to do with the money, and we'll talk again some other time." She smiled at him and said, "I've made coffee for us, but I would really like to go to bed and make love to you."

The sparkle returned to his eyes, and he stood pulling her up with him and said, "Forget the coffee."

The following day, David went to see Dan. Dan called out to him, "Hi David. How's the shrimper working?"

"It's really good thanks, Dan. The refurbished engine made all the difference." David looked around the workshop and saw a forty foot fishing boat for sale. "What's the story of the fishing boat over there?"

"What'd you want with one of those, David? Giving up shrimping and living a life of leisure?" Dan said wiping his hands clean on a rag.

"Yeah, right. I wish," David replied. "Is it reliable, or does it need work?"

"Yeah, it's okay for a runabout. Short trips—that sort of thing. I wouldn't take it out too far into the Gulf, especially in rough weather. It's a crossover—both bay and Gulf—but the make isn't that great. The guy that brought in in here wanted something a little bigger and faster so he could stay out in the really rough weather. He wanted to catch marlin. This boat couldn't hack it." Dan leaned against the side of the boat curious as to why a shrimping man would buy a small runabout fishing boat.

"Can I have a look?" David asked, before hoping up the ladder and stepping inside. At forty foot, the boat was roomy inside. There was a small cabin underneath where he could keep his diving gear and air tanks. The boat had a GPS on the dashboard, a ship-to-shore radio, and two 300hp engines on the back. This boat would be ideal to look for the treasure. He could have Ben captain the shrimper while he spent the time diving with this boat.

Dan came aboard the boat too and asked David, "Are you really thinking of buying this boat then, David? I'll see if I can make you a sweet deal if you are."

"How much?" David asked turning to look at Dan.

"Well, the guy who's selling was asking $185,000..00 It's only a year old, but to you, I'll see if I can get the price down to around $155,000.00 I'll give him a call if you're interested."

"Can I take it out for a test run?" David asked.

"'Course," Dan replied. "I wouldn't dream of buying something without testing it. Let's get it in the water." Dan attached the boat and trailer to his truck and backed it into the bay. David hoped on board and started the engine up. It ran as sweetly as he wanted. "Hang on!" Dan shouted. "I'll come with you."

They pulled away from the boat yard dock, and David opened up the engine and flew across the bay. She handled the swell on the water well, and as they crossed over from the bay to the Gulf itself the swell was bigger, but still the boat ran well. He could see why a sailor would need a bigger boat to stay out in rough weather, but, all in all, this would be fine for his purpose.

He smiled back at Dan who asked, "Is this what you want then, David?"

"I guess this will do for me," he said as he sped across the water back to the boatyard. "I'd like to haggle over the price."

"Dan looked at his friend and said, "I'm pretty sure I couldn't get it for less than $155,000.00 I'll try if you want me to, but I think you could lose the sale."

David hummed and hawed a little before nodding his head and saying to Dan, "Okay, go ahead. Tell him I'll pay cash for it."

"Come into some money then, David?"

"Not so's you'd notice," David replied.

It wasn't long before Dan came back and said, "The Dolphins Leap is all yours for the agreed price of $155,000.00 cash. I told him that $7,000.00 of that was my commission for selling it. Thanks, David. I appreciate the business."

"I'll be back tomorrow with the money," David replied with a smile. "Perhaps I'll take Morgan out for a run—and maybe even that silly mutt."

The following day, as David had promised, he returned to the boatyard with the money to buy the fishing boat. Dan put it in the water for them and David, Morgan, and Chowder boarded. With David at the helm, they went far out on the bay. Morgan had only been fishing with her grandfather once or twice, and now found she loved the water as she sat excitedly by David's side. Chowder sat at the front of the boat, his head raised and breathing in the scents held in the salty air, his ears flying back in the wind. David took them out as far as he thought the coordinates would take him, and they looked back to see no other boats around. "We've lost the smaller crafts, and so far there are no shrimpers out," David said. Chowder came and sat down at their feet as suddenly he found he could no longer see land and he was feeling a little unsure of himself. David swung the boat around and they headed home. He tied the boat up on his pier and they walked home talking excitedly about the boat.

When he returned later that afternoon to go shrimping, he went on board the Crimson Tide and retrieved his diving gear. He placed it in the cabinet of Dolphin's Leap and locked the cabin.

The Crimson Tide left harbor when the tide was full, watched by Morgan, Paul, and Chowder. She made a fine site in the late afternoon sun making her way across the bay, the sun dipping behind a cloud. David called Ben into the cabin, "Take the helm and guide us out to our usual fishing grounds, would you, Ben?" he asked.

Ben was really happy. He had once or twice before captained the boat and felt he was perfectly capable of the task. However lately he had not been asked. He thought of his ancestors who were slaves out in the cotton fields and wondered how they would feel about him captaining a shrimping boat.

David let the crew run the boat that night. He made no comments, and did not interfere with any decisions. The catch was large and all hands were needed, but David did not offer to help, and the crew wondered why. David just watched as the men did what they did every night, but this time under Ben's command. The following morning as they pulled into the dock, David turned to Ben. "You did an excellent job, Ben," he said. "Is your grandson, Jeremy still looking for work?"

"Yes, sir," Ben said. "He left school a good year ago, but he hasn't been able to find anything steady."

"When you go out this evening, you might like to include him in the crew," David said. "It might do him good to be able to learn something of the fishing industry."

"Thanks," Ben smiled.

"You know the tides, Ben," David continued, "and the fishing grounds. Take the Crimson Tide out with the crew on your own tonight. I'll be gone for a few days. Look after her and the catches and, I promise you, I will do the same for you." He turned and jumped down onto the pier, leaving the men with mouths wide open.

David returned to the cottage to find Paul fussing at Morgan. "I do not need any more help. I can do things for myself, Morgan, and, furthermore, I would like to return to my own home."

David stepped in to the fray, and doing his best to soothe the argument between Paul and Morgan said, "We would be happy to return you to your own home tomorrow, Paul. That will give us today to pack up all you've got here and take it with us. We'll also need to do some food shopping for you. Your fridge and pantry are empty. You tell us what you would like and I'll go and shop for you. How does that sound?"

Paul mumbled his thanks to David. "You see?" he rounded on Morgan. "One of you has got some sense. I always did say I liked this boy." He hobbled away to the sunroom and sat in his chair there, Chowder following in his wake and sitting at his feet.

Instead of going to sleep as he should, David went first to find Tyler and let him know that Paul was returning home. "I think he's had enough of Morgan fussing around him," he said with a smile. "She can be a little bossy with him, and I think he's had as much as he can tolerate. Perhaps you would be so kind as to spend a little time with him?"

"I sure will, Tyler had replied. "I'll also make sure to lock his doors when I leave."

"Thanks, Tyler. That will help enormously."

His next stop was in to Marylou's café. "I'm sorry, I don't think Morgan will be back to work for some time," he told her. "Paul is moving back home tomorrow, but then I need her for a little while," he had continued.

"That's okay," Marylou had said. "I took on a new young girl the other day and she seems fine. At least she seems to like the work and the clientele, so no big deal. I will take Paul some meals to put in his freezer. He still needs looking after."

"Yep, he does, and that's just what Morgan is doing right now—cooking some meals for him to take home and keep in his freezer. You are all amazing," he said. He left the café and stopped by the supermarket to get basic supplies for Paul. He went back to Paul's home and filled the fridge and freezer with his purchases.

As he left Paul's house, he saw a black, foreign-made car parked a little further up the road. Someone was sitting in the car, seemingly asleep, but David made a mental note of the car's plate before driving away. It was an out of state plate, which bothered David. However he had no one to ask to run a plate through the DMV for him and so he put it in the back of his mind and drove home.

Morgan had packed up the clothes they had bought for Paul and looking at Chowder lying on Paul's feet, she wondered if he should go with her grandfather, but then she changed her mind as she had grown to love the silly mutt who had obviously defended David's house.

They drove Paul home and David looked down the road, but the car he had seen earlier had disappeared. They settled Paul into his house, and he seemed to just crumple into his chair looking really happy. Morgan put a casserole into the oven for him and put the other meals she brought into the freezer.

"Are you sure you'll be all right, Grandpa?" she asked as she and David got ready to leave.

He patted her hand that was lying on his shoulder. "I'll be fine, Morgan. You have done a wonderful job looking after me, but it's time I was on my own again before I get used to all this fussing, and it's time you and David had the place to yourselves." He smiled gently at his granddaughter and then shouted, "David! When do you intend to make an honest woman of my granddaughter?" He turned his head to watch as David walked in from the kitchen.

David had a wide smile on his face when he said, "I have to make an honest woman of her?" and laughed as Paul began to splutter indignation from all sides. "Don't worry Paul. I'll marry her as soon as we can find a date for both of us and when your leg is healed. Morgan has told me she wants you to walk her down the aisle. I trust you'll honor us with doing that?"

"I was planning on it," Paul grumbled. "Make the date sooner rather than later. I might not last that long!"

Tyler chose to make an entrance at that time, so Morgan put another dinner into the oven for him, and David and Morgan escaped. She had waited to see if Chowder would stay with Paul, but he followed them out to the car, making it quite clear he was going home with them.

The following day, Morgan paid a visit to her grandfather first thing and made breakfast for him. "Yes, I had a good night, and there was no need for you to come 'round this morning," he replied to her inquiry. "I thought I had made it clear I want some time on my own," he grumbled as he ate the breakfast she had made.

"I won't see you again today, Grandpa," she commented. "So stop your protesting, and just eat the breakfast. I just wanted to know you had survived the night."

"Fuss, fuss, fuss. That's all you do," he grumbled back.

Morgan left as soon as she could knowing, that despite his complaints, her grandfather had been pleased with the visit.

Morgan and David planned to drive to Mobile as soon as she got back to the house. David was determined to dive again, but he needed more equipment than he had, especially if he was going to be digging in the sand. He also needed more guide rope to tie around the boat and himself, larger tanks of air, and maybe a better diving suit.

By the time they left the dive shop, the car was packed with diving gear and the essentials that David would need. He had again spent money from the stack he had in his safe, but he felt the investment was worth it. As the road cleared a little behind them on their way back, David checked his rear view mirror to see the same model black car he had seen outside of Paul's house the afternoon before. He said nothing to Morgan, but kept an eye on the car. By the time they got to Dolphin's Cove, the car was nowhere in sight. David wondered if it was all in his imagination. They drove straight down to the dock and David unloaded everything he had bought and placed it into the cabin of his new boat. Locking it firmly, they left to go home and get lunch.

They ate outside, enjoying the sun, and just as they were finishing, David had a call from John Standing.

"David! Good afternoon!" John said. "Good to know you're still around. You got home safely, I take it?"

"I certainly did," David replied. "Is there a problem? I didn't expect to hear from you for a while."

"Hmm," John replied. "It depends on what you call a problem." He hesitated for a second. "Did you know, David, that you were followed home from New Orleans and have been under surveillance ever since?"

David got up from his chair and walked as far away from Morgan as he could so that she would be unable to hear this conversation. "Well," he replied, "I've seen a black, foreign made car hanging around Oak Tree that I'd not seen before, and I believe it followed me home from Mobile today."

"Yes, it did," John cut in. "It's not even very good at what it's supposed to be doing."

"Are you in California?" David asked.

"Yes, I am," John replied.

"Then how in the hell do you know I am being followed and watched?"

"I have my own team down there trying to keep you and Morgan safe. Obviously you have not spotted them because you had no idea. But they report into me every few hours, and I wanted you to be aware of what is happening. I left a man keeping an eye on Paul too. It was a simply dreadful thing to have happened to Morgan's grandfather. I thought it might take your mind of that problem as it seems you do care for the old man."

"Look, David," John continued, "I really don't want to worry you, but you sold some of the coins that belonged in that Mason jar, and without a doubt, whoever you told about the coins is now waiting to see if there really are any more. You were out this morning at a specialized diving store, buying equipment presumably to go and see if you can find other jars. The people who were following you were right behind you. They even came into the store with you. You've bought a fishing boat, thank goodness with plenty of horsepower on it." John took a deep sigh before continuing. "At this moment, you are being very transparent in your dealings," John finished, "I am concerned for yours and Morgan's lives." He took a deep breath in which David jumped in.

"I really do appreciate your help, especially with Morgan's grandfather. He means a lot to both of us. He still hasn't got him memory back from that night and, honestly, I think it would be a good thing if he didn't remember. I took my smaller boat, Dolphin's Leap out the other day, but no one followed me of that I'm sure."

"Probably not then," John replied, "but they too were buying this morning. Of course my men could not stop them. It's their right to purchase equipment. But why would they be buying the same equipment as you? And I do know they have also purchased a similar smaller boat."

"I think if I flew in and talked to you, say, in two days, David," he said consulting his own diary and wondering if he could put some appointments off, "we could sort something out between us. You need more manpower and protection for Morgan both on the boat and at home. I don't mean to push myself forward but I think my men and I could be useful to you."

David reluctantly said. "I would like to think over what you've told me and come back to you."

John replied briskly, "That's okay with me David, just don't do anything crazy that will endanger any of your lives. Money is not worth it. Call me back soon." And he disconnected his call. John drummed his fingers on his desk while he was thinking. If David knew where the ship had gone down,

John wanted to be there for the find. He was not trying to dupe David out of anything, but if they could remove any further money from the ship, maybe it would be possible to bring the ship up from its watery grave. The more John gave thought to all of this, the more excited he got and the more determined he was to be there. This was history— part of the Knights of the Golden Circle and part Civil War. He was a philanthropist and a true Southern gentleman. He walked out to his secretary placing his glasses in his pocket asked, "Please cancel all my appointments for the next two weeks. If anything is urgent, tell whoever to contact me on my phone."

"Where should I tell them you've gone?" she asked.

"To hell and back," he smiled.

His chauffeur was waiting for him and took him home to pack. He telephoned the airport and spoke to his pilot and told him to make flight plans to Mobile, leaving in an hour. He informed his housekeeper, Mrs. Marsh, he would not be around for at least two weeks; therefore there was no need to prepare dinners for him. He made one last call to his daughter.

"I'm sorry, Annabelle. I won't be around for the next couple of weeks. Do you need any money or anything?" John asked.

"Really, Daddy?" she responded. "Adam is more than capable of keeping me in the style to which I grew accustomed when I married him."

"I know, Sweetheart. I was just checking in case. I'll call in once or twice while I'm away to make sure you and my grandsons are doing well. Give them my love." He disconnected his phone; he was ready to go.

When David's call was disconnected, he turned to find Morgan right behind him. "Could you please tell me what's going on?" she asked.

"That was John," he replied. He quickly made up his mind and repeated everything that John had told him.

"Someone's keeping an eye on my grandfather?" she repeated.

David nodded his head.

"And someone is following us?"

David once again nodded his head.

"John thinks it could be the person we sold the coins to or someone we told about the coins?"

David nodded his head once more. "It all comes back to one name doesn't it, Morgan?" he asked. "Gareth!"

"I wish I hadn't told him that story," Morgan whispered.

David put his arm around her shoulder and said, "We did, and now we have to face the consequences. But, now we don't have to do it alone if we don't want to. John wants to come here to talk and make suggestions before I go diving again. I thought I would start tomorrow, so, the question is: Should I put him off and go diving? Or should I wait for him to arrive? He says he's just trying to protect us, and I think he's being quite genuine."

Morgan nodded her head and replied, "I think maybe we should wait. It's only two days."

David placed a call through to John. "You've just caught me boarding my plane," John said "I'll be there in a few hours. Can you recommend a hotel anywhere near you?"

David gave him a name and said, "I'll phone them and make a reservation in your name."

"Thanks David. Make it for two weeks. I'll leave you alone tonight, but I would like to see you and Morgan, if she can stand business, tomorrow at ten, maybe at your home?"

The two men disconnected the phone call. Morgan returned to the house to clean.

Chapter 14

John Standing arrived at the house promptly at 10a.m. the next morning. He had hired a Land Rover for the duration of his stay, explaining he did not want anyone nosing around as they might if I arrived in a chauffeur-driven car. "I hope this will give me a little anonymity." He smiled at the two. "And who is this?" he asked as Chowder came bounding out of the sunroom to greet the stranger. He bent down to make a fuss of Chowder.

"Well, obviously he likes you," Morgan smiled. "He's supposed to bark when strangers come around. Please come in. I'm going to leave you and David while I go to see my grandfather for a while. I started to read a book to him when he was in the hospital and I haven't finished it yet. So today might be a good time. I've put coffee on and made some cranberry muffins. The sunroom is always a nice place to sit." She kissed David goodbye and gave a hug to John. "I'll see you both soon."

As always, Paul mumbled and grumbled when Morgan came in the door. Today's chief complaint was that he had to cook his own breakfast, and so Morgan offered to get him some lunch. "That'll do," he said.

"Grandpa, do you remember what I was reading to you in the hospital? It was a book written about the local people here in Gulf Shores, Mobile and surrounding areas and the fishing industry?"

"Yes, I do but you never finished it. Shame really, it was quite interesting," he said as he sat down in his chair, the sun shining on his face.

"Well, I have it here and I thought we might finish it today," she said. And sitting down opposite her Grandpa, she took the book out and began to read from where she left off.

Near the end of the book she came to a page that suggested very strongly that Jesse James had come down to a home in Gulf Shores known as Cooper's Landing. It was also suggested that he had an illegitimate son with a woman called Annie who had named her son, Jesse Mason James. He inherited Cooper's Landing and lived there with his wife, their children, and his mother for most of his life. Eventually, he sold the homestead, allowing his family to drift in and around the Gulf Shores area.

Morgan snapped the book shut to find her grandfather was asleep. Her mind raced with the possibilities but now she had somewhere else to start. Was it possible David was distantly related to Jesse James? Was Jesse James the founding father of his family?

Placing some lunch by her grandfather's chair, Morgan raced home to find a note from David saying he and John were down at the pier. She retrieved her computer and sat down with it in the sunroom. She typed in the name Mason-James, into the computer and at long last she was able to trace David's family on his paternal side.

Jesse James' son had stayed on at Cooper's Landing, and his son, David, was born there. David had eventually moved into Gulf Shores and worked as a fisherman—that was David's great, great grandfather. His son, Jack, had moved to Dolphin's Cove. That was David's grandfather, and here David was, two generations, later, still fishing. The names Jack and David were used repeatedly for the men in the families, from generation to generation. "How awesome to be related to someone so famous!" she thought. Just then, John and David came striding through the door. Morgan decided she would tell them what she found later. For now, she would get the men some lunch.

They sat at the kitchen table discussing the merits of the boat David had bought. "If the weather is good and the Gulf is not packing a punch anywhere," John said, "You could dive tomorrow and see if you can find the wreck again. But if digging equipment is required and we have to unearth the wreck, that fishing boat is just not going to hack it. We will need something far bigger. If at all possible," John added, "I want to pull the wreck up from the Gulf bed and ashore. That means having air bags down on the bottom of the Gulf to float the ship up, and we need a platform made to bring her from topside to the shore. It's not the easiest thing in the world to do, and it will take a lot of patience and time and a lot of good men to help."

David nodded his head. "I know a little of how to get wrecks out from the bottom of the Gulf, but honestly, would it be worth it if it was only a small ship? It could potentially cost you millions, John."

"I realize that," John replied. "But it's history. It's our past, and we're all a part of that." He had obviously already made up his mind.

John took them both out for dinner and asked Paul if he would like to join them. Paul refused, and so Morgan left Chowder with him for company. The restaurant was a nice one set on the bay outside of Mobile. They sat outside on the terrace as the sun began to set and watched as the white fluffy clouds drifted across the sun. The sun turned to a bright orange globe as it went down behind the water line, leaving a crimson sky behind it. "It will be another beautiful day again tomorrow," David remarked. "Perhaps even perfect enough to take the fishing boat out."

John's enthusiasm was evident. "We're leaving Morgan out of all this, David," he suddenly said. Perhaps we should tell her of our agreement." David nodded his head as John continued. "We have agreed to hunt for the treasure together. I don't know who you told of this treasure, Morgan. David won't tell me because he feels he is doing you a disservice. However, that person has hired others who are watching every move you and David make." He stopped while the clam chowder was put in front of them, and then continued. "I'm not going to dive myself. I'm leaving that to David," he said between mouthfuls of clam chowder. "This is really good," he muttered. Then he continued, "Whatever David finds in the way of Mason jars is his to keep and sell if he wants to. Of course I hope it will be to me. But first we need to find the ship that went down, and then, if possible, I want to remove the entire thing from the bottom of the Gulf." He finished his soup and put his spoon down.

David took up from where John left off. "I think it will mean weeks of work, locating the wreck as the coordinates I put in the GPS seem to be incorrect. Then I'm probably going to have to dig tons of sand. John is right when he says this is not a one-man deal. It will take a huge crew to do all this work, unless of course a miracle happens."

Morgan, who had been quiet up until now said, "I think a small miracle did happened today. I logged onto Ancestry.

com and traced your heritage, David. It all started with the book I was reading to my grandfather. The book talked of a place on the Bon Secour River near Gulf Shores called Cooper's Landing. The house belonged to a family—that of Annie Cooper—a mother to two children and a widow. It was said she had an illegitimate son born from an affair after her husband had died. The father of her son was thought to be Jesse James, and she called the baby Jesse Mason James. Mason-James became a double-barreled surname, which is the same as yours. It turns out you are the illegitimate great grandson three times removed of Jesse James."

Morgan pushed her plate away from her as she became animated about David's history. "According to the history books, Jesse James was an outlaw who robbed Union trains and banks. But it turns out he was also a member of the Knights of the Golden Circle and agreed with their philosophies of starting a second Civil War and reinstating slavery. If the South won the second Civil War, he wanted to retire somewhere in the South. Lore says it would have been Cooper's Landing."

"You found this out today?" John asked as David had gone totally silent.

"Yes, I most certainly did," said Morgan, leaning back in her chair as their dinners were placed in front of them.

"Is the site you got the information from pretty authentic?" John asked.

"As they come," Morgan replied putting pepper on her dinner. "It's how I made a living at the museum.

John looked over at David. "David you have gone very quiet. Did you know any of this?" John asked, taking a fork full of red snapper. "Oh my, this is delicious," he mumbled as he ate the fish.

David looked up and gave a wan smile back at the two looking at him. "I have some very old photos upstairs in the attic at home. I must get them down...... I've heard mutterings but nothing confirmed. Hmm. You're right, this red snapper is perfect." And he ate the fish with relish, thereby effectively closing that conversation for the time being.

It was when the restaurant had become a little quieter and they were sitting leisurely on the terrace drinking coffee and the men were smoking cigars that John bought the subject back up. "You know, David, if you are related to Jesse James, and it certainly seems as if you could be, you would have even more reason to help your town. If Jesse James was robbing trains and banks to help the cause of the Knights of the Golden Circle, and you have found some of their treasure, it would seem only right to help somewhere here in the south. Of course, it is up to you, but you have said that you are thinking about sinking money into the economy of Dolphin's Cove and Oak Tree Town."

"Let's see what we find first, and then you can advise me as to what, how, and where. It looks as if our lives are going to be crossing quite a bit in the near future, John. I hope that's all right with you." He picked up his brandy and said, "Here's to us and good fortune." The toast was taken up by all three of them.

The next morning bought warnings of a hurricane out in the tropics which could come into the Gulf waters in three or four days. The hurricane, named Erik was still a long way away but causing a lot of damage on the islands it hit. It stalled for a day over Haiti causing a tremendous amount of damage as the rains were so heavy. The wind not as damaging as it had come onto land as a Category One hurricane.

David and John took the boat out, and David dived down into the Gulf, but with no success. The waters became choppy and the waves a good five feet tall as the hurricane neared the Americas. As it swept into the Gulf Stream, the hurricane turned into a Category Three, and evacuation was becoming mandatory in most areas.

The day before the hurricane was due to hit land, John offered to fly David, Morgan, Paul, and Chowder out to his home in California. David had smiled back and said, "No thanks, John. I'm staying here to make sure no real damage is done, and to look after the old homestead here. My house is nearly a hundred years old and needs a little tender care. If Morgan and Paul want to go, please feel free to take them." But Morgan had said no, as had Paul, and John made plans to fly back to California alone.

They spent the day shoring up both houses and were a little surprised when John knocked on the door of David's house. He smiled at them both. "I was once in a pretty bad earthquake, but I have never been in a hurricane. A life experience I imagine. Can I stay here with you? The hotel has closed."

"Of course," David said and asked Morgan to make the third bedroom up for their guest. Paul was staying with them too.

When Erik hit, she lashed the house with rain and wind as everyone huddled inside. The electricity went out, but they all had flashlights. Morgan lit a dozen candles which cast a warm glow everywhere. They had a fire in the grate ready to burn if it was needed. They played cards for most of the evening, and David played melodies on his guitar. Although it wasn't very cold outside, Chowder remained curled up against Paul's feet, grateful he was not left outside to try to survive this horrible storm.

Two days later, the electricity was reinstalled and the Gulf once again as calm as a mill pond. The sun was shining and the sky was blue. Sand had been carried over the roads and highways and across the piers in the Marinas.

They cleared up the small amount of damage sustained on David's land—mostly downed branches from palm trees— and then Morgan had a request for the men. She wanted to visit Cooper's Landing with David—and John, if he would like to come along. They agreed that a day out might be nice. David went up into the attic and removed a box of photos that had been stored for many years. He spread them out on the coffee table, and they picked out the oldest ones they could find to take with them. They left lunch for Paul and Chowder, and set off in the Land Rover.

It was a hot day, and the sun shone brightly as they motored to their destination. They found the house called Cooper's Landing, and, just like Jesse James had done so many years ago, they decided to look around. The pier that Jesse had sat on had long since gone. However, the house and the two smaller buildings were still there, as were the oak trees that Jesse had sat under—the Spanish moss still hanging from them. A petite woman walked out and asked if they had come to find some plants from her garden.

Morgan walked forward and introduced herself. "My name is Morgan. This is David and John," she explained. "I think

David was related to a person who originally owned this property," she continued, "and we just wanted to come and look at what his ancestor might have seen."

"I'm Diane," the woman said. "Come on in to the house. My husband knows all the history of this house and the rumors concerning the property. He loves to talk about it," she continued as she walked back into the house. "Chick!" she called out. Diane turned back to the guests. "He usually gives tours around the property, but we don't have one scheduled today, so I know he would love to show you. Perhaps you would all like to stay for lunch?"

"Oh we didn't mean to put you out!" Morgan replied cutting across this very kind lady.

"It's no problem! I love to cook. I'll see what I can rustle up."

Chick appeared from the bedroom. He was a slim man with white hair and twinkling blue eyes. He took them around the main house, pointing out that the wood was original and had never been replaced, and that the first plumbing that had been installed was still functional, but had been upgraded to code over the years. He and Diane had tried hard to capture and maintain the integrity of the house. David removed the photos from his back pocket, and handed them over to Chick. He called his wife Diane to come and have a look and they were charmed to find the colors and styles of the furniture inside of the house was somewhat similar to what was there years ago. They looked at the pictures of the people in the photo and surprisingly, they found they had met David's grandfather.

"He's the one who told us about the original owner, Annie Cooper. Her husband died and it was rumored that she had a liaison with Jesse James and produced a son. His name was Jesse Mason James. The Mason was in honor of Annie's father. Later, the name became a double-barreled last name," Chick explained.

David smiled back and said, "It's my last name, and if Morgan and I have a son, it will continue in the family."

"It would seem you are related to Jesse James," Chick said. "I hope you find the history as interesting as we do. It is part of the reason we bought the house—because of the history attached to it. It seems to make living in it more exciting." He sipped his morning coffee and continued. "Come and have a look at the other buildings. One had been turned into a self-contained apartment, and it was this one that Jesse James was supposed to have slept in. We turned the other building into a large, professional kitchen where Diane runs a catering business."

As they sat down to a gourmet lunch, Chick explained, "The barn had fallen down slowly over a few years, and eventually was taken completely down after a hurricane collapsed the rest of the building. We didn't really need the building, so we never replaced it," he continued. "Otherwise the oak trees, other than being clipped every now and again, are pretty much what Jesse would have found when he visited—even with the Spanish moss hanging from them."

They took their coffee outside and sat on the same stoop Jesse would have sat on. It's unfortunate that over the years since Jesse James was here," Chick said, "some of the land was sold, and you can see a road has been put in place for the use of other houses. Now we don't have a pier that we can wander over to and fish in the river. The house itself is set about six hundred feet from the river, but already other people want to build on the little pieces of land left by the river. No longer does it give the appearance of the leisurely world it once was. The South must have been a great place to live in at one time, but now the pace of life is so much faster with modern technology that we all push forward too quickly. Sometimes it is nice to stop and smell the roses. This is why we bought the house, and why we give tours. Today is amazing for us because you probably were related to the original owners. That is very special for all of us."

John produced his cigar case from his inside jacket pocket, and the men smoked outside while Morgan and Diane went to the kitchen and loaded the dishwasher. "I can't tell you how much this means to us," Morgan said. "It actually sent shivers down my spine knowing where David's life really started. And all from Annie Cooper! Thank you so much for letting us in to your house and especially for providing us with lunch."

"Oh, Chick just loves to talk," Diane replied. "But even I was interested to meet a relation of the original owner. I guess Annie must have been David's great grandmother three times removed." She hesitated for a moment and then said, "I don't know if you would be interested in any way, but I do wedding receptions here and I think we could even manage an actual wedding. It would kind of be special wouldn't it?"

Morgan rounded on Diane enveloping her in a hug. "Oh my gosh! I wouldn't have dreamed of asking, but if you're offering, I think that would be fabulous! I have no brothers or sisters, and my parents are gone. I still have a grandfather, and I think David's parents and grandparents are gone, so there really wouldn't be too many people to invite. Oh, this would be the most amazing place! It makes me come out in goose bumps just thinking about it. Thank you, Diane. Really. Thank you!"

"Take our card before you go," Diane said, "And we can keep in touch and make all the arrangements." She walked out to the stoop with Morgan, just as the men had said it was time to go.

"Please sign our visitor's book before you go," Chick asked. "It's on the hallway table."

David signed the book, and slipped two hundred dollars between the pages to pay for their lunch. John smiled as he signed. David showed a lot of class sometimes, and he understood why Morgan wanted to marry him.

As they drove back to Dolphin's Cove, it was agreed that Cooper's Landing would make the most monumental place to hold the wedding. However, more detailed plans had to wait. It was time to start diving again.

David said, "I'm looking forward to going down, but there's something I want to try tomorrow."

When they returned, Paul insisted they take him back to his home. Morgan placed a dinner in the oven for him. Chowder made sure he jumped in the car with Morgan on the return journey. John offered to leave and go back to the hotel he'd had to vacate a few days before, but both David and Morgan insisted he stay. It would be more convenient when setting out for the diving in the morning, and, besides, they really enjoyed his company.

The following morning bought more sunshine and a little breeze. Morgan asked, "Can I come with you today?" and it was agreed that both she and Chowder could ride along. They set off across the bay in Dolphins Leap, as if they were on their way to a leisurely fishing day. David was behind the helm with John by his side. Morgan had chosen to sit at the front of the boat with Chowder. They had gone quite a way across the bay when David changed direction. He tried putting in the coordinates into the GPS by reversing two of the digits. John kept a sharp eye out and assured David that no one was following them. It wasn't long before David cut the engine and dropped the anchor. He took a look at the depth on the bottom finder and planned his dive for sixty feet for fifty-five minutes.

John helped David suit up and put the tanks on his back. They tied the rope around David so he could easily be pulled back into the boat. "If I give a sharp tug three times, I'm in trouble," David said. "If I pull once, reel me in just a little and stop as soon as I give one more. If I pull twice, make sure you give me more rope."

John nodded his head and warned David to be careful. "Remember we have communication; just push the button on the right hand side of your mask. Stay in touch. As you dive, give me a radio check as you begin your descent."

Morgan came over and gave David a kiss.

Between them they checked David's equipment again, he strode into the water when they finished. He entered the water, made a few quick adjustments and gave John the surface Okay signal and started his descent. As he descended David said, "Surface, this is diver. Radio check."

John replied, "Diver, this is surface. Reading you loud and clear. How do you read me?"

David replied, "Loud and clear, surface."

John and Morgan could see him diving down for just a few feet, and then even his fins disappeared. All they could see was the rope trailing behind him. John saw a small craft way off in the distance. It did not move, so he was not overly concerned.

David made his way down towards the bottom of the Gulf, seeing shoals of fish swimming around him and darting away from the strange creature sharing their water. He spotted a dolphin that swam around him. It seemed to be talking to him, and before long, when the water became murky, he found he was surrounded by at least eight or nine dolphins that seemingly had no intention of hurting him. He wondered if they were the same dolphins who had helped him before. They followed him all the way down to the bottom, where he landed with a bump. He waited a moment or two until the sand resettled from his bad landing. He turned on the light he was wearing on his head. It was enough to guide him, but was not that useful. He started his slow pacing on the bottom of the bed but found nothing. The dolphins talked back and forth between each other as they swam around him. He found they would not go in front of the light and so he turned it off.

The dolphins gradually, to his amazement, began to nudge him in a different direction. Because he was surrounded by them, he had no choice but to go where ever they pushed him. He saw no reason to distrust them. They had, after all, helped him the last time he saw them. Putting his arms above his head and kicking his fins, he placed himself in their midst and allowed them to direct where he went. After a few dozen feet, they rose above him and allowed him to sink back to the bottom. There was the wreck! And it was exposed far more this time. David shouted into his mask full of excitement. "Hey John, I found it. The wreck! I've found it and I'm going to look around and see what's here."

"Great, David, but don't forget to keep an eye on your bottom time and air. We don't want you running out."

David assumed the recent hurricane caused the Gulf bottom to shift, exposing more of the wreck.

The dolphins surrounded him again as he swam around the wreck. He found the mast from which he had snapped a piece, and he found an open side to the ship. He gently descended to the side of the ship and balanced himself on the rail. The sand in the ship was loose and would be able to be removed with a shovel for now. David had no idea where any treasure might be, or if any was there at all. He thought the most likely storage place would be below deck, so he began to dig and put the excess sand in the bucket around his waist. He emptied the sand a few yards from the boat, and went back for more. He continued to do this until he was exhausted.

He heard John in his ear piece asking if he was checking his air supply. He checked his tanks and saw he only had a little air left, so he ascended. He found he was not far from the Dolphins Leap and took a compass bearing back to the boat before he waved at Morgan and John, and swam back to Dolphins Leap.

Morgan had spent the time biting her nails. John had kept an eye on the smaller craft he had noticed earlier. It had crept a little further toward them, but had not tried to come anywhere near them. John held his hand out for David, and helped to haul the younger man out of the water. As they stripped David out of the wet suit, David told them of his find. "I'll get dry and warm first, but I want to go down again today before we return home," he said.

Morgan asked, "Will it be wise for you to go down again today, David? Why not go again tomorrow?"

John jumped in and said, "Morgan is probably right about going diving again. You maxed out on your diving time and you will have to wait on the surface for several hours before you could go down for any reasonable time at sixty feet. You should know that. You're actually trying to go in totally blind, David. We need to have some equipment that will detect whether there even is any other gold on the ship before you start searching blindly. Otherwise, the only alternative would be to get the ship off the bottom of the Gulf while it is still so visible."

"I'd like to look first," David replied immediately. "I have a feeling I'm going to find something else. I just need a little time." He drank thirstily from the water bottle water Morgan gave him. "Why don't you come and dive with me, John?" David gave a cheeky grin.

"Hmm." John replied smiling back. "I feel better in a business suit than a diving one, and better behind a desk than in the water."

"I thought you might like to know," said John as he sat down on the bench, "that small craft over yonder," and he nodded his head at the craft, "has been slowly creeping toward us." I sent the men I have down here to pick up the speed boat and they have been zipping around them for a little while now, just to see who they are and what they want. They followed us out here, but stayed at a distance. Any idea who they are?"

David took a pair of binoculars from the overhead bin on the console, and stared into them for a while. Passing the binoculars over to John, he said, "I have no idea who they are, and they are still too far away to see their features. If they are trying to fish, your speed boat will be annoying the crap out of them." He grinned. "One thing I can tell you—that's the Crimson Tide on its way out and we should go and meet her so I can give some instructions to Ben." He started the engine up and making sure he had the right coordinates locked in the GPS, they left the area and sped toward the Crimson Tide.

Pulling alongside the Crimson Tide, John took the helm, while David lithely jumped on board to be greeted by his crew. Ben turned off the engine so they could float alongside the smaller craft. "Hey boss, you ever coming back to work?" Ben asked with a smile. He was not the least bit worried whether David did or not. The catches had been good and they had sold all of them in Mobile.

"Just checking in with you," David said. "How's your grandson working out?"

Ben chuckled, "This is just what Jeremy needed, pulling him right back into shape here, Boss. Thanks."

"Glad to hear it." David smiled. "Now, I know your catch won't be as good as if you go out to the usual grounds, but I want you to shrimp a little closer into shore tonight, and while you are, I want you to tell me if that small boat creeps back out here tonight."

"What you up to, Boss?" Ben frowned. "Them people following you or something? I done told you I got a gun you can keep on board, and after what happened to Paul, I think you ought to."

"I'm not in any trouble yet, Ben. Hopefully, I won't need a gun," David replied. "I just want an eye cast over those men. I'll make up to you what you've lost in the catch. Good fishing!" He said as he jumped back aboard the Dolphins Leap. "I'll be down in the morning to see you all." And taking over the helm, he sped away from the Crimson Tide leaving an apprehensive Ben behind him with his crew muttering they never caught much out this way. It was a waste of their time shrimping here.

Chapter 15

The following morning saw the Crimson Tide come in with a huge catch of shrimp. David was waiting for them as they motored in. Ben came down the gangplank shaking his head, "How did you know, Boss? Best catch we've had in ages."

David smiled and said, "I'm glad it all worked out for us, Ben. Looks as if I need to come in to Mobile and help you sell the shrimp."

"That's okay, Boss. Jeremy is doing real good with that. He likes to go and haggle with the restaurants. That boat came out again last night and did some diving, but I don't think they would have found what they were looking for because they were miles away from where you were diving. You gonna tell me what's going on, Boss?"

"No I'm not, Ben. It's best you don't know for now."

"Whatever you say, Boss," Ben replied, and the two men passed knowing smiles. Out of respect, Ben did not pursue the conversation but walked back up the gangplank to help the crew with their tasks.

David watched as the chute came down from the Crimson Tide and filled the boxes on the dock with big shrimp. It was a good catch indeed, and the crew should be making a lot of money from it. He fervently wished they had an ice plant where they could pack the fish and shrimp and ship them around the world. Maybe that's what he should develop if he came into some more money. He had no idea how much it would cost to improve the facilities on the docks, but modern techniques were long past due.

He went back to the house to find Morgan cooking breakfast for them all. The coffee had just been brewed, and he helped himself to a cup. Sitting on a stool next to John, he turned to him and said, "I know what I want to do if we find more money down on the wreck."

John turned to him with a smile and said, "And all before breakfast. Sounds like a determined man to me."

"I want to put money into the docks here. We need proper packing facilities, and we need cold storage so that we can fish all year round and send shrimp across the world. We need dry ice as well as wet," he said more to himself than anyone else. "I could get Dan to build us more boats, and I could rent them out to the fishermen. It would help jump start the economy here, but I've no idea how to go about that without anyone else knowing how it was financed."

"Well," John smiled, "that's where my expertise would come in. As of yet, I know little of the fishing industry, but believe me when I say by the end of two weeks, I'll know all there is to know, and I would be only too happy to advise."

Morgan placed the breakfast on the table. Chowder crept underneath the table, just in case anyone sneakily fed him or dropped something he could snatch. They all sat down to eat and the talk was of how the economy would pick up if money was infused into the town and cove.

John had a phone call and excused himself from the table to take it. Morgan reached across and took David's hand.

"This is exactly why I love you," she said with a smile. "You're not thinking of spending that money on me or you but the town, and I think that's awesome. Please don't ever stop being the man I fell in love with."

David came around the table and, pulling her up from her chair, gave her a lingering kiss. Had they been on their own, they would have ended up in their bed. David looked longingly at Morgan and said, "I don't know how I came to be so lucky."

John came back at that moment, "Bad news, David. We need to get out on Dolphins Leap as soon as possible. The other boat is already out there. They have been going back and forth over the Gulf with a magnetometer." Seeing Morgan raise her eyebrows in question, he continued. "It locates metal on the Gulf bed. They are diving again a little closer to the wreck now. My men are out there in Sundancer, a bigger boat than they had yesterday, which has a lot of engine power, but the men who are diving have a big boat too. I strongly suggest we leave Morgan and Chowder here today. There could be trouble." He picked up his cup and drank the rest of his coffee. "I'll go and change into something more suitable for the boat." He did not have a need to do so, but felt it would be prudent to leave the two of them alone for a few moments.

Morgan gripped hold of David's hand, "What trouble?" She asked staring straight into his eyes. "Will these men out there try to hurt you and John? I want to come with you."

David smiled back down at Morgan and, stepping away from her just a little and holding her arms he replied, "No, Morgan, I am not taking you into any prospective danger." Morgan shivered at that moment because she has felt as if she heard two voices—David's and another one saying, "No Annie." Frowning, she looked back into David's eyes. He was continuing with his thoughts, "I think John may be just worrying you for nothing. Why don't you go and spend the day with Paul? You know he misses your company, and you could take Chowder with you. Find John's man and ask him into the cottage for the day. I wouldn't have to worry about any of you then, would I?" He kissed the tip of her nose to indicate the conversation was over.

Morgan was not happy, but she couldn't argue with David. When John came back downstairs, she saw that he had a gun pushed into the back of his jeans. That made her even more apprehensive of their expedition. Taking a deep breath, she took food out of the fridge and packed it up to take to her grandfather's house. She called Chowder, gave a wan smile to the two men, and left the house.

David and John went immediately down to the dock with the new equipment they had purchased the day before—a magnetometer, and more air tanks. David took Dolphins Leap around to Dan and asked for a full tank of gas. "Going out far?" Dan asked.

"Depends," David replied.

"Going into the charter business then, David?" Dan asked as he continued gassing the tanks.

"Nope, not really," David replied.

Dan nodded his head in reply knowing that David was not going to tell him anything. "Lot's a new people taking boats out on the bay. You be careful of those newbies. Don't look a lot like they know what they're doing," he said removing the pump from David's tank. He leaned a little closer to

David and said in a very quiet voice. "Not sure what those newbies are up to, but one had a gun in the back of his pants. Perhaps they're gonna shoot the fish to death!"

David paid in cash for his gas. He jumped back on his boat, started up the engine, and swung the boat around so that he was heading in the opposite direction from the smaller crafts he could see in the distance. He told John what Dan had said. John nodded his head and opened the cabinet, revealing his gun and spare clip of bullets.

"Just in case," he muttered into the wind. They sped across the water and anchored the boat on the far side of the bay. It was about an hour after they started fishing that the smaller of the two crafts began to make its way across to where they were.

David started up his boat and maneuvered to where they had anchored. "Any luck?" he asked to no one in particular. There were four men aboard, but no fishing rods. The boat was named Moonglo.

"No," the driver responded. "We seem shit out of luck!"

John's eyes raked over the boat, and he saw several diving suits and tanks in the cabin. "We just caught a beautiful red snapper," he said cheerfully, "but they are out of season, and we had to throw it back. I think we might go after some marlin now." And so saying, David, pulled the throttle back on the boat and they took off for the opposite side of the bay at full speed.

David killed the engine, anchored the boat, and quickly put on his diving suit and checked the air in his tanks. He strode off the side of the boat. John made a phone call and ensured the boat his men had taken out was moving closer to them. He then sat behind the helm keeping an eye on Moonglo.

As before, when David hit murky water, he was surrounded by the dolphins. They guided him to the side of the wreck which had tilted since he last dived and was standing more upright on its keel. Because of this, the sand had shifted again and the deck was clearer. "John, I'm on the bottom now and walking on the deck rail. Acknowledge please."

"All's fine here. Know where you are. Good hunting," John replied.

The dolphins chattered with excitement as they swam around David. He trod carefully over to the wreck, then flapping his fins, he rose up and landed on the deck. He swam around for a while until he saw there was a cover missing from one of the hatches. He dived down the opening to what must have been sailors' cabins. He looked through what he thought might have been the captain's cabin and tried not to disturb anything. If there was historical value in there, it should go to John. He opened all the cabinets by pushing on them and releasing any water pressure, hoping to find something, but came across nothing he was searching for.

Another cabin had obviously belonged to the crew. Hammocks swung lazily in the under current, and contained an entangled skeleton. A shoal of mullet surrounded him and, in a brilliant flash, swam on out of the ship.

A third cabin might have been for a passenger, and so David began to search through it. A tray sat on what could have originally been a desk or table. He picked the tray up and rubbed it clean and found that it could be silver. He placed that in the bucket he had bought with him. "John," he called out. "I think I may have found a valuable artifact. I'll bring it up with me."

"Acknowledged," John replied. "Pleased you're finding something. Watch your dive time, David."

Below the table where the tray had been was a cabinet with an old, rusted-through lock. David saw it was already opened and looked inside to find only empty drawers and shelves, but, looking down to the sandy bottom, he thought he saw a Mason jar top. He dug a little into the sand until the first few inches of the jar were exposed. It took all his strength, but he managed to pull it free from the sand. "Yes!" he shouted inside his mask. "Yes, yes, yes!" He put the jar into the bucket he had around his waist, and then saw the second jar. He pulled it out too. "We've hit pay dirt, John," he yelled.

He swam out onto the deck and pulled on the rope three times. There was no response. David tried again. Still, there was no response. Cautiously, by following the rope, he began to make his way back up to the surface. The dolphins followed him, although the chatter between them had stopped, and the water seemed eerily quiet. Out of the blue, a bullet swept by his cheek, making him lean back. The bullet completely missed David, but hit a dolphin's fin, causing the dolphin to scream in pain and terror. David immediately swam over to the hurt dolphin. Blood was seeping from the hole the bullet had created, but it had gone in one side and out of the other, and there was nothing David could do for the creature, except to go to its head and soothe the dolphin. The pod swam further down in the water to protect themselves as David made his way to the surface. He cautiously raised his head above the water line by the side of his boat. There were two speed boats chasing each other and firing bullets while John stayed firmly in the wheelhouse waiting for David. He had not been monitoring the rope because he could not get out on the open deck without being fired upon.

David needed to come on board as his air tanks were empty and he ran the risk of being spotted by the fast moving boats chasing each other around the bay. He caught John's attention by climbing back on board by the engines and wriggling across the deck. John pointed to the cabin, and they both scrambled inside. John helped David out of his diving suit. A bullet pierced the glass and flew through the window of the cabin, spraying shards of glass everywhere. David and John ducked as fast as they could, but a large shard of glass cut John's arm deeply, and blood rapidly began to pump through his shirt.

David grabbed the first aid kit from a bench in the cabin. He found a pair of tweezers, and, without looking at John's face, he pushed the tweezers into the wound and pulled out the shard. Still not looking at John's face, he took the bottle of iodine and poured it over the wound. He placed some gauze over the wound, then took off his shirt, and ripped a piece from the bottom. He wrapped the cloth around John's arm as tightly as he could. John tried to brush David away, but he knew the bleeding had to stop—it was no small cut and he could potentially bleed to death.

When the two smaller crafts moved away from the boat, David showed John his booty. "I need to go down again with a larger container, so I can bring all the treasure out. The ship is in a good place to be pulled from the bottom, if that's what you really want to do. It's shifted and now showing most of the deck. More of the sand has been washed away which is why I was able to get into the cabins. Of course you will have to get permits to raise it. One thing I did find was the name of the ship. It was known as the Bountiful Lady."

The smaller boats were coming back again, and John and David ducked back into the cabin. David grinned and said to John, "Did you see the Crimson Tide on the horizon? I'll take a bet that Ben saw we were having trouble and has come out to help. I'll start up this boat, and you take the gun, and let's see if we can't run these bastards off the bay."

Ben had put his gun aboard the Crimson Tide in case David needed it. He had heard gunfire when he was getting the boat ready for shrimping. He ordered the crew to discard as much extra weight from the boat as they could, and they took off at full speed. If they were lucky they could not only run this guy off the bay but get him stranded. Focusing on his bosses' new boat, Dolphins Leap, Ben leaned over the wheel of the Crimson Tide urging her forward. He was not going to let his boss be hurt.

John's men were not used to running a boat in and out of sand banks at full throttle. They followed the Moonglo nearer the shoreline where sand banks were obvious to the trained eye. They tried to stay in the wake of the boat in front of them until their boat, Sundancer, ended up firmly stuck in a sand bank. The only way they could get off was for one of the men to get out and push the boat from the bank. One man stripped down to his shorts and jumped in. Wading around to the end of the boat, he pushed with all his might until Sundancer moved and floated. He grabbed hold of the outside of the boat and hauled himself aboard again. "Let's go!" he shouted to the driver, who opened the throttle fully, making the wet and shivering man fall back in the boat. They leapt off the sandbank in hot pursuit of Moonglo.

Moonglo's driver, seeing that Sundancer was free, turned and drove his boat straight at them, in the hope that the men aboard would abandon it. They didn't. They kept in perfect line with them to hit head on, and the two boats swerved at the last moment to avoid one another, guns firing but bullets hitting no one.

Ben pulled the Crimson Tide alongside Dolphins Leap. "You alright, Boss?" Ben shouted. When Ben saw David nod and turn to head toward the other two boats, Ben leaned over from the helm and threw his gun onto Dolphins Leap.

David said into the marine radio, "Thank you. Make sure you keep out of the gunfire, Ben. Just keep around the edges of the battle!"

"Okay, Boss. If you're boat gets broken up, we're here to rescue you. We're not going to give up now. This looks like fun!" Ben pulled the boat back but kept in David's wake.

David opened the engines again and gunned toward Moonglo and Sundancer, still vying for position and firing guns at one another. He was surprised the Coast Guard had not come out on to the bay yet. Maybe, as there was no else around, the noise had not been reported.

John was by his side and shouted to David, "We have two guns now and I'm gonna load this baby up. We should both have one."

John loaded his gun with a clip, and put David's gun on the console in anticipation of being shot at from either side. They watched as, once again, Moonglo drove straight at

Sundancer. This time, without hesitation, Moonglo headed directly at the other boat and cut it in half. The security men on Sundancer were thrown into the Gulf waters, losing their guns.

David drew Dolphins Leap alongside the men swimming on the surface of the water, and John pulled the two of them out, costing them valuable time. Meanwhile, David kept an eye on Moonglo where the two thugs were fisting into the air at their victory. They had run further away and then turned making a direct line for Dolphins Leap. David glanced behind to make sure John had pulled the men aboard and then opened the throttle. He drove straight at the other boat, but swerved at the last minute. They were both heavy boats, and it took a while to get them back on course. David and John believed there were two people left on Moonglo and they now had four on Dolphins Leap, making it marginally slower. They were just making another pass when David was shot in the shoulder. His gun flew out of his hand into the water, leaving only John armed. John tossed his gun into the cabin and told David to make a run into shore. They turned to do so, and the engines abruptly stopped. David had run out of gas.

"I've been cut by glass. You're shot. The money isn't worth all this," John said.

David turned the ignition key off. John made sure that at least one person could pick up the gun by placing it just inside the cabin on the floor under a bench. The security men were not armed, having lost their guns in the water. As Moonglo came alongside, its men had guns trained on David, John, and John's men. It turned out that there were four people on board Moonglo. The other two had been hiding inside the cabin. Now they came up on deck also armed and boarded Dolphins Leap.

"Tie these three up," the tallest man said, pointing his gun at John and his security men. Then he pointed at David. "This one needs to be doing some work for us." His men did as they were told.

The tallest one grinned at David, "Now," he said. "Take us back to where you were diving."

"No can do," David replied with a smile. "You're shit out of luck. I've just run out of gas."

"You stupid fucker!" said the tallest of the men, and he hit David around the ear with the butt of his gun. Fortunately David had seen what the man was going to do and side stepped, deflecting the blow to a light tap. He looked at the man and said, "You must have been the one who hit Paul, that poor old man, around the head with the butt of your gun. Which one of these was with you?"

"I was," said a shorter man.

"Shut the fuck up, you idiot!," the taller man shouted. "Get the spare gas can from our boat, and bring it over here. NOW, Brandon!"

"Keep your shorts on," Brandon replied as he went to board Moonglo.

The tall thug turned to look at one of John's men. "You married?" he asked.

The man remained silent, and so the thug pulled the trigger on his gun and shot the security man in the leg. "Guess that was a 'no' then," he said, pushing the man over the side of

Dolphins Leap. John, unable to grab his gun, watched in horror as one of his security team had been shot and left to survive alone, floating in the water.

The security man who had been shot, kicked his feet and made his way behind Moonglo. He was able to pull himself aboard by the engines, and he hid in the cabin.

Brandon returned to Dolphins Leap with a can full of gas. David laughed, "That won't get us very far."

"It will take us to where you were diving. After that, it ain't gonna matter much whether there's enough to get you back to shore or not," Brandon replied. "Now get this fucking boat moving." He indicated to one of his men to get out and drive the Moonglo behind them.

Brandon was not as tall as either John or David. This seemed to annoy the man, and he viciously stuck the gun in the back of David's head and reminded him. "Get this fucking boat moving before I put a bullet into your head. Or, of course, I could do to you what I did to the old man." He laughed a mirthless sound. "We had so much fun putting our fists and boots into him. Did we kill him?"

David, aware that the intention of these men was to kill them all before they had finished, cheerfully said, "Oh yeah, right, you idiot. You fucked that up too, didn't you? Couldn't even kill a poor old defenseless man, could you? Is there anything you can do right?"

He received a blow across the back of his head for his retort, but they did not to want to kill him yet. He was too useful to them. They had seen him dive, and he thought they would insist he dive again.

David took them to a place about a mile away from where he had been diving and cut the engine.

Brandon asked, "Is this where you've been diving?"

"Yeah," David replied.

"Get suited up then," Brandon said pointing his gun at David's face.

"Well," David replied, "I would, but I don't have any air in my tanks."

"No problem," the taller of them said. "We bought some with us just in case you refused. You need to be doing some diving so we can get us some of those old dollars you've been bringing up."

John looked up and said, "Oh, Gareth told you to dive and get them, did he?"

The taller of the men looked at him and said, "You married?"

"Yes, I am." John replied. "Do you have a name?"

"Yeah I do. It's Butch. Who the fuck are you?"

"John. I know Gareth fairly well. He's from England. Been over here for ten or so years, I believe. How long have you been working for him?"

"Long enough, John," Butch said with a snarl. "Cut the crap, and let's get diving."

"Well really," John sighed. "I shall have to let Gareth know how you treat his friends. This simply is not right. I need to help David suit up," John continued, in the most pleasant voice he could find. "Would you mind if I do? You'll have to cut my ropes."

"Just get the fuck on with it. I've had enough of being on this fucking water," Butch replied, taking a knife and cutting John's bonds. He set the knife on a table nearby and was not quick enough to see John pick it up and tuck it down the front of his jeans.

John went around to where David was getting into his diving suit. He was being watched by both of the thugs, as they too were suiting up to dive with David.

John looked at David and managed to whisper through his teeth, "There's a knife down the front of my jeans. Pull it out, and put it into the arm of your diving suit. Do it when I reach up to adjust your mask. It should cover us both then."

David imperceptibly nodded his head. He knew what to do with a knife.

John looked over his shoulder and saw the Crimson Tide. She had moved closer to them, and he was hoping the others had not noticed. He was relying on Ben sensing what was going on.

David, ready at last, strode overboard along with the two thugs, who did backward flips. He came back up and washed his mask before resettling it back on his face. Smiling at the thugs, he disappeared under the water. The thugs swam behind David until the water became murky and they realized they could not see what David was doing or where he was going. They kicked their fins a little harder to catch up.

Just as they were doing so, a pod of Dolphins surrounded David and the thugs couldn't see him at all. They tried to put their fists into the dolphins to push and move them away, but the dolphins were too agile for them. The dolphins surrounded the thugs and began to attack them with their beaks. They pushed them and pulled them around until the thugs had no idea where they were. One goon had carried a gun in his waistband, and he pulled it out to try to shoot at the dolphins, but the dolphins pushed and shoved him until he dropped the gun. The gun sank and disappeared. The other goon took aim with the spear gun he was carrying, but it too was knocked away by the dolphins and lost.

The thugs didn't know which way was up. They were totally disorientated. Panic set in. They flailed at the dolphins with their hands trying to locate David, or alternatively get back to the surface. Both thugs found their feet touching the bottom and they tried hard to swim upward, but again the dolphins attacked them spinning them around upside down until they had no idea where they were. Both of them panicked, using up their air faster than they should have. Neither had any idea why the dolphins attacked. They were supposed to be such docile creatures. It was after fighting with them for about forty minutes, their air ran out. One of the thugs realized he had no air, so he took one last deep breath, removed his mask, and swam upward, only to be knocked back by a dolphin. Forgetting he had no air, he gasped and took in a huge mouthful of water. He sank toward the bottom, bubbles coming out from his mouth. The other goon tried to take the mask from his friend to see if he had any air left and succeeded in pulling in a mouthful of salty water. He coughed and spluttered all the while taking in more and more Gulf water. He too went down to the bottom of the Gulf. The dolphins left the bodies; just one dolphin went down and chewed through the weight belts, leaving the two thugs tied on the same rope ready for their bodies to float to the surface.

John was seated on a bench on the edge of Dolphins Leap. David could hear Butch and Brandon who had found the silver tray and Mason jars he had bought up earlier. "I wonder how much more they'll bring up? We'll all be fucking rich," he heard Brandon laugh. "Fucking rich!"

Morgan paced back and forth at home, wondering what was happening. She had returned from her grandfather's house hours ago, but had not heard from either David, or John. They were not answering their cell phones, and she had searched the bay with binoculars. In the distance, she thought she saw boats chasing one another. Knowing in her gut something was very wrong, she phoned the Coast Guard and told them she thought David might be in trouble.

Suddenly, there was a cry from Brandon.

"Butch, look over there!" Butch came running to the side of the boat. There, he saw two divers floating.

"Pull them in!" yelled Butch. "Which ones are they?"

"How the fuck do I know?" Brandon shouted. "They all look the same in those suits."

They gathered the end of the rope and began to pull on the rope hand-over-hand. "This is too easy," Butch said. "The rope is coming up too fucking easy. What the fuck is going on?"

David heard the commotion on board and took his opportunity. He quickly swam around to the stern. John saw the movements out of the corner of his eye. David looked over his shoulder to make sure that the thugs were still busy and slithered toward John. He cut John's ropes, and gave him the knife, whispered, "Get the Mason Jars and tray. Put them in a bucket and bring them back here. If you can, alert your security guy too." John made his way to where they had left the bounty, and putting it quietly into the bucket, he kicked his security guy in the leg warning him to be quiet and cut his ropes. They inched their way back to David.

Ben had been keeping a close eye on the boats and saw his chance to move in. The thugs had been so busy they had not heard him open the engine on the Crimson Tide, but David had. He heard the roar of the engines as Ben opened them wide, coming at full throttle toward them. He did not slow down or hesitate.

The security guard who had hidden on Moonglo crawled out of his hiding place and found the keys carelessly left in the engine. He turned it over and started it as Butch and Brandon looked up and saw what was about to happen. Not waiting to find where the treasure was, knowing they were in immediate danger, they jumped back onto Moonglo and Butch grabbed the wheel and pulled away as fast as he could. Brandon threw a fist into the security guy's face, knocking him into the water, but not before they struggled together and Brandon's gun went off and hit the security man in the shoulder.

Ben turned the Crimson Tide away from Dolphins Leap as soon as he saw what was going on, missing the boat by inches.

David turned the engine over on Dolphins Leap and, waving to Ben in acknowledgement, he opened his engines at full throttle and followed Moonglo across the bay. Dolphins Leap had larger engines than Moonglo, but Moonglo had cut right across the bay and was heading for the Inter coastal Waterway. David understood how dangerous the narrow channel could be, but Butch and Brandon did not. As the first boat entered the channel, they heard the Coast Guard siren. Neither boat driver had taken any notice of the 'No wake' signs and had hit the entrance at speeds of 50 knots. The Coast Guard boat turned in a swooping circle and followed in the wake of Dolphins Leap. A large coal barge was coming through the channel at them, and they split, one going to the left and the other going to the right of the barge, each hoping to gain a few feet on the other. The tug pushing the barge turned his sirens on both boats in warning. The Coast Guard continued to follow David who was gaining a few feet on Moonglo and pulled out behind the tug with just a few feet between them. John's security guy was urging David on and taking the one pistol left they had between them fired at the thugs on Moonglo. But Brandon anticipated their move and told Butch to swerve. Brandon fired at Dolphins Leap, putting a bullet through the hull of the Coast Guard boat.

The three boats went under a large bridge with restaurants on either side. Patrons watched in horror as the restaurants' floating docks rose in the swell the boats created before crashing back down onto the water, jostling tables and smashing glasses and plates. The boats continued on through rock walls on either side of the banks of the waterway, darting between pleasure boats, until they came out into the open again into an open area of water that went into small coves. Veering back and forth, Moonglo tried to find somewhere to hide among the boats docked at restaurants and bars but caused deep wake waves they could not hide. Dolphins Leap continued to chase Moonglo, with the Coast Guard following, their sirens still blaring in the hope people would get out of the way of this chase.

Butch could see that they were about to leave the Inter coastal Waterway and enter the Gulf. He had been warned that his boat was not a Gulf-going vessel, and the height of the waves frightened him. He spun his boat around in a tight circle and raced back up the Intercostal at break-neck speed. He swerved to miss a pleasure boat, and, misjudging his distance, hitting a rock-lined bank. He and Brandon jumped as the boat crashed sideways into the rocks, sending the boat up in the air in an explosion of flames.

David stopped his boat. The Coast Guard picked up the two thugs while David waited. By luck, he knew the Coast Guard captain well and called out, "Mike! There are two more bodies on the bay. I'll show you where if you want me to."

"Just remember, I'm following you, David. I'll want to talk to you soon. Really soon."

David waved in acknowledgment and the two cruised at a sedate pace back to the bay where David saw the Crimson Tide not far out. He called Ben on his marine radio.

"Good to hear you, Boss. You okay?" Ben didn't wait for a reply, but continued, "I picked up the bodies, Boss. Yeah, I'm afraid two are dead the other injured but not too badly. I'm laid up waiting here for you."

David pulled alongside the Crimson Tide, and the Coast Guard boat pulled up on the other side. David clambered aboard followed by John and the security guy.

"Hey, Boss, you're looking a little pale."

Detective Lawson hailed from the Coast Guard boat. "May I come aboard?"

"Sure," David replied. "What are you doing out with the Coast Guard?"

"We were told there was a bit of trouble out on the water. These two men have been spotted out on the bay following you for a couple of days. We were informed today they were armed and dangerous. It seems our informant was right as we heard gun fire. I'll check to see if they have licenses for guns of any kind, but I doubt it. We'll book them on unlawful possession of a firearm for now. We have a bullet from one of their guns lodge in the Coast Guard boat, I also want to test their DNA and see if they were the people that unlawfully entered Paul's house and caused the poor man to lose his memory. We'll take the two dead men back with us for the coroner's examination. Do you know anything about any of these thugs?"

John said, "You might want to question Morgan's ex-boyfriend at the museum in New York, Gareth Hunt. I think he sent the thugs. It appears he was unhappy his girlfriend had found someone else."

"And you are?" Detective Lawson asked, looking at John.

"Friend of the family," John replied with a smile.

"Do you normally go into the water fully clothed?"

"Not usually, no," John replied with a smile. "It just looked as if it was the right day for it today."

"You've obviously been hurt and by the look, David has a bullet hole in him. So has that man over there. I'll need to see all three of you tomorrow. I want an explanation of what went on, why three smaller crafts went out on the bay and why only one is returning." Detective Lawson cast a quick eye around Dolphins Leap and the Crimson Tide, but could see nothing out of place except for the four very wet men. "Okay. I'll leave you for now, but I'll make sure there is a sergeant waiting on the docks for you so that he can accompany you to the hospital. He'll stay with you until you are discharged and I've talked to you. I'm going back to book these thugs." He jumped back on the Coast Guard boat.

The captain of the Coast Guard boat, Mike, looked up at David with a grin. "Good fishing, David," he wished him. "Bring back a huge catch on Crimson Tide next time you take her out—you and yours need it. Let me know if there is anything else we can do for you." And with wave to Dolphins Leap, he swung his boat away from them and with sirens blaring made for shore.

David's energy suddenly left him, and he sat down hard on a bench. He rubbed his eyes and found his hands were shaking. John sat down next to the younger man. "You did well today," he told David. "I was very proud of the way you handled yourself in such a stressful situation. It's not everyone who could turn their hand to a violent situation the way you did. Congratulations. You also saved the Mason jars and the tray. We'll have to go diving in the next few days. At least we know there will be no one else chasing us around the bay. Now you and I need medical attention, as does my security man over there. So do you think you could tell Ben and the crew to turn around and take us to shore?"

Ben secured Dolphins Leap to the back of Crimson Tide and turned for home. Before he docked he came over to David and asked, "Well, Boss, you gonna tell me what the hell was going on, and why you got a fishing boat and done be chasing those other boats across the bay with gunfire and all?"

David shook his head at the older man. "Just know that if I could, I would tell you, Ben. I promise I will make all this up to you and the crew one day. I promise you, I will."

"You've been shot, Boss, Don't you think you should have told that Detective Lawson why they followed and shot you? Those thugs should pay for what they did to you, John, and that man over there," he said pointing to the guard.

David nodded his head and said, "I will sit down and talk to him tomorrow. I just didn't want to today. I know it sounds inane, but all I could think of was getting back to Morgan. She kept me safe and she wasn't even here. I need to thank you as well, Ben. I knew you were watching and wouldn't let us get hurt. I could see the sun reflecting from your binoculars."

Ben smiled at the younger man and replied, "I've been with you for years now, Boss, and I can read your mind as easily as I read your pop's. I done told you I wouldn't let you get hurt. Not on my watch."

David nodded his head, wondering how he had ever been able to get such respect and loyalty from his men. But right now, he didn't want to wonder. He just wanted to see Morgan and was pleasantly surprised to find her on the pier waiting for the Crimson Tide to dock, along with the sergeant promised by Detective Lawson. As soon as the gangplank was lowered, she ran onboard. She threw her arms around David's neck, hugging him as hard as she could until she saw him flinch from pain. It was then she realized he was hurt.

"John too, and his security guy," David said. "Any chance you could take us to the hospital?" Both had lost a lot of blood, and Morgan could see they were pale. She ran back along the pier to her car and drove it right onto the pier below the shrimping boat.

Asking no questions, she drove to Mobile as fast as she dared; followed by the sergeant in his car, zigzagging in and out of the traffic and taking risks she normally would not. She didn't understand that her erratic driving was causing them all pain. She drew up outside the hospital emergency room doors and slammed on her brakes. The three men gingerly got out and she said, "I'll park the car, and I'll be right back."

On entering into the hospital, the men were taken straight away into the emergency room. John discreetly asked if David's bill could be put on his. He figured David had no insurance.

David was wheeled away to the operating room, with Morgan by his side. "I'll wait here, David. I'll be right outside the operating room until you come back out."

David managed a woozy grin and replied, "Go and find John, See how he's doing. They're gonna knock me out, and I won't know a thing until they call you."

"But...."

"Go, Morgan. John needs you, too. I love you."

"I love you, too." With tears trickling down her cheeks, Morgan made her way back to the emergency room as the nurses wheeled David into the operating theater.

She found John sitting on a bed being stitched up. The doctor looked up as she walked into the room. "How's the patient doing, Doctor?" she asked wiping the tears away with the back of her hand.

"Never better," the doctor replied. "Thankfully, somebody knew a little about first aid and cleansed this wound as best they could. There was no glass left in there and so we've just had to stitch it up. There, that's the last one. You need to come back here next week for me just to check, John. If you're leaving town, go to your own doctor and have the stitches removed. I'll give the nurse a prescription for pain pills. Make sure you take them for the first two days. After that, it's up to you. I'll also prescribe an antibiotic which has to be taken for ten days. Please make sure you finish the course. Any questions?" As there was just a shake of the head from John, the doctor continued, "Well, in that case I'll leave you. The nurse will be back in a minute with your discharge papers, prescription, and instructions." He shook hands with John and walked out of the room, leaving the door wide open.

John looked a little shaken, and Morgan asked, "Are you really okay, John?"

"Let's see," he replied. "I've been in two or three boat chases, had my arm severely cut, watched helplessly as my security guy was shot and pushed into the Gulf, had a gun thrust in my face and threatened to be killed, swum in the Gulf—

237

and I hate swimming—and been rescued by a shrimper and questioned by the police, all that in the past twelve hours." He looked at Morgan and with a smile said, "I'm just fine. How is David?"

"They took him up to the operating room to remove the bullet and clean the wound. The doctor assured me he'll be okay. They've taken your security guy into the operating room too, and he is doing well."

The nurse came with papers for John, and after he signed them, she told him he could go.

Morgan and John wandered the corridors until they found a coffee machine and a waiting room. She offered to take John home, but he shook his head, and, instead, they sat in the waiting room. Two hours later, they were told that both David and the security guard were out of surgery and doing fine. Both would be asleep and resting for the rest of the night, so Morgan and John left the hospital. John was still woozy from Morgan's driving earlier and insisted on driving. Chowder was waiting for them in the sunroom. Exhaustedly they all made their way to their bedrooms.

John phoned his daughter and made light conversation, saying he would be home in the next few days.

Morgan grabbed a sweater of David's and holding it near her face, fell into an exhausted sleep with Chowder sleeping right next to her bed.

John Standing's House
In Los Angelese
California

Chapter 16

The following morning found two patients in the hospital chomping at the bit to get out. John made several phone calls and arranged for all three of his security guys to fly back to California to recoup from their injuries and experiences. Morgan phoned David to tell him she was picking him up from the hospital a little later. Detective Lawson was David's first visitor.

"All right," he said looking at David as he walked into his hospital room. "I want to know what the hell is going on and why. You had better be answering my questions this morning before I charge you with obstruction of justice."

David looked up and saw the grim look on Detective Lawson's face. "What have those two thugs told you?" he asked.

"Absolutely nothing! It's up and over to you now. I want the truth."

"Okay," David sighed. "Here's what started all this. I got an old trunk down from my attic to look for some photos to show Morgan and at the bottom were some old coins. I had no idea what they were but, Morgan, with her museum experience, determined they were old and wanted her ex, Gareth Hunt, to verify they were of some value. We knew Gareth wouldn't necessarily help me, so Morgan concocted a story about her grandfather. We went to New York and Gareth seemed excited about the coin and asked if we had any more. Morgan, so she would not be bothered by this asshole, told him she was selling them from her grandfather's collection of coins to pay for her grandmother's funeral. It turns out it was a stupid thing to do. The coins themselves were not worth much—just a few thousand dollars. We ended up selling them to a friend of Gareth's before we came back to Dolphin's Cove. It seems that Gareth must have thought Paul had a lot more coins. I believe that's why Paul was attacked."

"Why the hell didn't you tell me that before?" Detective Lawson demanded.

"Because I had no proof," David replied. "I still don't, but I'm hoping you find the connection from these thugs to Gareth Hunt. I would really like to see him behind bars." He swallowed some water from a glass and then continued. "Anyway, my friend John was visiting from California for a few days, and we wanted to do some fishing while he was here. So John bought two boats from Dan. One was for his security guys, and the other was for us. We went out for several days fishing for marlin and the like—I might add without much success except the snappers we caught and put back."

Detective Lawson rolled his eyes, and said, "Just get on with it."

"Well those thugs—whoever they were—followed us for two or three days, or at least we think they did. John and I also did a bit of diving, looking for old wrecks, but were also unsuccessful. Anyway, suddenly out of the blue, those guys came speeding over the water and driving their boat directly at John's security guys."

"Who the hell is he that he'd bring security with him?" Detective Lawson asked.

"He's a very wealthy business man who just might pump some money into this place if people would just stop firing bullets at him and his security team!" David replied indignantly.

"If he's that wealthy, David, how come you not only know him, but became friendly with him?" Detective Lawson asked.

"John came here a few years ago, and we bumped into each other in a restaurant in Mobile. He bought me dinner and we have been friends ever since.

"At least you and John are consistent in your stories. It's pretty much what he told me earlier when I saw him at your house and asked John some questions on what went on yesterday." Detective Lawson replied with a small smile on his face. "I would really hate to call you a liar, David."

David's eyebrows rose an inch on his face before he decided to totally ignore the remarks thrown at him. "Anyway, to get back to the story, the same thugs eventually boarded Dolphins Leap, and shot one of the security guys and pushed him overboard. I honestly thought they were going to kill him, but they just shot him in the leg. It was an act of intimidation of course. They then insisted we take them back to the place we had been diving. It turns out they thought we were diving for treasure, we were just trying to spear some fish instead of returning empty handed to shore. But of course we caught nothing. We were shit out of luck all day. I don't know what happened to the two thugs who died. I lost them in the murky bottom of the Gulf and swam back to try and find them. I dived several times, but could not see them. Of course, I came to believe they were not experienced divers and had got into a heap of trouble."

Detective Lawson cut across him and said, "The bodies were examined for a cause of death last night, but no obvious indication of foul play was found. They are to be autopsied today."

David nodded his head. "Well, when they eventually came floating up in the water, the other two thugs tried to haul them in, which gave me an excuse to get the security man and John off the boat and into the water. With all the commotion, the thugs didn't hear the Crimson Tides engines opened at full throttle. Ben said he had seen we were in trouble and this was the only way he could save us, and thank goodness he did. I swear those thugs were going to use those guns on us, and the ridiculous thing is, it all stemmed from finding two coins."

Detective Lawson was checking the time on his watch and smiling at David. "I expect you would have liked to have been there, but Gareth Hunt was arrested two minutes ago by the New York police and will be waiting extradition here on charges of conspiracy of fraud and attempted murder of four people. He'll be locked away for a long time."

"Well," he continued. "I think I have everything I need from you for the time being." He rose from his chair to leave. Turning back, he said, "You know David, if you had told me all this when Paul was attacked, we could have saved you from what followed. Anyway, good luck to you and John, and keep out of trouble." He left the room, passing Morgan on her way in.

"Get me out of here," David said as a way of greeting.

"Well, good morning to you too," she said. "We can go as soon as the papers are signed." Morgan threw herself on the bed and hugged David. "I thought I had lost you," she whispered. "What would I do without you, David? I love you so much." "God, all this happened because of the stupid story I told Gareth. I wish to heaven I never had concocted it." Tears flooded her face.

David pulled her in as close as he could whispering words of love and comfort until the nurse came in. "Oh sorry," she said. "I bought your discharge papers with me. I didn't mean to disturb you."

Morgan quickly wiped her eyes and sat up. "He's ready," she replied. Much to his indignation, David had to be wheeled out to the exit door in a wheel chair by a nurse. At least Morgan had bought him in a fresh set of clothes to wear. The nurse reminded David to keep his arm in the sling for at least a week.

David awkwardly got out of the wheelchair as the valet got Morgan's car. When it arrived, David held out his hands for the key. Morgan just laughed and took them from the valet. She told David to get in the passenger seat. He was going to be a difficult patient.

When they got home, John was snoozing in the sunroom with Chowder fast asleep at his feet. As it was now near lunch time, David demanded a beer and John joined him. It wasn't long before the talk turned to retrieving the rest of the Mason jars, but neither patient seemed inclined to go out on the water today. They both fell asleep in the afternoon sun, and did not wake up again until the evening. "Must be the medication," they both said.

Three days later, David and John headed to Mobile to replace all the equipment that had been destroyed. Just short of the prescribed week in a sling, David cast it off. After recuperating for two more weeks, David and John took out Dolphins Leap to attempt to retrieve the treasure from the bottom of the Gulf.

John gave David a hand suiting up. Although the hole in his shoulder was healing nicely, David knew it was going to hurt like a bitch when he got in the water. As soon as David stepped overboard, the dolphins surrounded their friend and took him down to the wreck. They were chatting away to themselves and waited above while David retrieved Mason jars from the sand. His load was heavy, and so John pulled them up two or three at a time and then sent the basket down again. David pulled on the rope for John to help with his ascent. While he was waiting, the dolphin that had been shot came around David's face. He recognized the dolphin because of the hole in the fin. The dolphin rubbed his body around David and gently pecked his cheek. David stroked the top of its head. Without warning the dolphins formed a tight pod and swam away together. David felt the pull of the rope and ascended to the surface, with two Mason jars intact. There were nine in all. With the two they had pulled out the other day and the one he originally found that made a total of twelve. Suddenly David realized he was rich.

Now it was John's time to take charge. The first thing he did was to give David a check for half a million toward the price of the Mason jars. He had the plane ready to fly to California two days later and the flight plan already logged. He had graciously asked Paul to fly with them and spend a little time with him at his home, but Paul looked at him and muttered something that sounded very much like, "I don't condone my granddaughter flying around the country with David and her not married. It ain't right. So 'till she walks down the aisle with him, I ain't going nowhere with them." And that was that.

Tyler told Morgan, "I'll be happy to look after Paul until you come back." Morgan got to work making meals for Paul's freezer. At least he and Tyler wouldn't starve.

Before he left, David went to the hospital where Ben's disabled son had most of his therapy sessions, and where Ben had purchased or leased the expensive equipment his son used at home. He asked what Ben's outstanding bill was. The hospital was reluctant to let David know, but when he explained he would like to pay for whatever Ben owed, the entire bill, they told him. David wrote a check for the outstanding amount on the condition that it was kept confidential. He then went to the nursing home where Ben had placed his parents. Quietly he said he would like to pay a year in advance for them and would continue to do so every year on the condition no one else knew of the arrangement. They happily agreed. It was good to have the money in the bank.

David then asked John to run a few errands for him. First, he sent John to the Mighty Shrimp.

John remarked to Patch, "The crew saved my life out on the Bay that day David and I were in the boat chase, and I cannot thank them enough. Do you think that if I left a thousand dollars that you could open a tab for me. If the bill goes higher than that, I'll settle with you later when I come back again. Or, of course, David could settle for me. I think the crew would be able to have one really good night each month with that, shouldn't they?

"As long as I'm included" grinned Patch.

No one would ever know or guess the money had come from David.

Next, David had John go to the café and give Marylou enough money for a dinner party for everyone in the town. John explained, "Paul is a dear friend of mine, and I cannot thank you and the townspeople enough for all you have done for him."

Pleased that this had infused the town with a little of his money already, David was ready to leave with John for California. Morgan took Chowder to her grandfather's and asked him to look after the dog until she came back. He was more than willing.

Morgan had never been on a private jet and was surprised at how comfortable it was. John was wearing a suit for the first time in a while, and he looked at ease and at home in the luxuries that surrounded him. Morgan did not know why, but she could not stop looking at him. David had closed his eyes. It made no difference to him that they were in a luxurious plane—he was in the air and did not like it one little bit.

John took several phone calls and at times seemed cross, and at other times happy. He constantly took his glasses out from his pocket to read papers he was referring to in his conversation. Periodically, he would look up and apologize for being so busy. "I've been away a while and now have to catch up," he said as his cell rang again. Morgan noticed as they got closer to their destination that John was commanding, demanding, and generally got his own way, but never once raised his voice. He continued to use the voice of reason. He was, she thought, one of the world's nicest men. She continued to look at him as he talked on the phone, noticing for the first time how handsome he was, how his face went from a smile to a frown and back again, and then she reprimanded herself because he was old enough to be her father. However, she could understand why women of all ages could be attracted to him.

John looked up and caught Morgan staring at him. He raised a quizzical eyebrow at her and asked, "Is there anything wrong, Morgan? Can I get the flight attendant to get you a drink or something?"

For the first time in a long time Morgan blushed. "No I'm sorry. I was watching you work and I was half asleep really," she replied.

"Okay," John replied. "As long as you're all right." And he went back to his paper work.

Morgan looked out of the window as John glanced up from his work and stared at her. It had been a long time since any woman had piqued his interest. But then he looked at David who seemed as if he was asleep, but still holding Morgan's hand. John dismissed the idea.

A limousine ride was waiting at the airport. They drove back to John's home where he insisted they stay with him. "You can live in the guest wing," he had said. The housekeeper greeted him on the steps and as he walked through the door, and then a beautiful young lady ran to him, throwing herself in his arms.

"Daddy! You've been away so long!" she pouted.

"Well I'm back now. Where are my grandsons?"

"In the garden playing. They've missed you too. I thought you were only going to be away for a little while. It's been ages." On seeing David and Morgan, the smile fell from her face, she asked, "Who are these people?"

John smiled and said as he put his arm around his daughter, "Annabelle, I would like you to meet David and Morgan."

Anabelle quickly looked them up and down. She did not hold her hand out to shake but rather stared at the two rather unfashionable people and said a quiet and unenthusiastic "Hello."

The housekeeper, Mrs. Marsh, had stood aside while the introductions were made and quickly stepped into the silence that had followed. She said, "Sir, Ma'am, if you would like to follow me, I'll show you to your rooms."

"Dinner at six, Mrs. Marsh!" John shouted as they went up the stairs.

"Yes, sir," she answered.

"I'll see you two in the library for drinks at five-thirty then," John said as they ascended the stairs.

Morgan admired the opulence of the house as Mrs. March led them to their rooms. She showed them into the right wing of the house where they had a bedroom, bathroom, and a sitting room furnished with the best of everything. "Thank you for showing us the way, Mrs. Marsh," Morgan said.

"I hope you will be comfortable here. Let me know if there is anything I can get you that will make you time here more enjoyable. I shall be bringing tea up at three and I will come and fetch you and show you where the library is just before five-thirty." As David put the cases on the bed, she said, "Sir, I can unpack those for you. It will be a little later if you don't mind."

David smiled back at her and said, "We can take care of that, Mrs. Marsh. I'm sure you already have a lot to do, but thank you for offering."

She nodded her head and left the room. Morgan looked out of the window which overlooked the tennis court and some beautifully kept gardens and in the far distance the ocean. "Oh, David, come and have a look out here," she sighed.

David came and stood by her looking out the window. "It's beautiful, Morgan. But me, I love the Gulf, and no matter how many tennis courts and flowerbeds you have outside, it is not the same as seeing the ever changing bay we live by. But if you want that sort of life, well maybe we could move out from Dolphin's Cove and look somewhere else." He moved away from her and started to hang up his clothes. He had no doubt he would be expected to dress for dinner and shook the only jacket he had bought with him to try to get the creases out. He too had noticed the opulence in the house and wished they had chosen to stay in a hotel. It made him feel uncomfortable. He liked nice things, but he also liked the simple, uncomplicated life.

Morgan lingered by the window a little longer. When she had been younger, this had been her dream—to live in this manner—and she was torn. She turned and looked at David and her heart jumped. He had taken off his shirt to shower, and she saw the rippling muscles and the scar on his arm from the bullet wound, and she knew exactly where her heart lay. She walked over to David with mischief in her eyes, but there was a discreet knock on the door, and Mrs. Marsh was there with a tea tray and cookies. "I'll be back later," she smiled, having seen David without his shirt. But the mood had been broken. David took his shower while Morgan drank some tea, and nibbled on a cookie.

They were led down to the library at exactly five-thirty. Morgan had showered and had changed into a simple long cotton dress, and David had put on slacks and an open neck shirt with his jacket. John was waiting for them, dressed in a beautifully cut suit, and with a glass of scotch in his hand. "What can I get you two to drink?" he asked.

David would have loved a beer, but in these surroundings, felt that was too low brow, so he said he'd have what John was having. Morgan had a vodka tonic. They sat down in the well-appointed library with a huge desk and leather arm chairs surrounding a coffee table by the window. The books caught her eye, and she stood up again to have a better look. They were all leather bound, and many of them first editions. John saw her looking through the titles and said, "If there is anything of interest there, I'll have Mrs. Marsh take it up and put it by your bedside so you can read it, or, of course, you can come in here at any time to sit and read."

Morgan smiled back at John as she accepted her drink. "Thank you. That's really nice of you, John."

John looked back at David, and said, "I hope Mrs. Marsh made you both comfortable upstairs."

David smiled back and replied, "I don't think there is anything else we could ask for. You seemed to have thought of everything to make your guests comfortable."

John just smiled back. The silence stretched out just a little too long for Morgan to feel comfortable and so she said, "This house is huge, John, and the grounds, from what I have seen are really beautiful. Your wife must have her hands full trying to keep up with everything."

John looked down at his glass which he rolled between his hands. Looking up, he said, "My wife died ten years ago from cancer. It was she who loved this house and insisted I buy it. It has ten thousand square feet and, of course, separate quarters on the grounds for Mrs. Marsh. When my wife was alive and my daughter was here, we had guests coming and going all the time, and the house never felt more alive. My wife died, and my daughter married, and now the house is empty, except when my daughter and grandsons come over. They live just a few miles away, but they have busy lives. This house needs a family. I guess I've just got lazy and haven't thought about selling it."

Morgan said, "I am so sorry about your wife, John. Have you thought about getting married again?"

He laughed out loud replying, "No, I really haven't. There are enough young ladies around here that would like to take my wife's place, but I had a good solid marriage and, honestly, I have not seen nor found anyone I think would be interesting enough for me. It's not all about the bedroom, it's about the joining of the minds and hearts, and I'm afraid, I'm just a little picky!"

Mrs. Marsh appeared in the doorway to tell them dinner was served.

John turned and, with a smile, offered his hand to Morgan to pull her up from the chair. Then he offered her his arm, and he led the way. All the while, his eyes never left her.

They had a wonderful dinner of three courses—pate de fois gras with toast, consommé, and roast beef with roast vegetables and potatoes. Morgan seemed completely at home with everything, and David felt more and more at a loss. He liked to eat in his sunroom with his meal on his lap and not worry if he spilled food down his front, and he liked to wash it all down with a beer.

Mrs. Marsh announced that coffee had been served in the library. "Is there anything else I can do for you this evening?"

John had replied, "No thanks, Mrs. Marsh. Dinner was amazing, as always. We'll see you in the morning." He stood up to lead the way to the library again, but Morgan suddenly felt she should, if nothing else clear the dishes from the table.

Mrs. Marsh smiled a genuine smile when she saw Morgan's intention. "Thank you for thinking of that, Ma'am," she said. "I've got it, and really, it will all go in the dishwasher."

David was more ardent that night than he had been in a while. Their lovemaking was wonderful, and she turned over to David and said, "I think we should buy us a mattress like this. This is so comfortable and cozy."

David said, "You can have whatever you want, as long as I know you still love me."

"Of course I still love you, David. Whatever would make you think I didn't?" she asked snuggling contentedly up in his arms.

He pulled back a little from her and looking into her eyes, replied, "You're not even a little bit in love with John and his way of life?"

She looked back at him and didn't quite know how to answer, and sighing, she said, "I love what John has, but would it make me happy? I don't think so, David. Maybe if I had met him under any other circumstances, I could have loved him. But he is almost as old as my grandfather, and even though he is handsome, I look at you and know where my heart belongs. It belongs to you—a man who had not loved anyone in years, hardly ever spoke to anyone, but plucked up the courage to talk to me and ask me out because you saw something in me that you liked. You love the water and living by it, and so do I. You like simple and so do I. If you really want to know where I would like to live, it's in Cooper's Landing, and maybe one day when my grandfather has left us, and, if the people who live there now would like to sell it, that's where I would like to be with you, David." He pulled her closer to him and held her tight for the rest of the night. No more words were needed.

The following morning after breakfast, David and John closeted themselves in his library. John had once again bought all the coins sight unseen, and David was looking to invest his money. John had called in a few of his financial advisors and together that morning they invested eight million dollars for David. They advised that he put the rest into a bank account where he would have liquid funds to pay bills for the time being while his accounts were being set up. David passed two million dollars of the money back to John to start a new company for him. "I want to buy a tract of land near the pier and build a freezer unit for the shrimp and fish," David said. "I want to be able to deliver shrimp around the country and, eventually, around the world." He took a deep quaff of water as he continued. "The company we set up would need to purchase three new shrimping boats to be built at Dan's Marina in Dolphin's Cove. I would also like to make a donation to the football team at the local high school to buy equipment they need, plus a new swimming pool. I also want to make a donation to the local library to keep that open, and to purchase new books." He continued, "I had no idea what all this will cost, but hopefully I will have enough money to do all this and never have to worry again. The shrimp alone should make me and the other shrimpers extremely rich over a period of time."

The advisor had no problem with what David was asking.

They also advised David very strongly that if he wanted to stay anonymous and was never to be recognized as the benefactor to so many in Dolphin's Cove and Oak Tree, he must have an estate drawn up for himself, instead of a will. The estate would make his transactions undiscoverable.

"I'll call in my attorney tomorrow." John had immediately said. "He was the one who set my estate up. It will protect you and Morgan, of course, if you do intend to marry her. If you do, she needs to be here tomorrow."

The two men stared at each other for a few moments and David wondered how fond John was becoming of Morgan. From time to time he had seen a look between the pair. However, he was sure they had not acted on the attraction, and he quickly dismissed the idea his friend and benefactor would betray him in any way. He replied, "We will be getting married at the earliest date Morgan can set when we get back." John nodded his head and made the phone call.

Annabel, John's daughter, had arrived that morning in time for breakfast and ate with them. "Where are my grandsons?" John had asked.

"At home with the nanny, Daddy Dearest. I couldn't bring them with me because you wanted me to take Morgan shopping, and that would be impossible with two small children."

John handed his credit card over to his daughter and David helplessly asked Morgan how much she wanted. She told him she would put whatever purchases she made on her own credit card. They agreed and Annabel and Morgan set off for a day of shopping, leaving the men to a day in the library.

Annabel made no effort at all to make conversation on the journey, and so Morgan had kept her comments limited to the scenery. She thought to herself, "Annabel is a mean-spirited, selfish, little witch." They parked near a row of shops and went into a large well known store. Annabel picked out several outfits for herself and burned quite a hole in John's credit card. Morgan had quietly looked at the prices and refrained from trying on anything, although she picked up some slacks for David, two shirts, and a jacket.

"There must be something you like," Annabel sulkily said in the end. "Daddy told me you could have anything you wanted, and he'll be cross with me if you go back with nothing."

Morgan had about enough of this churlish woman, and replied. "I can afford to buy my own clothes and don't need your father to do so. If there was anything I had wanted, I would have bought it." She turned away and walked to the furthest end of the store, leaving a stunned Annabel with her mouth open.

It was a good fifteen minutes before Morgan heard a small voice say, "Are you interested in my dad?"

Morgan turned and looked at Annabel and asked, "What do you mean 'interested'?"

"Would you get involved with him?"

"No, Annabel I would not. I am engaged to David, and I will be getting married to him as soon as we get back to Alabama. I love David very much. He truly is my heart and soul."

"I'm sorry," Annabel said hesitantly. "I thought my father had bought you back here because he liked you, and I've seen the way he looks at you. He hasn't done that to any woman since my mom died." Morgan shook her head.

"I've never really gotten over my mother dying," Annabel continued. "She and I were attached at the hip, so to speak. I had no brothers or sisters, so I turned to Dad. I guess I must seem a little too attached to him."

There was silence for a few moments while both ladies searched through racks of clothes. Annabel suddenly spoke up again. "I like you Morgan. Can we start again? I'm Annabel." She held out her hand for Morgan to shake. But Morgan didn't take her hand. Instead, she opened her arms and took the younger woman into an embrace.

They stopped for lunch and tried another store with Annabel now as animated as a young woman normally was. As they walked through the store, Morgan came to a dead stop as she saw a floor length dress on a mannequin. "It's stunning!" she thought to herself. It was plain white with long lace sleeves that came to a point of the hand. It had a round neckline that dipped just low enough over the bust. It was caught under the bust line with a dark green sash and fell in folds down to the floor. On closer inspection she saw there were flowers embroidered all over the dress in a cream color." She picked up the price tag and nearly fell over. She had never in her life paid that amount for one dress—nor even for 20 dresses.

Annabel was watching Morgan with interest and walking over to the dress she picked up the price tag and looked. She smiled at Morgan and said, "Do you know Daddy paid thirty four thousand dollars for my wedding dress? This is so pretty and would suit you really well, and Daddy could buy it as your wedding gift." She called a sales assistant over to help and had the dress bought to them in Morgan's size. Annabel insisted that Morgan try it on.

Morgan had resisted all the other clothes but the moment she had seen this dress, she wanted it as her bridal dress. Temptation won, and she went to the dressing room and put the dress on. She looked into the mirror and saw the white of the dress showed off her freckles and red hair, and the green sash made her eyes pop. She walked out to show Annabel and the assistant who both gasped. "You look beautiful Morgan!" Annabel cried. "I hope you're inviting me to the wedding." It was decided at that moment. This was the dress.

Morgan changed back into her street clothes and came out of the dressing room to pay the bill only to find that Annabel had already paid. Her dress was packed, and they were ready to go.

By the time they arrived back at the house, John and David were playing with John's grandsons. "What are you doing, Daddy?" she asked.

"Playing pirates," he answered, as his eldest grandson lunged at him with a pretend sword.

"Well, I'm taking them home because that seems just a little violent to me," she snapped back.

"They're fine, Annabel. They're just playing little boys' games," John answered back. "Stay and have dinner with us. I'll get Mrs. Marsh to whip up something for the boys."

"Thanks, Daddy but no. Their nanny can see to them when we get back. She shouldn't have bought them here this afternoon. I didn't instruct her to."

"No you didn't," John replied. "I wanted to see them, and so she bought them out so we could swim and play games. That's what grandfathers and grandsons do."

For a moment Annabel relented and then said, "We'd have to have Donald over for dinner too and that isn't going to work because you dislike him so much, Daddy." On a quieter note she continued, "Maybe another time in the not too distant future, Daddy. I don't see enough of you, nor do the children and we all love you very much."

John just nodded his head and when she was ready to go, she whispered into his ear what they had done that afternoon for Morgan. "Thank you, Annabel for being so nice to someone else."

"I like her, Daddy, I really do. Will you take the boys and me to the wedding?" she asked.

"If that's what you want, I would be happy to."

David hadn't showered from swimming yet. "Let me shower, Morgan he said. "You go ahead to the library for a pre-dinner cocktail with John."

She did not want to spend time alone with John, but she didn't know exactly what to say to David, so she went. Annabel had said John was attracted to her, and she too was feeling very attracted to him, although she had no idea why.

In the library, John greeted her as he always did with a smile and got her drink order while she looked out of the library window. She did not turn around but said, "I have to thank you for my wedding dress, John. Annabel had already paid for it on your credit card before I had time to dress again." It was only then she realized that John was right behind her with her drink, and she turned to take it from him to find there was hardly any room between them.

"You're welcome," he said looking directly into her eyes. "You're sure a wedding and David are what you want, Morgan?"

She looked down at her drink and softly said, "Yes, I think so."

He never moved but continued to stand there until she looked back up at him. "Am I imagining something happening between you and me?"

Biting her lip she replied, "I didn't say there was nothing happening, John. There can't be anything. I love David. I really do."

He nodded his head. "Then stop looking at me with those puppy dog eyes that now have tears in them. I didn't mean to make you cry." He lifted his hand to wipe the tears away but instead, gripped her chin. He lowered his mouth to hers and gave her the gentlest kiss she had ever had. There was so much love and tenderness there it took her breath away. John looked down at her, realizing what he had done, and he balled his fist and walked to the door of the library. "Tell David I have an emergency meeting with two of my management team tonight and will see him tomorrow." He walked out softly closing the door behind him. Morgan stood with her fingers on her lips as John walked away, stunned by what had just happened and the intensity of both their emotions.

David accepted the news that John had an emergency meeting and would not be dining with them with a little relief. He felt more at ease without his very proper host overseeing their comfort for the evening. They dined with Mrs. Marsh seeing to their every whim.

Mrs. Marsh said, "I told Mr. Standing that he works too hard and with having visitors here, he should cancel late meetings like this one. But as always, he does what he has a mind to, but he asked me to remind you that he is looking forward to taking both of you out tomorrow for a night out on the town before your return to Dolphin's Cove."

Taking a walk around the grounds before they retired to bed, Morgan was anxious to show David how much she loved him and asked if they could retire early.

Morgan felt guilty that David never questioned why John didn't join them or why Morgan suddenly seemed really anxious to go home. "I want to get married as soon as we get home," she told David. "That's if you haven't changed your mind."

"I love you Morgan, and that's why I put that ring on your finger. You never asked me where I got the ring from. Aren't you even the least bit curious?"

"I thought you must have bought it from an antique store," she replied with a frown, looking down at the ring on her finger. "I've never taken it off since you put it on my finger."

He stood by her side, "You should. Have you seen the initials inside the ring?"

Morgan slipped it off and inspected the inside of the wide band. There inside, barely able to be seen, were the letters A for Annie and a heart and a J for Jesse. The letters had been scratched there so many years ago and lovingly worn by so many different women since, that the initials had almost worn away. Morgan looked at David and said, "I'll take it into a jeweler when we get back and have them etched in again."

David smiled at her and said, "When I got the ring from my father, I had no idea who the initials stood for, but now it seems eerily right that you should have the ring. If it pleases you, have the initials carved a little deeper if the gold will support it". He nodded his head. "It certainly is antique. The ring must have been my great, great, grandmother's and has been passed through the family for generations. On the day we get married, I have something else I want you to have and wear. It also has been passed down in my family, but you'll have to wait and see what it is because it is still in the safe in Dolphin's Cove." He smiled down at her as he slowly unbuttoned her blouse, planting kisses on her neck and face. "When do you want to get married?" he asked between kisses and caressing her breasts.

"Now," she answered as she took a deep breath.

"As soon as you can arrange a wedding, when we get back," he whispered continuing his journey of kisses down her body. I love you, Morgan."

"I love you too, David. I really want to be your wife. I'm tired of being your other mistress."

He shot up and stared at her. "I don't have a mistress, and you are my finance, not my mistress."

"Yes you do," she grinned. "You told me the first day I met you the Gulf was your mistress. Until you marry me, my grandfather says that's what I am to you—your other mistress." She was by now openly laughing at his stunned face, and realizing she was just teasing him, he picked her and threw her on the bed.

"Then behave like a loose woman," he growled whilst trying to grab her as she laughed out loud and he began to tickle her. It was not long before the two were making love.

They spent the next night out on the town, dinning in the most expensive restaurant and going onto a casino and gambling. The champagne flowed and money was thrown away as if it was just paper to be burned. They listened to a band that played contemporary jazz, and Morgan loved every minute of their time there, but as they undressed to go to bed, she looked over at David, and said, "I want to go home—to our home."

Chapter 17

Morgan sat in the sunroom with Chowder by her side. They had been back for two days and David was already shrimping. His crew had been happy to have him back—none more so than Ben, who had been amazed when he went to pay some of his bills at the hospital to find a benefactor had paid them all. "Boss, you have no idea the things that have happened since you left," he told David, who listened and smiled, but said nothing.

Morgan watched as the Crimson Tide left harbor and travelled far out into the bay with the sun setting in front of her. The sky was filled with warm colors of reds, oranges, and yellows, heralding a bright, sunny day tomorrow. She had never been happier than she was right now. "Oh," she thought to herself. "The short time we spent with John was fabulous. The lifestyle he has is amazing, but since I came back, I know this is the right thing for me. David is right for me."

She found the card that Diane had given her from Cooper's Landing and made her first phone call. "Would it be possible for you to cater a wedding for twenty people?" she asked.

"I would really love to, "Diane had replied, and the wedding was set for four weeks hence.

Morgan had bought back the white dress and took it to her grandfather's house. When she had walked through the door, Paul had looked at her and said, "I thought you'd left us and departed for different shores."

She smiled back and said, "No, Grandpa. I've come back to get married to David, and we are going to live right here in Dolphin's Cove, so you'll have to put up with me for a while longer yet."

"Well," he replied. "You've got no parents left, so who's gonna give you away?"

"I was hoping you would, Grandpa," she said with a look of concern.

Morgan saw a flash of tears in his eyes as he got up from his chair and, putting his arms around her, he said, "It'll be my honor, Morgan."

"Grandpa," she asked, "Have you got your memory back, yet?"

"No. I remember most everything, but nothing about what happened to me. Maybe it's all for the best."

"Did you know that the two men who did this have been arrested, Grandpa?"

"Yes. I knew. Detective Lawson came to see me several times, but I still can't remember that night or what happened to me, so I was no help to him at all. But I hear David had something to do with them being arrested. I always did say I liked that man. Good thing he decided to marry you. It's about time!"

"Well, I'll have to take you out and get you a decent suit to give me away in, Grandpa, and maybe you'd like Tyler to come to the wedding too."

"When's it gonna be then?" he asked.

"Four weeks Grandpa. Not much time to arrange everything, is it?"

"That's ridiculous," Paul replied. "Do you even know where you're gonna hold the wedding?"

"Grandpa," Morgan soothed. "I want a very small wedding and as simple as it comes. I'm going to be married at Cooper's Landing on the Bon Secour River. I hung my dress up in the closet upstairs, and now all I have to do is invite the people I want to come. David and I are paying for the wedding, so all you have to do is give me away."

Paul nodded his head and sank back in his chair. "Is there something wrong, Grandpa?"

Paul looked at his granddaughter. "I keep forgetting things. You'll have to remind me when the wedding is. I'll forget otherwise."

"It's okay, Grandpa," she replied trying to make light of this news. "I'll probably be over every day, and you'll be sick of seeing me. When you're ready, you know you can come and live with David and me, don't you, Grandpa?"

"Now, now. Stop fussing. I ain't ready for a nursing home yet," he replied with gruffness but a hint of tears and relief in his voice.

Morgan returned home to cook a late lunch. David was still asleep upstairs. She poked her head around the bedroom door to see David arms akimbo and Chowder lying on the bed with his legs spread to the four corners of the world. Both were snoring. She shook her head and made her way downstairs again and started the lunch. When it was all simmering, she returned upstairs and, creeping over to the bed, she leaned down and gave David a kiss. She was just raising her head again when his arm snaked around her neck and pulled her back for another one. "I didn't know you were awake," she smiled.

"That was the idea," he replied as his lips found hers again, and his hands wandered over her body. "Do you miss me when I'm shrimping?" he asked raising his head from her stomach and looking at her.

"Sometimes," she whispered back wishing he would go back to what he had been doing.

"Do you want me to give up work, Morgan?"

"Not if you don't want to," she replied.

"Well……."

"David, shut up. You're talking too much."

David had looked over the ground for sale by the pier in Dolphin's Cove and found a tract he thought would be eminently suitable for a freezer factory. He had emailed John who had, in turn, purchased the tract in David's new company's name—Dolphins Pod. Local contractors would start building in two weeks.

The high school had been ecstatic over the money donated by the new company in town. The football team already had new uniforms and equipment, and the pool and football field would be installed during the summer vacation.

The library was scheduled to close for three weeks while

it was being refurbished. Shipments of new books arrived every day.

Dan had called David into the Marina the first morning he had seen him back from California. "This is crazy, Man. A company called Dolphins Pod has ordered three shrimpers to be built here at my Marina. They paid a third of the money down so that I can buy what I need and hire some men. This is really crazy stuff. Who the hell is going to be captaining these? You should apply for a job with them! Wow! Really crazy shit! Hell, I hear there's to be a freezing plant built over yonder too. Can you imagine the difference it will make? I think all this activity will put this place back on the map." He turned with a big smile on his face. "Well, I might add you don't seem very happy, David? Something wrong?"

"Absolutely not," David replied. "I'm as happy as everyone else. I hope it brings this town alive."

"Well it should with all the money that's being pumped back into Dolphin's Cove and Oak Tree Town. I wonder if there will be more people moving back here again? I can remember when there was so much here. Perhaps someone will re-open the bowling alley and the movie theater. It would really be cool to have these things back. Anyway, for the first time in a long time, I'm pleased to say to you,......... 'I have to get back to work!' I can't spend all day talking to you!" He laughed and slapped David's back as he turned to go back into the Marina.

He didn't see the big grin over David's face as he made his way home. David could smell the breakfast as he walked up the drive and entered the kitchen, "You know this is all I'm marrying you for, don't you?" he teased Morgan. "I think I should keep you barefoot and pregnant and chained to the kitchen sink!"

"Well," she said sashaying toward him, "We could always keep trying on the pregnant bit. That would involve the bed, and you haven't been there for at least twelve hours." And putting her arms around him, she kissed his neck and shoulders.

He threw his hands up in the air and said, "How do you expect me to eat the breakfast you just cooked me?"

She stood up quickly and laughing she replied, "You stink of shrimp anyway. Eat and shower."

The more time she spent with David, the more convinced Morgan became that John would not have been right for her. She loved David—loved his body and his mind. She loved the simple life they led, and, as she cleaned the plates away into the dishwasher, she made up her mind and ran upstairs. Stripping off her clothes, she joined David in the shower.

Coopers Landing 2013

Morgan and David's wedding day arrived with sunny skies and temperatures predicted in the upper 70s.

Diane walked swiftly to hug Morgan and her grandfather as they stepped from their car. "Where's David?" she asked.

Morgan laughed at Diane as she said, "It's my wedding day today, and my grandfather insisted I stay at his place last night as tradition dictates. That's why he drove me!"

Diane laughed replying, "Well, he is very traditional, I'm sure. I'll bet he never lived with his wife before they got married back in the day."

"Oh look," Morgan said, looking over at the driveway to a delivery van that had parked there. Those are the roses for the men's lapels. Personally, I am really happy you offered to pick my bouquet from your garden this morning." Morgan took the roses from the driver and placed them inside the main house.

Morgan stepped back outside to help Diane place cutlery on the table. "I have no idea what David has decided to wear," she continued, "but I hope just a suit. I've sort of mentioned a suit to him once or twice. I don't know if he's taken up my suggestion or not. I couldn't imagine him in a tux. He would be so uncomfortable, and that is not what today is about."

Diane went into the house and came back with mimosas for the two of them as they continued to transform the outside of the house.

Morgan went on to say, "John flew in last night and, much to my surprise, he has bought his daughter and grandsons.

They are staying in a hotel in Gulf Shores that has a swimming pool for the children."

"Sounds sensible to me," Diane replied.

"David has tentatively told me he had asked John to be his best man, if I did not mind. John has not at any time been back to the Gulf since we left California. Gosh, Diane, if I had met that man at any other time........," she drifted off for a second. "But thankfully any infatuation I had felt for him has left me. So I was able to smile at David and say that I really didn't mind. It will be nice to see him again."

Diane placed an arm around Morgan and smiled up at her, "I don't really think you had strong feelings for John and if you did, well, they are gone now. I can understand why you did. He is an attractive, charismatic man. I saw that for myself when I met him. But he is too old for you, and it wouldn't be long before it would tell in your relationship. I think David is far more suited to you."

The two women hugged and smiled. Since Morgan had come back to the Gulf, they had become like sisters, and both hoped they would not lose the friendship that had blossomed between them.

Morgan smiled as she went on to arrange some flowers in a vase, "Of course I should have known John better than to just be a visitor. He is having two cases of champagne sent here for our wedding and is providing a stocked bar and a bartender. He is a very generous man."

Diane's mouth dropped open. "We were just having wine! I guess now we aren't."

Diane, Chick, and Morgan spent the rest of the morning getting Cooper's Landing ready for the wedding. Chick had built an archway and covered it in white blooms from their garden.

It was time for Morgan to go and get ready for her wedding. Diane had put aside her bedroom in the big house for Morgan. She showered first, and when she finished, she sat at the old fashioned dressing table which had triple mirrors standing on it. Morgan looked at her reflection and reached for her face cream. When she looked back up, there in the mirror was someone else's face, her hair almost the same color as Morgan's, with beautiful flowing locks of red which she was twisting into curls. She smiled at her reflection, she seemed as though she was getting ready to welcome someone. The reflection pinched her cheeks to put color into them and gently bit her lips. The face in the mirror looked so pretty, and Morgan knew who she was—Annie. Morgan was not in the least bit afraid. She moved just a little, and the woman's reflection disappeared. Morgan reached forward to try to get the woman back but she was gone. Why had she come here today? No one had ever mentioned to Morgan that this place was haunted.

Morgan put her make-up on with no sight of Annie again. She brushed her hair until it shone and then gathered it up to cascade down her back in simple curls. The dress was next. Morgan let it fall over her head and onto her body. Morgan looked into the long mirror Diane had put there for her, and lo and behold, there was Annie's reflection. She looked beautiful in a simple dress which was strikingly similar to the one Morgan had on. Morgan watched as Annie straightened the folds of her dress. Smiling at her reflection, Morgan whispered. "Annie? You look so beautiful."

For one brief second Annie's eyes held Morgan's and she smiled and whispered back, "It's my wedding day today. Jesse isn't here yet. I hope he won't be late. I've waited so long."

There was a movement behind Morgan, and Annie faded away again. Morgan's grandfather had come to collect her and walk her down the aisle. "You look beautiful, Morgan. You remind me of your grandmother when she and I got married." He shook his head at his own memories. Morgan pinned a cream rose into her hair.

"Is David here?" Morgan asked, surprised to see the time had gotten away from her.

"Everyone is here that matters, Paul replied. "You sure this is what you want, Morgan? It's not too late to back out."

"No, Grandpa. I'm not running anywhere. I'm ready if you are." Morgan smoothed the folds of her dress and looked in the mirror to see a slight shadow behind her.

"David asked me to give you this to wear today," Paul said and gave Morgan an old box.

Puzzled, Morgan opened it to find a beautiful topaz threaded on a delicate gold chain nestled in the middle of the box. "It's so beautiful!" Morgan cried.

"Apparently it has been passed through the generations of David's family from father to son," Paul replied.

"Can you do it up for me, Grandpa?" Morgan asked.

It took him a moment of fiddling with the clasp, and as Morgan replaced her hair and looked in the mirror, Annie looked back at her holding the topaz. Morgan smiled at her and turning to her Grandpa, she said, "I'm ready now, Grandpa."

Morgan's grandfather walked down the stairs in front of her. They stood together in the open doorway and Morgan looked at the sight in front of her. There on the platform behind the archway with the minister, stood David, dressed in a well-cut suit that made him look so handsome. Beside him, John looked equally as handsome, but her eyes came back to my future husband. "I love that man so much my heart feels as if it will burst," she whispered to her Grandpa.

The music struck up on the piano and Morgan's grandpa started to walk her down through the chairs as people stood for her. But her eyes focused on something behind David. It was a fleeting shadow, and maybe Morgan imagined it, but she didn't think so. It was a cowboy, his hat in his hand, dressed in a suit. He was as handsome as David. They looked so alike. Morgan's eyes focused back on David, and the shadow disappeared.

"You look beautiful," David whispered to Morgan as she stood by his side.

The minister started to speak, and Morgan didn't see anything else unusual until she and David began to recite their wedding vows. Morgan felt Annie step by her side saying the same vows to her cowboy, and Jesse James stood by David's side, repeating his vows to Annie. Morgan blinked and in the instant after their "I do's," and the apparitions disappeared again. David placed the wedding band on Morgan's finger and she placed one on his. In that instant, real or imaginary, Jesse and Annie were married too. Annie's soul belonged to Jesse's as Morgan's did to David.

David gave Morgan another gift that afternoon—the deed to Cooper's Landing. He had listened when she told him where she wanted to be, and had taken Morgan at her word. Diane and Chick were not going to leave for about a year unless they found another place they really wanted to buy sooner, but David had paid them enough to buy any property they might like in the area.

Morgan asked Diane later that afternoon if she had ever seen a ghost in the house. Diane smiled with curiosity and asked, "Like who?"

"The original owner—Annie," Morgan said.

Diane smiled back at her, shaking her head. "Not by me," she replied, "except I had a feeling today.......but then I expect I'm just being silly."

It was wonderful to see their friends that day and celebrate the most fulfilling day with them all. John asked Morgan for a dance later, and they went up to the platform that Chick had built, and they danced to a slow song. "Are you really as happy as you looked this afternoon, Morgan?"

Morgan looked up into this very dear and familiar face and smiled. "Yes, John. I really am that happy."

He nodded his head and demanded, "If anything ever happens to David, you must tell me straight away, Morgan, and I promise I will look after you. I'll be around for a while. I've obtained permission to raise the Bountiful Lady from the bottom of the Gulf." He looked over at his daughter who was dancing with David and continued. "My daughter has told me she is desperately unhappy in her marriage and has moved back in to my home in California. The boys love the pool and having a man who spends a little more time with them. I think they even enjoy the discipline I mete out! I will probably bring them here with me."

"Annabel is beautiful, John, and I'm sure it won't take her long to find a more suitable husband, and perhaps one who you can approve of."

The wedding was over. David and Morgan sat on the porch of Cooper's Landing enjoying the peace and quiet of the evening. Chick and Diane had loaned them the house for the night and left for a hotel. David and Morgan were going to sleep in the carriage house. There was a small breeze carrying the insects away from them as they sat under the beautiful star lit sky gazing at the moss in the old oak tree that was swaying in the breeze. They needed no words; they were in love. When they had their fill of the evening, they made their way to the carriage house hand-in-hand. The bedroom had a beautiful stained glass window without drapes. The moon shined through, casting shadows and colors over their bodies. David slowly undressed Morgan whispering words of love. As she unbuttoned David's shirt, Morgan heard the merest whisper of Annie and Jesse. She smiled as she remembered that Diane had told her it was in this house that Jesse and Anne had celebrated their love. As David lavished love on her body, she closed her eyes and ears to the whisperings of the house and of Jesse and Annie, and celebrated her own love of David

Epilogue

Morgan sat uncomfortably in the chair outside of the house in Dolphin's Cove. She had watched the four shrimpers going out last night, and now they were coming back in. She had asked David the past two nights not to go out in his new shrimper, but to stay with her.

David had caressed her face and said, "Maybe tomorrow. You're just panicking, it's not time yet."

The past nine months has seen growth in the town. The once sleepy town on the bay had become busier. The football team won many of their games, and was talked of as an up-and-coming championship team. The swimming pool encouraged the growth of good swimming teams and divers.

Dan's Marina had taken on many workers and had built three sound, solid, shrimpers. As his reputation for good workmanship spread, Dan picked up new contracts from many fishermen for miles around, and he was talking of expanding.

The local library had also opened up a coffee shop, and the locals drifted in and out all day.

The coffee shop activity did not seem to hurt Marylou's. The restaurant had expanded its menu and hours and started serving wine and beer. No one knew where the money had come from to build the economy in this once sleepy town, but it had happened all at once. There was even talk of having a movie theater somewhere near the town center.

Morgan smiled as she saw David walking up the hill toward the house. As he came nearer she stood to welcome him home and her water broke.

"Hi, she laughed. "My water's just broken and you need to get me to a hospital. I've been having contractions for a while."

By the time David had a quick shower; Morgan went back to her original idea and asked him to drive the back roads to Cooper's Landing. In the carriage house, with Diane assisting her, she gave birth to her beautiful healthy son. David cut the cord. "We have a son," he said holding him up. "What should we call him?" As Morgan looked up she saw Annie, her arms held aloft to hold the baby, a smile lighting her face.

Morgan took the baby from David and looked down into his little face and saw David and his grandfather—his entire ancestor's right back to Jesse James. "Annie wanted us here, David—here at Cooper's Landing. It's time this legend had a happy ending and I think you and I made that happen. We'll name him Jesse Mason-James What else could we possibly call him?"

Look for other books by Katharine Carter on amazon. com or barnesandnobles.com or on my web page, www.katharinecarter.net

Music Beneath the Waves.

The Fluteplayer

In the Blink of an Eye

Twisting in the Hands of Time

Twisted Inside Out

Magnolia Manor

The Haunting of Magnolia Manor

Fire in Magnolia Manor

Blues House on the Hill

Katharine Carter

I was born in Royal Berkshire, England and lived there for the first thirty nine years of my life. My husband and our children moved to Wisconsin due to my husband's business. We lived just outside of Green Bay in the country. We have since moved to Gulf Shores in Alabama. I enjoy writing my books while over-looking the blue/grey waters of the bay of Bon Secour. My writing comes from the experiences I have gained from each country and states I have lived in and those I've visited.

This is the first time I have collaborated on writing a book and I think the end results are amazing. Both John and I are excited about 'The Legend of Coopers Landing' and hope that you, the reader, enjoyed the book, and thank you for buying it

John Rottger

A Former Navy SEAL Lieutenant, Stunt coordinator and Technical Advisor, and Dive Operations coordinator.

I grew up in Yonkers, New York, and joined the Navy conducting special operations all over the world. While working in different special warfare commands, I became a SEAL Instructor.

On leaving the Navy I created a second career working in Movies and Television coordinating stunts both in water and on land. I have worked in many movies and television and television series. This is my first foray into writing but hope it will not be my last.

The Legend of Cooper's Landing

A spellbinding, fictional novel of adventure, love and treasure! The action packed love story spans across a century from the civil war to a devastated Gulf Coast spill in 2010.

A true page turner worthy of reading, filled with mystery, intrigue and plenty of action.